TRUST
MISPLACED

a Paul Dodge Novel

TRUST MISPLACED

a Paul Dodge Novel

CHRISTOPHER FLORY

Light Messages
Torchflame Books

Durham, NC

Published 2021, by Torchflame Books
an Imprint of Light Messages
www.lightmessages.com
Durham, NC 27713 USA
SAN: 920-9298

Paperback ISBN: 978-1-61153-430-6
E-book ISBN: 978-1-61153-431-3
Library of Congress Control Number: 2021913189

For my brother, Jeff,
who might not have approved of the content,
but I am sure would have applauded the accomplishment.
I miss you.

For my wife, who told me to get a hobby.
This is what happened.
Thank you.

Love you both.

CHAPTER 1

THE MAN SAT IN THE SMALL ROOM, admiring what had taken him nearly a month to assemble. First, he built the room without the landlord catching on or neighbors complaining about the commotion. The noise had been his biggest worry. Landlords rarely just dropped in, but people recognized construction racket, and neighbors called and complained about sounds of hammers and saws coming from surrounding apartments. Working in the evening, mornings, and weekends was out of the question. Too many families were home. He had a four-hour window during the day to work unnoticed. Battery-operated devices were wrapped with a damp towel to deaden the whine from the electric motors. He smuggled construction materials in using the maintenance stairway in the dead of night, away from prying eyes.

Once the man finished the construction, he needed to decorate the room. Two more weeks passed before he found the appropriate items. Not obvious, but not so out of the norm to be absurd. He didn't want people to be dismissive and chalk it up to a Ripley's Believe It or Not! moment. A thousand eyes staring. None too memorable, except her. She was the key. They had to pick her, or this plan wouldn't work.

One last look at his work. The job was nearly finished. He just needed to wipe every available surface for fingerprints. It wouldn't take long, as he made a habit of wearing latex gloves. He never used the bathroom in the apartment for fear of leaving DNA. A quick check for items out of place. He saw nothing.

Smiling at his accomplishment, he headed out the door, wiping the handle as he left.

—⁓—

The sound of his phone ringing shook him from a dead sleep. The ring was irritating, like nails on a chalkboard. That ring meant Detective Renquest, and if he was calling, they had caught another case.

"This is Dodge."

The voice on the other end was unfamiliar. "This is Officer Jenkins with Metro PD," the voice said.

"Officer Jenkins? Put Renquest on the damn phone."

"Detective Renquest asked me to call you and told me—"

Dodge cut him off. "What do you want?"

The man's voice crackled nervously. "The detective asked me to call you, sir."

Dodge waited for the officer to offer more information. "I need to know where you're at, son."

"Yes, sir. Sorry, Agent Dodge." The young officer gave him the location and told him where to park once he arrived at the scene.

"Tell Renquest I'll be there in twenty minutes. I need to stop for coffee." Dodge didn't enjoy morning calls. They always involved a corpse. A dead body and Detective Renquest having a street cop call to mess with him made for a terrible day. Wearing only boxer shorts, he crawled out of bed and trudged to the bathroom to take care of his morning business.

In his bed, covered in a blanket, a woman awoke.

"Who was that?"

Dodge had a mouth full of toothpaste, which he spit out before answering.

"Dodge, who was that?"

"It was Renquest," he said. "I have to meet him downtown."

"Another case?"

"Looks that way."

"Why can't people wait until after lunch before starting their workday?"

Dodge agreed. There should be a gentleman's agreement stating neither party will cause any drama until after noon. The idea didn't seem unreasonable to him. Heads of criminal organizations and the police department could meet in an unassuming warehouse by the docks to make an agreement. He knew this wasn't realistic, but a guy could dream.

"Do you still want to meet tonight?" she asked.

"I'll call and let you know once I know what my role will be."

Sometimes work with the task force dragged late into the night. It wasn't uncommon for him to walk through the front door well after midnight. Working sex crimes was a dirty business. Because many sexual crimes happen at night, like rape and sexual assault, it was late-night business. The exception to that rule was when a child was involved. Many times, the people that call the police on child sexual crimes are custodians and teachers, people that see the victim during the daylight hours.

"That's fine."

Dodge nodded.

"I'll let myself out," she said.

Clothed and clean-shaven, he reappeared from the bathroom. There were two pieces of toilet paper stuck to his face to stop the fresh shave cuts from bleeding. He sat on the bed to put his shoes on, then reached onto the bedside table and pulled out his duty weapon and badge.

Sitting up, the woman grabbed Dodge's arm. He leaned over to kiss her on the forehead. She plucked the pieces of clotting material stuck to his face. He flinched.

"Thanks," he said.

"Be careful."

"Always."

With that, Dodge walked out. He thought of her lying in the still-warm bed, knowing she would be watching his car's taillights fade from the window. Being a parole agent gave him a trust factor of just above freezing, so the thought of leaving anyone alone with his personal property twitched a nerve. It made him feel uncomfortable. But it was different this time. He and this woman were linked by an event neither of them asked to be part of. He hadn't heard from her in a couple of years. Then, out of the blue a week ago, she had walked into the parole office and asked to see him. The two talked for an hour over coffee.

Kelly told him how she had left the streets and gotten clean over a year ago. She was taking classes at the local community college at night. She said there were daytime classes, but night classes gave her something to do at night, a check-and-balance approach. She needed to have something to hold herself accountable so she didn't slip back into old habits. He liked her. He had always wanted her. Then, last night happened. It was easy. She felt comfortable to him. The good and bad memories flooded back. He shook off the thoughts in his head as he approached the area of the crime scene.

Dodge pulled up to the address the police officer had texted him. A standard apartment, the building wasn't the worst he had processed. Crime scenes were often in places most people never wanted to visit, but this one didn't appear to be such from the outside appearance. The building had a brown brick façade with a set of concrete stairs leading up to the front door. A second set of stairs, down and to the left, led to a service entrance built for unloading coal used for heating. The building was originally built for upper-class business owners who couldn't yet afford the high cost of home ownership in the downtown area. Apartments allowed businessmen and their families to live near downtown for convenience and status. Now, the building was mixed housing, with low-income apartments.

Walking up the front steps, Dodge placed his half-smoked cigarette in his pocket after extinguishing it on the sole of his shoe. It was a habit he learned in the Air Force, not leaving trash on the deck. That day, it was crime scene integrity. DNA pulled from a butt left behind could match a suspect in days. No need to muddy the waters with his DNA and give a defense attorney a chance to poke holes in the case. As Dodge approached the front door, a street cop nodded. He nodded back.

Upon entering the building, he began climbing the stairs. People rarely died on the first floor, especially overweight folks. He was told once there were always three medical examiners for bodies on the second floor and above. One to do the examination and two to carry the gurney. Dodge didn't notice a medical examiner's van when he arrived. Maybe they weren't on scene yet, or they had finished. Hopefully, the detective on scene had waited for him before releasing the body to the coroner. An examination of the crime scene with the victim present made it easier to determine what exactly had happened. Lack of a body made a tough job more difficult. His anger started to build as he stepped onto the second-floor landing.

Working sex crimes wasn't new to Paul Dodge. He spent ten years in the Air Force as an SP, the Air Force's equivalent to a civilian police officer, where he ran into more than his fair share of rapes and sexual assaults. In fact, a case he worked with local law enforcement, for which he received an accommodation, helped him get his current position as a state parole agent working with convicted sex offenders and his spot on the local sex crimes task force. He had never wanted to work in this field but realized he had a knack for it the same way some people excel in sports. A good shortstop can tell which way a batter will hit the ball by his stance in the batter's box. He will pick up on a weight shift from one leg to the other or a quick glance to the outfield by the batter and adjust his defensive stance. That was how Dodge was with a crime scene. He looked at a scene and noticed what others missed. He noticed tiny nuances seasoned detectives with years more experience than him had not seen. He turned the corner and proceeded past the third floor.

Active listening was an important skill in his work. He found that by paying attention to what others around him were talking about, he could extrapolate pieces of information, analyze what he had heard, and use that information to learn what interests a person had. Once he knew what someone cared about, it was effortless to do the research and insert himself into a conversation. People talk about what interests them. They want acceptance. This is a genuine flaw of human beings and the best way to exploit them.

Dodge continued past a uniformed officer stationed at the landing between the fourth and fifth floors. On the fifth-floor landing, he encountered two officers in full uniform. The first officer made eye contact as Dodge moved off the last step and onto the small landing. Dodge knew the officer and didn't care for him. He guessed the feeling was mutual.

"The detective is in there," the officer said.

Dodge handed the first officer his empty coffee cup of coffee. "Two creams and one sugar, and don't fill it too full," he said, entering the apartment.

"Screw you, Dodge! Who does he think he is?"

The second officer cracked a smile. "Don't worry about him, Jimmy. He's an asshole. No one likes him, not even the detective, but he has to call him because of politics."

The first officer shook his head and tossed the coffee cup on the ground. "Yeah, screw him and his coffee."

Dodge continued past without giving the comments a second thought. He entered the crime scene and into his world.

His examination of a crime scene was routine. First, visually inspect the entire room. What stands out? Are there drugs on the coffee table or a digital scale on a windowsill? Second, check for computers and other digital devices that may contain evidence of a crime. It was common to find emails, text messages, and photos on personal cell phones that documented the hours or minutes before someone died. He saw nothing. There wasn't even a body. Why the hell was he called?

A voice booming from the far corner of the room broke Dodge's concentration.

"Dodge, it's about time." It was Detective Renquest. "You look like hell, man."

He ignored the comment. "What do we have here?"

"We got a call from the guy down at the Center for Missing

and Exploited Children saying they had information on a kiddie porn distribution site."

Dodge again glanced around the room. "I see no one in handcuffs. Is a victim being questioned or a body lying under this trash?"

"There was no one home when we arrived. A preliminary search has turned up squat."

Dodge shrugged. He had still not heard why they called him.

Detective Renquest continued, "The analyst received an invitation into a chat room where he met our guy."

"What guy, and how did you arrive at this specific apartment?"

The two men had worked together long enough to know he liked to tell stories. He even tried to imitate voices. All the voices sounded the same, but Renquest got a chuckle out of it.

"After the chat room, the suspect asked for a meeting to swap kiddie porn movies. This is the address he proposed. Once here, HQ instructed me to call you and have you take the lead on the investigation."

This surprised Dodge. In his experience, PD always took the lead. His role was always supportive, aiding with profiles and technical knowledge in areas where the detectives were less familiar. Why did the brass defer the investigation to him? The parole agent knew he wouldn't get an answer from Renquest and turned his attention back to the crime scene.

"Why meet in person? Why not share the files over a secure connection through peer-to-peer software?"

Renquest shrugged. "We got the call from the tech and set up the sting here."

Everything appeared wrong to Dodge. It was too risky for peddlers of child porn to meet in person; in that, Renquest was correct. Files traded online using untraceable user names and paid for with bitcoin was the norm. It was quick, and no one saw your face. Why the change? He looked around for Renquest, who was instructing an evidence technician on the proper way to work a crime scene. For all his faults, Renquest was as good as it got for maintaining crime scene integrity. He paid attention to the little details and ran his scene like a general commanding a troop of soldiers in battle. Precise and efficient.

Dodge noticed something different at this crime scene, besides the lack of a body or computers. The place was a trash pit. Whoever had been living there had not made use of either the trash can or recycling container in the kitchen. Food containers and old pizza boxes littered the floor. It was impossible to take a step without hearing the crunch of plastic underfoot. It was one of the filthiest places he ever had to work.

"Get your gloves on," Dodge said.

"Do you think it will matter?"

Renquest had forgotten his gloves in the car, and his partner handed him an extra pair.

"No gloves, rookie mistake."

As the two men rifled through mountains of garbage in the room, Dodge wondered why a person who dealt in kiddie porn had no computers. It was uncommon for a child porn offender to not use multiple computers and phones. Dodge reached into his pocket and pulled out his cell phone, selecting an app that picked up Wi-Fi and Bluetooth signals within ten feet. The program ignored any weak, public, or intermittent signals.

"Hot date?" Renquest asked.

"I wanted to test out a new app I installed."

He walked around the room with his phone held out in front of him, like an old-fashioned Geiger counter.

"Find anything?"

Dodge slipped the phone back into his pocket. "No Wi-Fi signal. How did he plan to trade the material, VHS tapes?"

"Maybe he took the computers with him."

Dodge was quick to dismiss this theory. Why take his equipment with him if he didn't know the meeting was a setup? And why didn't anyone notice a guy carrying multiple computers down five flights of stairs? An evidence tech appeared from the door leading to the bedroom, breaking his concentration.

"You two need to come in here."

The bedroom resembled the rest of the apartment home. Half-eaten sandwiches and empty gas station fountain soda cups covered the floor. There was a small path cleared through the middle of the room, where the techs and evidence team moved items on the floor, being careful to photograph each piece before placing it in an evidence bag for examination later. It reminded Dodge of a documentary he had watched on one of those animal channels about a colony of ants in the South American jungle, the worker ants foraging for food to bring back to the queen and feed the larva. The worker ants cut a mile-long path through the jungle and devoured everything that got in their way. Evidence techs were the worker ants, and Renquest was the queen.

"What a shithole," Renquest said.

"If you and Agent Dodge will follow me to the closet, I'll show you what I found," the tech said. "Please try to stay on the path."

The excavated path wasn't big enough for both men, and neither cared. They both ignored it, making a beeline straight for the closet.

"Detective! Agent!" the tech begged. "Stay on the path, please."

The two men stood in front of the closet. The doors were economy sliding doors that folded into themselves when moved to the side.

"Don't worry about the rest of the room," Dodge told the crime scene tech.

"Why?"

"Whatever we are searching for will be in this closet," Renquest said.

It was an organized closet. Clothes appeared sorted according to season from left to right, with T-shirts first. Next were long-sleeved dress shirts. Last were sweatshirts and light jackets. Everything faced the same direction. Each hanger was spaced with a one-inch gap between it and the next one.

The tech shook his head, got on his knees, and disappeared

under the dress shirts into the closet. Dodge knelt to one knee and heard a voice echoing from the back wall.

"You're both wrong. Everything we need to find isn't in this closet. It's through the closet."

The back wall was fashioned into a sliding door using a system of rails and counterweights. A slight amount of pressure in just the correct spot on the door caused it to slide to the right, revealing its secret. Dodge peered up and back at Renquest, who had a puzzled expression on his face.

"What?" Renquest asked.

"It's a hidden room."

"A hidden room?"

"Yeah. It's built into the back of the closet." Dodge turned his attention back to the closet, reached into his pocket, and turned on a flashlight, shining it toward the discovery.

"While you check out the spank room, I'll hang out here and make sure the crime scene guys get things wrapped up on time," Renquest said.

"Of course," Dodge said as he crawled through the entrance, and the light from his flashlight illuminated more of the space. He and Renquest had been correct. The closet was the key.

CHAPTER 2

THE MORNING SUN FOUND ITS WAY through the curtains, shielding Dodge's bedroom from the world. It was a crisp fall morning. A single ray of warm light focused on Kelly's cheek as she tried to fight the urge to wake up. Kelly didn't enjoy mornings and thought it was one thing that Dodge liked about her. He typically woke up at five in the morning, using that time to catch up on his casework. Kelly remained in the bedroom, allowing an overworked man to have his time. He would bring her a cup of coffee at half-past eight. They would then decide on plans for that evening.

Kelly wasn't a fan of Dodge's job. This was mainly because their relationship could never evolve, as he was a parole agent and she was a former call girl. But also, because the daily work with sex offenders wore on his psyche and made him paranoid. She used subtle hints to point out these disadvantages about his job and the toll she saw it taking on him.

A firm sense of duty, instilled in him by his service in the Air Force, meant he would never quit. But it also involved ego. Dodge didn't trust anyone else to do the work. The risk was too high to allow someone else to watch over the rapists, child molesters, and sexual deviants he had on his caseload. What if another agent screwed up and someone got hurt? Living with that would be too hard, he would tell her. It was all ego. Deep down, she knew that.

After about five minutes, Kelly opened her eyes and welcomed in the morning. She sat up in bed and saw her robe on the floor, right where it had fallen last night. Looking around for slippers to ward off the shock of the chilled hardwood, she considered not staying in bed. A glance at the clock on the bedside table alerted her that it was time to get her day started. The clock read 9:07 a.m., almost mocking her for being lazy. Kelly forced herself into the bathroom, where she washed her face, brushed her teeth, and tied her hair into a ponytail. Her hair was often in a ponytail during the day. She only styled it for evening activities. When unmotivated, a baseball cap with her ponytail pulled through the opening in the back worked well. Dodge liked the ballcap look, and she wore her hair that way from time to time to please him.

After putting on clean clothes, she ventured into the kitchen for a cup of coffee. The pot was empty. Kelly reached for the coffee beans and remembered they had meant to pick up coffee filters before returning home, but Dodge had not wanted to stop at the store. She looked around for a coffee filter substitute. Once, she tried to use a piece of paper towel in place of a coffee filter. The only thing that experiment accomplished was clogging the machine and forcing coffee to spill out on the counter.

"I guess I'll go to the corner store and grab a cup to go." Kelly grabbed her purse, along with a key ring containing the front-door key. She turned north toward the caffeine dispensary she desperately needed. Kelly noticed her phone vibrating through the sides of her designer purse. She wasn't expecting a call.

"Why do I keep throwing it in there?" she said. It was a question she had the answer to. The couple had had this conversation a few weeks ago after dinner at Micki Angelo's, an Italian restaurant downtown. Dodge and the owner had attended the same high school. He always made sure they received a table with a view of all the exits. Kelly didn't understand Dodge's obsession with facing the doors in a restaurant. She asked him about it once. He told her he just liked to see who would dine with them that evening. She knew it was a lie and never questioned him about it again.

A shout came from behind her. She felt a firm grasp on

her left arm, right above the elbow, and a force pulling her backward, forcing her to shout in pain. Before Kelly could turn around to see who grabbed her, a bus approached. In an attempt to free her arm from the man's grasp, she jerked it back, losing her balance in the process. Her right foot slipped off the curb, and the bus's rear tire caught her ankle, pulling her under the two sets of rear wheels as the bus passed.

Crowds of onlookers gasped at the gruesome scene. One man attempted to provide CPR, but too much blood was pooled in her mouth and nose. She was dead. Her chest had been crushed by the massive weight of the bus tires rolling over her body. Her neck was twisted, facing the wrong anatomical direction. Her neck looked like a towel that had the water rung out of it. It was a quick death.

In the back of the crowd, a man stood with his phone in the air. Every bystander was looking at the woman. No one had paid any attention to him at all. His repeated practice had paid off. Reach out, make contact with the arm, appearing to grab but pushing slightly, and the bus would do the rest. He had underestimated the force of the initial blast of air as the bus passed. The strength of the blast almost knocked him off balance. He stood still while the crowd reformed over the dead woman's body. Most of the witnesses had their phones out. Everyone was snapping pictures of the gruesome scene. He did the same. A picture wasn't required for the transaction, but it couldn't hurt. Then, he slowly backed away toward the alley.

Once around the corner, the man reached into his pocket and pulled out a different cell phone. He dialed and waited for an answer.

"Yeah, it's me," he said. "It was the girl…I got close enough to smell her perfume. That's how I know. It's done. I'll expect payment as agreed upon."

The man disconnected and dropped the phone on the ground, smashing it with his shoe. His heel ground the device into a pile of broken plastic and glass, then he disappeared down the alley.

CHAPTER 3

The beam from the flashlight jumped across the walls of the tiny room. Hundreds of faces—men, women, and children of all ages and ethnicities. Finally, it focused on a single photo. The face was pale. Her deep brown eyes stared back at Dodge. The face of the teen girl reminded him of Kelly.

The evidence tech interrupted the silence. "Agent Dodge, have you ever seen a room like this?"

"I doubt anyone has."

The tech set up a portable lamp, lighting the entire room with the flick of a switch. Photos covered every wall. What appeared to be an unused mattress lay in the middle of the room. While the rest of the apartment was a trash pit, this room was pristine. Based on what Dodge thought this room was used for, it should be considered a hazmat zone.

"You suppose that is where he assaults his victims?" the tech asked, pointing at the mattress.

"Not likely. It looks as if no one has slept there."

"Maybe this was his spank room."

"Possibly."

Pushing with his hands, Dodge spun on his knees and crawled out of the room.

"How do you want me to handle the pictures?"

"Bag and tag them. Have a courier send the box over to my office, and I'll take a longer look at them today." Dodge paused. "Make sure you photograph everything before removing any pictures."

The tech nodded.

Once in the bedroom, the parole agent stood up. His knees popped, causing him to sigh. He could hear Renquest in the living room, barking out orders to the other crime scene techs. He took one last glance at the bedroom, then joined Renquest.

"What did you find?"

"It looks like a spank room, but I'm not sure what to make of it."

"Is something in particular making you so indecisive?"

Dodge paused. "The room was spotless. The mattress appeared to be new."

"There was a mattress in there?"

"Yeah, surrounded by hundreds of pictures on the walls."

"Any kiddie porn?" Renquest asked.

"Not that I saw. There also wasn't a pattern regarding age or gender."

"That's strange. Could the perp be victim neutral?"

"Most sex offenders have specific victimology," Dodge said.

Renquest nodded because his partner was correct. Most sex offenders had a type. Many offenders prefer prepubescent children, while others choose teens. Still, others picked the elderly. Dodge knew a few offenders that didn't conform to a specific age group when selecting victims. Both men were rapists, where power was the real gratification, not sex. Both were still in prison.

"If you want the evidence, it'll have to clear command staff, but I don't think that'll be a problem," Renquest said.

"Call me if you pick up the guy who lives here. I want to be present for the interview."

"You can do the interview."

"Let's wait until we know what we have. For now, I'll plan on just observing." Dodge needed to check in at the office and brief Chief Johnson on the case.

It was ten in the morning when he arrived at his office. The parking lot was full of offenders reporting to take drug screens before going to work. It could be hard for people with felony convictions to find work. Assisting in the job search was one of a parole agent's primary duties. Most of the offenders who reported in the morning worked in the food service industry. Restaurants, from McDonald's to the most luxurious steakhouses, needed bodies to cook, clean vacated tables, serve food, and wash dishes. Restaurant managers didn't care about criminal records or prior drug use, and State Parole provided a steady flow. This was the population that kept the parole office humming during the late-morning hours. Many restaurants didn't open until between 11:00 a.m. to 1:00 p.m., and parolees could drop a drug test on the way to work.

Taking the last drag from his cigarette, Dodge pinched out the cherry, put the butt in his pocket, and entered the front lobby.

"Morning, Agent Dodge," the security guard said.

The metal detector beeped as he walked between the sensors. The walk-through metal detectors had been purchased after an offender tried to bring a gun into the building when his parole agent filed a violation report concerning his poor performance on supervision. Dodge was in the lobby when the offender arrived and noticed the bulge in his jacket. The guy's hand never touched his gun. The well-trained agent pulled his duty weapon and had sight alignment before the offender finished sweeping his coat for an unobstructed draw. It ended there. The offender was arrested and returned to prison with new convictions for good measure.

Pulling his jacket back, Dodge revealed his weapon. "Morning, Stan."

The elevator doors opened to a chaotic scene involving offenders and agents. It was a battle of wits and stamina over how long the offender could hold out before the agent caved. Dodge didn't love the struggle but thrived on the chaos. Chief Johnson was talking to two suits in his office as Dodge made his way through the myriad of desks.

"Good Morning, Chief," he said, passing the chief's office.

The chief had his usual expression of displeasure, and

Dodge was sure it was his fault. The two men had a tenuous relationship. Each respected the other's abilities, but neither of them excelled at communicating how they felt. The lack of open communication between them often led to arguments on how a parole agent should do his job.

"Where the hell have you been, Dodge? Crap's hitting the fan, and my office is a suit toilet."

"Came straight from the call out this morning, Chief. What's with that?" Dodge nodded toward the two men in the chief's office.

"They are waiting for you. The suits are U.S. Marshals here to talk to you."

"To me or about me?"

"Well, you weren't here, so it was about you."

Chief Johnson didn't enjoy working with the Feds. There would be consequences for the responsible party.

"Any chance you just tell me now?"

"Not a chance in hell. If I have to talk to them, so do you." Chief Johnson had one rule. If he was in the shit, so were you.

"OK. Let me grab a cup of coffee."

Chief Johnson returned to his office, while Dodge poured a cup of coffee and watched the men in the office before joining them. The two men must have had other plans because they headed to the elevator before he reached the office. As Dodge entered Chief Johnson's office, it seemed every eye in the place was on him. He shut the door behind him and pulled the cord hanging by the window. The blinds let out a screech as they dropped to the windowsill. Dodge sat on a sofa across from the chief's desk.

"So, what did they want?"

"They got word of your call out today," Chief Johnson said. "One picture on the wall set off an alert in the Marshals Office."

Dodge was surprised. He had not mentioned the hidden room to anyone since leaving the crime scene.

"How did they hear about it so fast? I came straight here, and the techs were processing it." Not enough time had passed to finish collecting the evidence. Besides, Renquest always called when the techs finished, giving a timeline for processing the evidence. "They haven't even finished bagging the place yet," Dodge said.

"The deputies didn't say, and I doubt they will share the name of their mole with me," Chief Johnson said.

How had the Feds learned about the room, and what implications will it have on my investigation? Dodge wondered.

"The picture was of a teenage daughter of a local federal judge."

Chief Johnson's words snapped Dodge out of his thoughts of marshals and police moles. "What the hell is a picture of a federal judge's daughter doing in that room?"

"That's what they hoped you would be able to answer."

It had surprised Dodge that the U.S. Marshals Office asked for his help. He had had a run-in a few years ago with the local marshals over a fugitive parolee arrested in a bordering state. The marshals had not wanted to pick up and transport the offender due to a clerical error on the arrest warrant, so he used his local media connections and got the story on the nightly news. The story snowballed to a national level. When the cable news outlets picked it up, DC got involved, and the local Assistant U.S. Marshal ended up with egg on his face. They ordered him to transport the prisoner and bear the brunt of the cost. The name Paul Dodge had been a curse word at the federal courthouse since that day.

"What is it they think I can do besides work the case?"

"Do you remember a few years back when the Feds were using actual Department of Corrections offenders to teach profiling techniques to their academy trainees?"

"Yeah. The Feds hit up Smith at Rolling Meadows and, uh, Fernandez at Taylorville," Dodge answered.

"Well, during that experiment, they met an inmate they think may help with this case," Chief Johnson said.

Dodge knew Smith and Fernandez, and they were of no use. What other inmates did the Feds talk to who were intelligent enough to use in a profiling case? Then, it hit him. He felt acid in his stomach rise to his throat. It burned and caused him to clear his airway.

"Are you fucking kidding me?" The chief held his hands out, signaling Dodge to relax, but he was furious. "I won't talk to that narcissistic fuck. Not for anyone!"

Chief Johnson leaned back in his chair to try and de-escalate the tension. Dodge recognized the gesture, took a deep breath, and stretched out his fingers to let the blood flow to his extremities. He had not even noticed he was making fists so tight his knuckles had turned purple. He gave Dodge a moment.

"That's what I told them," he said.

"What else did you tell them?"

"I told them I wouldn't make you go, and the department, nor anyone else, couldn't force you to either. Because of your poor attitude and penchant for disobeying orders."

Dodge forced a smile because he didn't know what to say.

"Just give it some thought and give me your decision tomorrow," Chief Johnson said. "Either way, I'll support your decision."

"I haven't said no, but hell, it's not even lunchtime."

"Minor victories," Chief Johnson answered.

Upon returning to his office, Dodge was reminded of the work he had to do by the pile of files he needed to review before appointments started reporting in.

CHAPTER 4

TRUTH BE TOLD, Dodge had no intention of driving three hours to meet with Grayson Heller. The only contact the pair had had since his conviction was at his last parole hearing. Dodge attended to remind the parole board of Grayson's violent past and protest his release. Being a victim, as well as the one who caught him, his testimony carried more weight than normal with the parole board. The board members kept Grayson right where he was, in a six-by-twelve cage. The one thing they could count on was that Dodge planned to attend every parole hearing to make sure that never changed.

After meeting with three of the five parolees scheduled to report that day, Dodge talked to Chief Johnson again. Something concerning the earlier meeting with the marshals was eating at him.

"Hey, Chief. Got a sec?"

"I have a few minutes before a phone call with the regional director. What's on your mind?"

"What did you ask for in return for my talking to Grayson?"

"You know something, I forgot to ask for anything. I'll make a note of it for later."

Chief Johnson, a traditional law enforcement guy, played the game well. He always worked an angle when it revolved around Dodge and a task force case. This angle dangled Dodge as bait for a favor returnable at a later date.

"Now that I get screwed with my pants on, what do they want me to talk to Grayson about?"

"My best guess is the marshals were watching the house. When the first cruisers arrived on scene, they started monitoring police bands on the radio," Chief Johnson said.

"I am still not sure how one missing girl in a room with hundreds of pictures popped that quickly in the missing person database."

"That's the odd part."

"What do you mean?"

The chief hesitated. "The girl isn't missing. She is home and safe with a marshal's detail."

"Was she ever missing?"

"Nope. Changes things a little, doesn't it?"

Dodge was quiet for a moment. He understood the Feds wanting to keep a judge's daughter safe, but they didn't need him or Grayson. The daughter would no doubt have a protective detail assigned to her and would no longer in immediate danger.

"How did they manage a match of the picture so fast?"

"Someone in the police department recognized the girl and tipped off the marshals would be my guess. It is not the first time local police leaked information to an outside agency for personal gain."

Command Staff at the local PD leaked information to anyone they thought gave them an edge in the public relations game, and Dodge knew it.

"OK, let's say I buy that explanation. Why Grayson?" he asked.

"Because they have zero leads and a father who is on the federal bench. You think the almighty Marshals Service wants our help? Your help? They want answers before going to the judge to explain they don't have shit."

Now Dodge understood. The marshals protect the judge and his family. To allow a stalker close enough to get pictures of his daughter was bad. People got transferred to Alaska for the rest of their careers for mistakes such as that. He was the patsy if everything went to shit, but something still bothered him.

"Does the timing make sense to you, Chief? I left the scene

an hour ago, and marshals are in your office before I can get back."

"This entire thing leaves an itch I can't scratch. Every time I get involved with the Feds, I get stuck with the shitty end of the digging stick."

In the past, Dodge and Chief Johnson had worked multiple cases with the Feds. State agents did the legwork, and the federal agencies swooped in to make the arrest. News cameras were everywhere with no shortage of Federals willing to describe their part in the successful capture of a dangerous felon. They left DOC swinging in the wind. Not a single mention of their role in the apprehension. Both men held grudges to this day.

"True story. But before I beg for information from that sociopath, let's see what I dig up about who lives in that apartment," Dodge said.

"That's what I was thinking," Chief Johnson stated. He looked into the bullpen and pointed. "You want me to put Robbie on it?"

"No, I'll have an analyst from the task force do it. It is what they get paid for. Once the pictures and other evidence gets here, have them scanned into the database and see if we get any other hits. It might give us a lead on who this guy is if he has ever been in the prison system."

The chief looked at his subordinate. His eyes grew narrow. "You have one live girl on that wall. My question is, how many are dead?"

The same thought bounced around Dodge's head as he turned to exit Chief Johnson's office. He stopped before leaving and turned to face Chief Johnson. "This might end up being a real shit sandwich. All I'll be able to eat for a while."

"Like you have done any actual work here in the past six months."

On his way out of the office, Dodge stopped by the technology office to tell forensics to expect evidence boxes later. The forensics technician, Robbie, wasn't part of the task force, but Dodge got approval for funding, providing a stipend when

Robbie worked on non-DOC cases. Robbie liked the challenge, and Dodge enjoyed not relying on the police lab for forensic results.

"Hey, Dodge," Robbie said. "What can I do for you?"

"Expect a package of photos and other evidence delivered by courier later today."

"From the thing this morning?"

"Yes. And I want to be the first person you talk to if you find something."

"Roger that, Dodge," Robbie said.

"Good. I don't want to hear anything on the news. The Feds breathing down my back because of a leak is the last thing I need."

"You're my first call."

"Thanks," he said.

After reaching the elevator, Dodge pushed the button for the lobby. It had been an interminable day so far, and he needed coffee and a smoke before formulating a plan to deal with Grayson Heller tomorrow. He did not want to show up at the prison and just wing it. Grayson was too smart for that. Dodge needed control of the entire interview from start to finish.

———⁓∿⁓———

When Dodge arrived home, a patrol car and an unmarked cruiser were parked in front of his townhouse. The unmarked vehicle looked like every other unmarked cruiser in the city: a late-model sedan tagged with out-of-state license plates. The windows were tinted darker than the law allowed for civilian vehicles, and a small round GPS tracking antenna was attached to the roof. *Who do they think they are fooling with these cars?* he thought. *They might as well be in a black and white.*

A uniformed officer sat in the marked unit. He was concentrating on his smartphone and didn't see the truck until it pulled up next to his driver's side door. The unmarked unit had two people inside. Dodge couldn't tell if they were wearing uniforms but assumed the two would be in plain clothes—likely cheap suits bought at the local dress clothes store during a buy-one-get-three-free sale. Cops made a small salary, and most couldn't afford to have more than one custom-tailored suit. Dodge pulled up next to the unmarked unit and rolled down his window. The driver of the car did the same.

"Do you mind moving your vehicle? You're in my spot," Dodge said.

"Are you Paul Dodge?" the man in the car asked.

"Who is asking?"

The man opened his door and stepped out into the street. "I am Detective Hanson with the county sheriff's office homicide unit."

Dodge turned on his hazard blinkers, got out of the truck, and walked over to Detective Hanson. The other detective stayed inside the vehicle, appearing to pay little attention to what his partner was doing.

"I'm Paul Dodge. What can I do for you, Detective?"

Detective Hanson shifted his weight, reached into his pocket, and pulled out a crinkled business card. He handed the card to Dodge, who immediately recognized it. It was one of his own issued by the Department of Corrections.

"This is my business card. Where did you get it?" Dodge asked.

"We found it on the body of a woman downtown. We were wondering how she got your card."

Dodge paused before answering. He didn't give up many details about anything without knowing where it was leading to. "As you probably saw on the card, I am a parole agent with the Department of Corrections. I give out hundreds of my cards every month. Where did you find this one, on a junkie?"

At that moment, the other detective exited the car and stood next to his partner. Detective Hanson took a step back.

After an awkward silence, the other man spoke. "I am Detective Keller. I work in the Vice Squad." Dodge said nothing. Detective Keller continued, "I received a call today from

Detective Hanson concerning a woman hit and killed by a city bus this afternoon."

"Since when does a homicide and vice detective get called to a pedestrian-bus accident?" Dodge asked.

"By city statute, the sheriff's office investigates any accident resulting in death on or by city property. The intent was to assign those cases to an outside agency for transparency," Detective Keller said.

Makes sense, Dodge thought. "So, it takes two detectives to investigate a pedestrian-bus accident? It seems to me to be a poor allocation of resources."

Detective Hanson stepped forward. "I was the original detective assigned to go to the scene to determine if what happened was an accident, or if we would need more investigation. Several witnesses said a man grabbed the woman and tried to pull her back before the bus hit her. The funny thing was no one could find him. He left before the cops arrived."

Not liking where the conversation was headed, Dodge said, "What does this have to do with me? Like I said, I have handed out many business cards throughout my career."

"I called Detective Keller after I realized who the woman was from her driver's license." Dodge said nothing. "Her name was Kelly Gosling. She was a known prostitute in the area. We ran her rap sheet, and she came up clean over the past five years. Not a single bust for drugs or turning tricks. Yet she had your business card in her wallet. Care to tell us where you were today around noon?"

The news hit Dodge like a sledgehammer to the chest. He concentrated on holding his composure. "I was at a crime scene all morning. You can call Detective Renquest with Metro PD. He will verify my whereabouts."

"We will," Detective Keller said. "Why did she have your business card?"

"She could have gotten it from someone on parole. Sometimes our cards get passed around like currency. You see, parole agents have lists of community resources. We often help citizens not on supervision. But Ms. Gosling had my card because I knew her, and since you said you recognized her, I am guessing *you* knew that already."

"We read the story about you rescuing her from that psychopath. What was that, about ten years ago?" Detective Hanson asked.

"Almost eleven," Dodge said.

"Well, we just needed to cross a few things off the list before we go public with the findings," Detective Hanson said.

"So, you think it was an accident?"

"Witnesses said she had her face buried in her phone right before it happened. She probably didn't see the bus coming. You know how it is these days. People walk around like zombies, their eyes glued to their phones, afraid to miss the next great tweet or whatever."

"What about this Good Samaritan? The guy witnesses said grabbed her."

"We couldn't pin him down, and none of the witnesses could say for sure if they saw him push her," Detective Keller said. "Detective Hanson will gather any video of the incident from camera footage in the area. I'll search the internet for any videos that might have been uploaded from the accident scene. But for now, it is looking like an accident."

Dodge thanked the two detectives and parked his truck in the empty space left by the black and white. He sat in his truck, staring out the windshield. She had just been in his bed, not twelve hours ago. He decided not to tell the detectives about their new relationship. He had nothing to do with her death, and they didn't get to know the details of his personal life. Besides, being a suspect in a death investigation wasn't something on his bucket list.

Once inside his house, Dodge poured a glass of bourbon, swallowing it in one gulp. He poured another, downing it like the first. With his arms hanging empty by his sides, he sat on the couch and glanced into the empty bedroom. He had known her for ten years but had been intimate with her for a few weeks.

Suppose the wrong people found out he had been keeping time with a former prostitute. He wasn't breaking any laws, but he knew the optics were terrible. At the current time, only his chief and Renquest knew about the relationship. And even they didn't know if he had slept with her yet. He had complete trust in both. He didn't have the same feelings concerning Detectives Hanson and Keller. If they found out, it could be the end of his career.

CHAPTER 5

ROLLING MEADOWS WAS ONE of the oldest prisons in the state. A fifteen-foot-tall stone wall topped with military-grade razor wire encased the grounds. Inside the walls, warehouse buildings, each half the size of a football field, were surrounded by stone paths and manicured lawns with signs declaring off-limits green spaces. Towers lined the perimeter wall where guards with assault rifles watched over the recreation yard.

Dodge entered the man trap after being searched by the corrections officers working Pod D that day. The first door shut behind him, but a minute passed before guards opened the second door leading into the tier section. He always hated the sound of the heavy clank as the doors locked behind him. It was an eerie feeling of being under another's control, unable to leave until that person released you. He wondered if that was how inmates felt, or if they had become immune to the routine. Dodge shuddered. He understood the risk of walking too close to either the outside wall or the cells. The cell blocks were three decks high, and moving further from them opened him up to having urine or feces tossed on him from the upper tiers. Walking near the bars of their cells allowed inmates to reach through and grab you or wipe substances on you. Again, the thought sent shivers up his spine.

As Dodge approached the end of the tier, a man in a suit with a corrections officer trailing close behind appeared. It was the warden, who greeted him with a handshake.

"Dodge, good to see you again. I hope your drive was pleasant," the warden said.

"I always say I'll buy a piece of property down here. Then I come here and remember why I hate this part of the state."

The warden smiled and gestured for to follow him. "It's not all bad."

They entered another man trap. Man traps are built by enclosing a small section of a hallway with a locking door on each side. An inmate or guard must enter the enclosed area, no bigger than a jail cell, and close the door behind before the second door will open, providing access to the other side. The door buzzed, granting access into another secure space away from the general population warehouse pod. Two inmates were mopping the floor. The air smelled of bleach. The warden pointed to a dirt smear on the floor as one inmate quickly moved to wipe it up.

"We have one of those fancy sushi places now."

Dodge tried to visualize the town and where a sushi restaurant might be. The entire town was one stoplight at intersecting highways. There was a laundromat, a dollar store, and a gas station. No bank or schools he could remember. It was literally the middle of nowhere.

"Where on Earth would they put a sushi restaurant in this town?"

The warden smiled. "It's at Clive's."

"The gas station?"

"Best food in town."

"Gas station sushi should be a reason for being locked in here."

"You don't know what you're missing."

The men navigated one more man trap and stopped in an area that contained individual interview rooms. A man was shackled to a metal table inside one room. It was Grayson Heller, but he looked older than the last time Dodge had seen him. His hair was gray and thinning. He had lost weight, maybe fifty pounds. He had excess skin, its elastic components unable to do the job of holding his skin tight. He looked old and feeble. Not the man who tried to kill him ten years earlier.

Before signaling the guard in the control pod to open the door, the warden warned Dodge. "Don't let his appearance fool you. He is one bad hombre and will shank you faster than you can blink."

Dodge thanked the warden for his insight and grabbed the door handle, waiting for the electronic lock to activate.

"Remember, he leaves the way he arrived. Catch my drift?" the warden stated.

"I won't be in there long enough for anything to happen," Dodge said.

The warden shook his head and motioned to the camera overhead to open the interview room door. A buzzing sound started, ending with the click of a lock. The room was compact. It had one window that let in faint amounts of natural sunlight. A metal table sat in the middle of the room with its legs bolted to the floor and a hardened steel chain linking the table and Grayson's chair. The chain had enough slack to allow the chair to slide backward. The legs to Dodge's chair were not tethered and made a screeching sound against the concrete floor as he pulled it out. Grayson spoke first.

"Agent Dodge, how nice it is to see you again. I wish they had told me you were coming."

The air was thick with the stench of sour breath and sweat. It was apparent Grayson hadn't showered. Dodge was sure Grayson did it to throw him off. The odor of soiled linens might force a quick end to an interview for most investigators, but it wasn't anything the grizzled veteran hadn't been exposed to thousands of times.

"It is a pleasure to see you here."

"Where else would I be?"

"Nowhere, and that is right where I plan to keep you."

The smile faded from Grayson's face. Dodge's strategy to control the interview was working. He doubted his bosses in the administration building would have approved of his technique.

For over a decade, the department had moved to a kinder and gentler way of dealing with offenders, one that promoted affirmation with positive feedback in place of negative reinforcement. The theory came from research that showed a higher chance of offender assimilation back into the community if agents were more positive during interactions. Dodge had read the study and was skeptical of the data and methodology. He believed politics dictated DOC policy, not science and data.

"What, no smartass comment?"

Grayson examined the cuffs and chain securing him to the table. "Few people have spoken to me that way, and those who did regretted it shortly thereafter."

"Threatening a parole agent. That's a bold choice. Not the direction 1 would have gone, but ten more years on your sentence should give you plenty of time to think about it." Dodge continued pushing. A little more. A little harder. "You know what your weakness is? You are predictable."

Grayson opened his mouth to speak, but was cut off before he could say anything.

Dodge continued, "Me, 1 don't give a fuck about how many people like me. Especially a bottom-feeding child rapist and murderer."

Grayson tilted his head to the side, a sign he was becoming irritated. 1t was time to slam the door shut on the meeting by coming full circle. "1 told the Feds you were full of shit, but they wanted me to come anyway. Now I've talked to you. Why don't you take a shower? 1 am sure you have made lots of friends in there."

Grayson leaped halfway across the table, forcing Dodge to use his legs to propel himself backward beyond his reach. The chains were tight with pressure, forcing the cuffs to dig into his wrists. A foamy drop of spit hung on the corner of his lip. The noise from the chair legs sliding on the concrete floor must have alerted the guards outside because they were yelling as they tried to open the door. Dodge motioned to the guards that he had it under control. They backed away but continued watching through the window. Grayson relaxed his body, and slack formed in the chains again. He laughed a hard, deep laugh that made his adversary uneasy.

"I told them you were a waste of time. Just a lonely fat old man who compensates his sexual inadequacies by raping women."

"I don't rape women," Grayson shouted.

"Keep telling yourself that." Dodge signaled the guards to open the door and took one last look at the room.

"Enjoy your stay. You not being able to do what I am about to is all I need to be happy."

"And what is that, Agent Dodge?"

"Walk out of here a free man," he said, half laughing. "Have a pleasant life. What's left of it."

Walking away, Dodge could hear Grayson's shouts echoing behind him as the guards rushed into the room to subdue him. The screams faded as he entered the man trap at the far end of the hall and the door closed behind him. A smile appeared on his face as he headed for the parking lot. His goal had been accomplished. He honored his word to the marshals by meeting with Grayson Heller, and it ended the way he had expected. Grayson didn't know anything concerning the judge's daughter, or he would have used it to keep Dodge in the interview room longer.

As Dodge reached the city limits, his phone buzzed. He had been out of cell phone range for an hour during the drive home, and someone had left a message. The number on the little screen showed *Unknown*. He hit the button preset for voicemail, and a voice came over the speakers of the truck.

This is Detective Hanson with the sheriff's office. We spoke briefly yesterday about the bus fatality. Uh, I just wanted to let you know that we have had several videos of the accident come into our possession over the past twelve hours. Several videos were from witnesses at the scene and not very useful. However, there was an ATM camera with a fisheye lens that caught the whole thing. I can't reveal too much during an active investigation, but the man witnesses described as grabbing the victim by the arm is known to us. He is not the "helping a stranger" kind of guy. We are keeping the file open and investigating it as a suspicious death. I just wanted to let you know. If you have questions, please call Detective Keller or me. You have our numbers.

Dodge felt the blood rush out of his face. Who would want to hurt Kelly? Did something from her past get her killed? This was the reason she had left her old life, why she had gotten clean. Over a year had passed since she last worked the street. That was a long time for someone to wait for revenge.

Dodge's face flushed, and he felt anger building in the pit of his stomach. The clock on the radio showed the time as 16:23. Most staff left his office by four-thirty or five. He was still a half hour from the office in this traffic. Besides, he needed a drink and a shower to wash off the stench of the prison. Then a thought entered his head. It was like a light bulb suddenly turning on in a dark room. His and Kelly's past was shared by one more person. Grayson Heller. Dodge wondered if he had gotten even with Kelly for testifying against him and sealing his fate? Did he have the reach outside the prison walls to pull off a murder? He looked at his jacket and could still smell Grayson's breath lingering on his clothes, forcing a gag reflex. First things first, a shower.

CHAPTER 6

THE LAST REMNANTS OF SUNLIGHT had crossed the floor of the living room, and light from streetlamps took over where the sun left off. Dodge sat at his makeshift desk in the dining room of his townhome. It was littered with photos and old case files. The parole tech had received the evidence boxes with all the pictures found at the scene over twelve hours ago and delivered them to him as instructed. He attempted to organize the photos into piles based on approximate age and gender to narrow a victim typology. *It should make identifying other potential victims easier,* he thought.

He created two piles on his desk, one stack for males and one for females. After sorting the pictures by gender, he divided the images by age. One group contained any photograph where the victim appeared to be younger than twenty-five. The other contained the pictures of where the person in the image appeared to be twenty-five or older. By maintaining the gender status, he had four easier-to-manage stacks of photographs.

Dodge knew one photo contained a live underage victim, the judge's daughter. Again, he wondered what the purpose was of the room full of pictures. Nothing about the case made sense. Currently, too many unknowns remained to draw any conclusions about the suspect or his motivations. Dodge looked at the picture of the judge's daughter. She was a pretty girl but looked older than she was. She appeared to be happy in the photo, but something was off about the scene in the picture. He couldn't quite place his finger on what was bothering him. He put the image on the table, turned away, and closed his eyes, trying to blank out his thoughts like a pitcher on the mound trying to shut out the crowd noise. A few minutes later, he picked up the picture again and studied the image thoroughly. He still couldn't see what had bothered him and decided to set work aside, pouring himself another bourbon.

He stared at the bedroom door before walking into the room. The smell of Kelly's perfume lingered in the air. Looking at the bed, he thought, *I should wash the sheets.*

Dodge became so engrossed in stripping the bed that he didn't hear the knocking on his front door. *Bam, bam, bam.* The loud bangs got his attention the second time. He assumed it was just a courier dropping off another box of evidence. Dodge shoved the sheets into the washing machine then answered the door. The person standing on his stoop wasn't a courier. It was a woman. She had long, semi-curly black hair. A short red dress hung at knee level, and bright red lipstick with red painted nails finished the ensemble. He approximated her age between twenty-five and thirty years.

"Can I help you?"

"I'm Anna. I am, or uh, was a friend of Kelly's," she said.

"How did you get my address?"

"Like I said, I was her friend. She once told me if I ever needed anything and she wasn't around, she knew a guy that might help me."

"And she gave you my address?"

Anna smiled. "No. She gave me your name. I have a client that works at the motor vehicle office, and I asked him for a favor."

Dodge said nothing.

"I hope I haven't done anything to make you mad. It's just when I heard about Kelly, I didn't know what to do. So, I found you."

Thoughts of Kelly hit him as he stared at the woman standing in front of him. Kelly was the person who tried to help others. Her career choice aside, she was a thoughtful woman.

Kelly was also loyal. She didn't give Anna his address and always talked to Dodge before giving out personal information like phone numbers and addresses.

"Why don't you come inside and tell me what is going on." He held the door open as Anna stepped inside. He watched her as she lightly brushed up against his midsection, then led her into the living room, offering her a seat on the couch. She remained standing.

"Can I get you something to drink?"

"What are you having?" Anna nodded at the empty lowball sitting on the desk.

"Bourbon, but I also have a beer and some wine."

"Bourbon will be fine."

Dodge noticed Anna staring at a display that hung in a shadow box behind the couch. It contained a small flag folded in the traditional triangle pattern. A gold medal attached to a red-white-and-blue sash below the flag sat next to a commendation letter from the U.S. Army Central Command. He had won the award for his work on a joint Army-Air Force group investigating civilian rapes in Iraq. The case involved several Special Forces lieutenants accused of sexual assault. Their base was attacked with rocket-propelled grenades every night for months, and they believed someone in the village had information. After several days of terrorizing villagers, the officers had found two sixteen-year-old Sunni girls walking home from the market. After convincing the adolescent girls to follow them to an empty building, the soldiers took turns raping the girls. One girl died from her injuries, and the other came to the base for medical help. The nurse who saw her recognized what had happened to her and called base commanders to report the abuse. They called Dodge to interrogate the suspected soldiers and write a report on his findings. He broke both men in one day, and they pled guilty to rape and murder and were discharged from the service. He received a medal for his efforts.

Dodge retrieved an extra glass from the kitchen cabinet. The floorboards creaked under Anna's light footsteps as she moved around the living room. "You sure have a lot of awards."

When he returned from the kitchen, he was carrying an empty highball glass in his hand. Embarrassed by the comment and unsure what to say, he turned to the bottle of bourbon perched on the edge of his desk and began pouring a drink. First hers, then his. As he turned to offer her a glass, it surprised him to see her standing within a few feet of him. Handing her the drink, he noticed a pair of red high-heeled shoes in her left hand. While Dodge was in the kitchen, she had removed them. She took the glass, and he noticed her deep blue eyes. They were the color of tropical waters, and eyes don't come in that color. *They must be designer contact lenses*, he thought. She was beautiful.

"So, what is it that is bothering you?" Dodge said as he walked to the couch and sat down.

Anna followed him and sat on the opposite end, keeping a reasonable distance between them. "Do you know she died?"

"She was hit by a bus while crossing the street."

"Did she suffer?"

"I would like to think death was instant. I'll know more after the autopsy."

Tears welled up in her eyes. He handed her a box of tissues that was sitting on the end table.

"Thank you," she said.

He gave her a few minutes to collect herself before asking why she came to see him.

Anna stared at the floor, then looked at Dodge. "I don't think she walked out into traffic like that."

"What makes you say that? I mean, people get hit by cars all the time in the city. Statistically, it is just a matter of time before it happens to you or someone you know," Dodge said. "If you know her as well as you say you do, you would know she has a habit of burying her face in that phone of hers, and the world disappears. I have told her many times myself to pay attention to where she was going."

Anna nodded.

Dodge waited for her to answer.

"Did you know she was being followed?" Anna said.

"By whom?"

"She didn't know. She told me she just had this feeling she was being watched but would turn around, and no one would be there."

Dodge knew Kelly could be paranoid. She'd had a rough life, and sometimes she fed off his own cautious approach to people. Being a parole agent meant working with some of the most violent people in the community while living in the same neighborhood as those he supervised. It wasn't uncommon to leave a restaurant because he saw a parolee dining at the same place. Better to be cautious than dead. So, he wasn't dismissive of Anna's claims concerning Kelly. But he would need more than a feeling before taking her concerns to Detectives Hanson and Keller.

"She never mentioned a name or that she could snap a picture of someone she thought might tail her?"

"Not to me. Like I said, it was just a feeling Kelly had. But then I hear she is dead, and I remembered what she told me about you. So, I found your address, and well, here I am."

"Did Kelly keep a journal?"

"You mean like a diary?"

"Yeah. A notebook she wrote in or a work document on her computer where she might have talked about her fears and her locations when she thought she was being watched."

Anna looked up as if trying to recall some distant memory buried deep in her mind about Kelly. After a minute, she shook her head. "I don't know."

"Well, what you told me doesn't give the police much to go on, but I'll pass the information on to the two detectives working the case. Is that all right with you?"

Anna nodded.

"Do you need a ride home?" Dodge asked.

"No. I can call a cab."

"Are you sure? It isn't a problem at all for me to take you home."

Anna dialed the number for a taxi service, and the dispatcher told her it would be about ten minutes before a cab could be dispatched to her location. The two sat on the couch in silence, waiting for the taxi to arrive, which happened exactly ten minutes from the time she placed the phone call.

On her way out the door, Anna mentioned to Dodge that she had a spare key to Kelly's apartment. Kelly would let her crash in the spare bedroom sometimes when the apartment complex Anna lived in was having maintenance work completed, making sleep impossible. She handed the key to him and said she couldn't go back to the apartment. Too many memories. Anna then got into the cab, and he watched as it pulled away and drove south toward downtown. It was late in the evening, but he guessed Anna was going to work. Downtown was where the hotels with fully stocked bars and business people in five-thousand-dollar suits stayed on business trips. One client could pay a month's rent. *Everybody has got to eat*, he thought.

After closing the door, he walked back to the dining room table and stared at the pictures neatly arranged into four piles, trying to concentrate. But thoughts of Kelly kept creeping into his head. Anna's visit caused his curiosity about the phone call he had received from the detectives working Kelly's case to spike. He remembered what Anna had told him about Kelly's fear of someone following her. At first, he had chalked it up to paranoia, but now, thinking about it, along with what the detectives said about the suspect having a criminal past, made him wonder if there was a connection between the two. Dodge wasn't a believer in coincidences. *Where there is smoke, there is fire.* He needed to go to Kelly's apartment to have a look around. Maybe he would come across something to help locate the man in the video at the accident scene, the supposed Good Samaritan. If his efforts didn't turn up anything, he would hand the key to the detectives tomorrow. *Seems like a reasonable plan,* he thought.

The drive to Kelly's apartment on the north side of town took about twenty minutes. The traffic was light at that hour, but at night the red lights stayed red longer when waiting on a side street crossing the main road. He hit three red lights. Each one lasted four minutes, adding an extra ten minutes to his trip. He was going to stop and get a cup of coffee but decided against it; he still had to work on the task force case in the morning and needed to get a few hours of sleep to keep his mind sharp.

The apartment building Kelly had lived in was like dozens scattered across the city: brown brick with concrete adornments. A staircase with wrought-iron railings led to the main entrance. Once inside, Dodge located Kelly's apartment from the piece of masking tape she, or Anna, had placed on the key with the apartment's number, 2D. He climbed the first flight of stairs and scanned the doors for 2D. The first door at the top of the stairs to the right was 2A. The door in front of him had the number 2B written on a piece of masking tape. The entrance to the left was 2C. He walked the small hallway to the left, and in the back, on the street side, was 2D. Back at her door, he inserted the key into the lock, and the tumblers turned until the click of the deadbolt signaled it was no longer engaged. Dodge took a quick look around. He didn't see anyone watching, and he entered the apartment.

The apartment was clean but sparsely decorated. There was a hint of bleach in the air, and it caused him to sneeze. The living room contained a small couch butted up against the outside wall. An empty coffee table sat parallel to the sofa. In the far corner, next to the couch, was a reading chair with a floor lamp positioned beside it. He could almost picture Kelly sitting in the chair reading a book, her pale skin reflecting the glow coming from the light. He smiled. The kitchen was galley style and separate from the rest of the apartment. Every available wall was covered with cabinets. The builders must have known the small kitchen would be a negative to renters, so they included as much storage space as possible. There was a bedroom on each side of the living room. The first bedroom must have been the guest room. The bed was made but looked like it hadn't been used in weeks. A small dresser sat under the room's only window. Dodge opened the drawers one by one. Each was empty. Next, he searched the nightstand. It was empty. The closet contained empty hangers and a spare set of sheets and pillows for the bed.

Having found nothing of significance in the spare bedroom or living room, Kelly's bedroom was next. He stopped about two steps into the room as his senses started working overtime. Her perfume lingered in the air, but it was the condition of the room that first caught his attention. The room was a mess. The king-sized bed wasn't made, and clothes were scattered about the floor. The closet door was open with all the hanging garments pushed to one side like someone had searched for something. A dresser stood against the wall to his left, its drawers half-open with shirts and socks and underwear scattered on the surrounding floor. Someone had been in this room, and they were looking for something.

A glance back into the living room revealed it was spotless. The spare bedroom was the same, as was the kitchen. Dodge returned his focus to the main bedroom and placed his hands in his pockets so he wouldn't touch anything. Then, he walked carefully to the en suite bathroom. A glance inside revealed the room was as it should have been. Nothing seemed out of place. Whatever the person who had been here was seeking, they somehow knew it would be in Kelly's bedroom.

Dodge retraced his steps back through the bedroom, into the living room, past the kitchen, and into the entrance. He wiped the door handle on the way out and locked the door with the key. He then wiped the key and placed it on top of the door frame where no one could see it unless they were eight feet tall. An average person would have to jump to get to the height to see the key.

After walking down the stairs and out the main entrance, he crossed the street and climbed inside his truck and sat there, thinking. What could Kelly have had that would be so valuable to someone? She wasn't wealthy. Call girls were seldom rich.

She worked to pay the rent and put food on the table. She wasn't into drugs. He was sure of that. *But you never know a person as well as you might think.* Maybe she stole something, or perhaps she had been with a married man and he was worried about his wife finding out about his prostitute on the side? There were a million possibilities.

He may have made a mistake denying his and Kelly's relationship. A good investigator would uncover the truth sooner rather than later, but it seemed like a good idea when the detectives thought her death was an accident. A suspicious death changed everything. He may have to come clean and tell the detectives about their relationship. But not yet. He wanted to do some digging on his own. He needed to know what Kelly had been doing during the last year. Who did she met in rehab? Who did she owe money to? Rehab would be more challenging because of HIPAA requirements. He would start with her finances. But first, he needed to know if Grayson Heller was involved. He would check the prison visitation records and cross-reference any names with friends or clients he came up with. He thought of the woman who came to his house—Anna. She might know some of Kelly's old clients or if she was ever strong-armed by a pimp. It wouldn't be the first time a street girl was killed by a greedy hustler.

Dodge yawned. It had been a long day, and he was tired. The emotional drain of the day had taken a toll on his faculties. It was time to go home and get some rest. He had just set a high bar for the next few days. Sleep would be scarce from here on out.

CHAPTER 7

IT WAS A WARM FALL MORNING. The low-pressure front pushing up the coast had stalled. After dropping abnormal amounts of rain and producing below-average temperatures, the front had passed offshore, and the following high-pressure front brought late-summer daytime temperatures. Most residents welcomed the change. It was unseasonably warm, and he couldn't remember a warmer week this late in the season in past years.

The man who owned the coffee truck called his name. Dodge raised his hand, making his way through the crowd to retrieve his first of many caffeine doses for the day. Most mornings, he stopped to order a cup of coffee from this truck. It wasn't the best, but the truck parked near his work, and he usually needed a refill by the time he arrived downtown. While sipping his coffee, a black SUV pulled up and parked in front of him. Both front doors opened, and two passengers climbed out into the street. He recognized them immediately as the men from the U.S. Marshals in Chief Johnson's office the other day. The driver didn't shut his door, causing traffic to slow to a crawl while vehicles maneuvered around the obstacle.

"Deputies," Dodge said.

"What in the hell do you think you are doing?"

"Isn't it obvious?" Dodge said, holding his coffee. "Would you two like a cup? It's probably not as good as the coffee you get down at the federal building, but it will put a little pep in your step." He threw up two fingers to the coffee truck owner, who nodded. Then he leaned slightly toward the two agents. "Actually, the coffee is awful, but I don't have to pay for it."

The second deputy spoke. "Why the hell would we want to drink shitty coffee? Why would anyone?"

Dodge remembered the driver's name: U.S. Deputy Marshal Fisch.

"You see that guy over there." Dodge pointed to the man tucked inside the coffee truck. "His name is Benito. He has a daughter. I suppose she would be about twenty now. Well, when his daughter was about fifteen or sixteen, she had this piss-ant, nineteen-year-old wannabe boyfriend named Paco. At least that was his street name. Anyway, Benito didn't care much for young Paco and didn't relish the idea of some young gangbanger taking liberties with his daughter."

Agent Fisch crossed his arms over his chest. "What the hell are you talking about?"

Dodge ignored the question and continued, "One morning, as I ordered my coffee, I noticed something bothering Benito. I asked him what was wrong, and he told me the story of how his daughter had run off with this nineteen-year-old gangbanger. Apparently, she slipped out her bedroom window and rendezvoused with Paco at the end of the block. A few days had gone by without hearing from his daughter, and he became impatient and angry, as is understandable. He considered hiring someone to both find his daughter and deal with Paco."

"Does this story have any semblance of a point? Christ, I'm getting older over here," the second agent blurted out.

Running his hand through his short hair, he assured the deputies a point would show itself if they would allow him to continue.

"Get on with it," Deputy Fisch said.

"Thank you. Paco had no job and zero money. He drove a piece-of-shit, twenty-year-old Honda that wouldn't get the star-crossed lovers far. In reality, Benito's daughter didn't have a future with Paco. So, I told Benito that his daughter would tire of the mope lifestyle and return home in the next couple of weeks. The only genuine concern I had was if she came home with a minor surprise. Women will do strange things when a child is involved. But she didn't get knocked up and returned home to a grateful father after a week."

"You said there was a point to this story," Deputy Fisch asked.

"The point is you asked for my help. You wanted me to talk to Grayson. I did, and it was a waste of time. Just like Benito paying for someone to find his daughter would have been a waste of resources." Dodge sat his coffee on the top of a small retaining wall behind him. "Grayson didn't have any information and is back in my life. That is something I blame on you and the Marshals Service. This exercise has done nothing but make an unpleasant situation worse, and on top of that, I now have to play his fucking game."

"You think this is a game," Deputy Fisch asked.

"I think nothing to do with sex crimes is a game. In fact, I take that seriously."

"Then why did I get a call from the warden?"

"The warden called you after I talked to Grayson?"

"That's right. Apparently, after your chat, he ripped his cell apart and even got his hands on a guard. They had to move him to solitary."

Dodge understood Grayson as well as anyone. He had been in prison for going on eight years, not including the deuce he did in county awaiting trial. In that entire time, Grayson caused the jail staff zero problems. Not a single write-up. He had been a model prisoner. Why now? Why mess up by assaulting a guard? Some inmates hit their breaking points while serving out their sentences. The constant fear of having to watch their back and the pressure to join a prison gang for protection all turned out to be more than some inmates were able to handle. But Grayson was different. He was a cold, calculated sociopath. Every move he made furthered a larger goal. Grayson's goal was to get paroled as soon as possible, and Dodge knew that. Up to this point, he had made all the correct choices to sway a parole board to grant him his freedom early. Assault on a guard would add ten years to the end of his current sentence. Any parole will get denied for years.

"They placed him in solitary for attacking a guard?" Dodge asked. Grayson had a spotless inmate record. He had never even looked sideways at a guard, no infractions of any kind, which is why Dodge showed up at his parole hearings to advocate against his release. Why would he risk his privileges now? Grayson Heller always played the long game. If he was in solitary, it was because solitary was where he wanted to be.

"That's right. Because of what you said," the second deputy said.

Fisch gave his partner a stay-in-your-lane glance. "How the hell are we supposed to get him to cooperate now?"

To be honest, Dodge didn't give a shit about Grayson cooperating. He was sure Grayson's involvement solely related to their history. If he woke up tomorrow and Grayson was gone from the earth, he would have a drink and go back to sleep. "He doesn't have any knowledge about your girl. You are being played."

"Now we may never know," Fisch said.

An idea popped into Dodge's head. He needed a reason to talk to Grayson again. He could use that as a cover. No one would need to know he was working Kelly's case on the side. He needed to think fast.

"Look, Deputy Fisch. Grayson and I have a history, as I'm the one who put him in his cage. Everything he has done to this point has been to assure his release on parole." He paused to take a drink from his coffee. "He will come back to the table. But that still doesn't mean he knows dick about your victim."

"What makes you think he won't just hang himself with a bedsheet and call it a day when he finds out we are on to him?"

"Grayson would never commit suicide. He is a survivalist, and by that, I mean he will do anything to stay alive. Anything. It is a narcissistic view that he has something more important to accomplish on this earth."

The two deputies just stared into open space, as if looking past him to something in the distance. He wasn't getting through to them, but he knew something about them. They needed to see this out to the end, or at least until Grayson proved no longer useful. The Feds had gone all-in on a pair of deuces and were fully invested in the pot. Dodge figured the next logical play would be to bluff their way out of a bad hand.

"I don't care what kind of fucked-up fetish you and Grayson have for each other," Deputy Fisch said, stepping into the parole agent's personal space. Dodge's muscles tightened. His heart rate accelerated. He fought the urge to reposition himself into a more tactical stance. He stood with one foot placed slightly in front of the other with his hands out front at waist level, ready to block any attack. Deputy Fisch stuck his finger in Dodge's face. "If you fuck this up, you won't be able to get a job mopping the jizz room at Bobby B's strip club."

Deputy Fisch was a smoker. His finger stopped close enough for Dodge to smell the odor of tobacco and notice the slightly browning skin between the second and third knuckles. Dodge wanted to reach up, snatch the finger out of the air, and use it as a makeshift lever to force its owner to his knees. However, if he went on the offensive, he would have to contend with marshal number two, who wouldn't stand by as his partner was taken to the ground. Deserved or not, a suspension would follow, and his place on the task force would be lost. He decided honor was the better part of valor, took two steps back, and wished the two marshals a pleasant day.

"It's been fun, fellas. I'll be sure to fill you in on how it turns out with Grayson, but I don't want to be late for work."

"You make sure you do," Deputy Fisch said as he turned away from Dodge.

The two deputies walked in stride back to the black SUV they had left running parked halfway in the street. Deputy Fisch jumped into the driver's seat. The vehicle moved before the second marshal could get all the way in, forcing Fisch to stop and wait for his partner to regain his balance and shut the door. Dodge watched the vehicle until it made a right turn and disappeared out of view. He began the brief walk to his office.

It took about five minutes to walk to his building, and he had plenty of work to do. He also knew a drive back to Rolling Meadows to talk to Grayson awaited him. He currently had the upper hand with Grayson but didn't want to switch from offense to defense, which could risk swapping power. He also needed to meet with Renquest, so he pulled out a clamshell flip phone from his pocket. The task force had not upgraded him to a smartphone as of yet. He opened the phone, pushed the button on the top right, and scrolled through the list of personal and work contacts. The list grew every year, and it took him longer to find the name he wanted every year. When he saw the name he was searching for, he hit the call button and waited for an answer.

CHAPTER 8

DODGE STOOD ON THE SIDEWALK around the corner from the parole office. His first call went to voicemail, so next, he dialed the personal cell number. It rang several times before being answered.

"Parole Agent Robbie Shaw. How can I help you?"

"Rob, it's Dodge. Is the chief in yet?"

"Hey, Dodge. Where are you at?"

Dodge was in sight of the building but didn't want to venture closer, as someone might notice him.

"I am heading over to PD to talk to Renquest. Is the chief there yet?"

"Haven't seen him this morning. I think he may have had a unit head meeting this morning at District One. Let me check the board."

The early morning buzz of the office could be heard through the speaker as Robbie walked through the maze of cubicles and desks to the whiteboard. The board was used by everyone in the office to sign in and out. Its chief goal was to keep the secretaries up to date on every agent's location.

"It looks like chief is in a meeting and won't be back to the office until after lunch."

"OK. Can you put me in for around 1300 hours?"

The after-lunch arrival would give Dodge plenty of time to meet with Renquest and plan his next move concerning Grayson. His other duties would have to wait. Besides, he always hated sitting at a desk. He saw himself as a "kicking doors in" kind of guy, even though his job didn't need him to use his legs and feet as battering rams much anymore. Times had changed. But fieldwork beckoned him just the same, and he was always eager to knock on doors.

"Sure thing," Robbie said as he moved the little red magnetic dot next to Dodge's name from "Off" to "Field."

"Oh, and, Robbie, can you check the system and see who has visited Grayson Heller in the past six months? I also need you to check the disciplinary records to see what other inmates have been in solitary over the past couple of weeks. If someone has visited him or bunked with him, I want to know about it."

"I'll call you as soon as I get something," Robbie said.

The whiteboard, or sign-in board, was a mixed bag for Dodge. As the office safety officer, he pushed other agents and staff to use the board. If something happened, everyone would have a rough idea of an agent's location and use the board to direct local law enforcement to an agent in distress. This seemed practical and made perfect sense to him. However, he also understood the board to be a tracking tool for management, used to micromanage agents and their caseloads. Academics and correctional organizations had been pushing the research-based social work approach for about a decade. It wasn't until the last couple of years the new initiatives had gained national traction and hit the department. He was an accomplished agent who worked from instinct. If something felt wrong, it probably was wrong. When the woo-woo hairs on his neck stood up, it was for a good reason.

A person could read all the academic journal articles in the world on human behavior, but people learned through experience. He believed it was the sole reason he had not ended up on the wrong side of a bullet on at least two occasions, once in the Air Force and once as an agent. There may have been other times, but those two pointed directly to the hairs on the back of his neck and avoidance of death. That was enough evidence for him.

He entered the state-owned parking garage from the south

entrance, which was in an alley next to the building containing his office. None of the DOC staff used the back entrance anymore because of an attack that happened two years ago. A homeless man had jumped an employee as she was smoking a cigarette during her morning break. The homeless man, who had severe mental health issues, asked the woman for a cigarette. When she refused to give him a smoke, he punched her in the face, ripped the purse from her shoulder, and kicked her once in the stomach for good measure. No one in the office noticed she was missing, and an hour passed before anyone went looking for her. Staff found her lying unconscious in the alley with a broken rib and a dislocated shoulder. Two things happened after the attack: using the whiteboard became mandatory, and no one used the alley entrance to the garage. For Dodge, using the back entrance meant coming and going unnoticed.

Twenty minutes later, he was pulling into the parking lot of the police station. His frequent interactions on cases with the police department earned him a parking pass in the detectives and administration lot. Typically, Dodge would have denied the pass since it appeared he was receiving special treatment. His relationship with the rank and file had been excellent. More than once, he had needed the help of a patrol unit when making an arrest or serving a search warrant. Being seen as a special friend of management by uniformed staff meant they might not rush to answer his call. After all, he wasn't one of them. A parking permit assured that he didn't have to drive around the block for fifteen minutes looking for a street spot and fight with DOC for reimbursement of parking fees. He felt this made it worth it. The parking lot attendant raised the gate after Dodge flashed his credentials, and he passed under the retractable arm and entered the parking lot. It was early, so finding a spot close to the building's entrance proved easy.

Detective Renquest was on the phone, standing with his back to the door when Dodge stepped into his office. Two piles of files covered his wooden desk, one pile on each side. One stack had about four or five files stacked to a height of about eighteen inches. The other stack had seven or eight files haphazardly piled on top of one another, with some facing one way and others a different way. No order to its mayhem. Both chairs and a couch were also impromptu file cabinets, leaving no room to sit.

Renquest turned and noticed him standing in the doorway. He motioned with his free hand for Dodge to enter. He pointed at the chair directly in front of the desk, the one covered in case files, forcing him to remain standing.

Renquest returned to his phone call. "Yeah, I know, sir." The voice on the other end was loud enough that anyone within twenty feet could hear. It was like how Charlie Brown's parents sounded in the cartoons.

"I'll talk to him, sir." Renquest paused as the voice on the other end increased in volume. "Today, sir . . . Yes, sir, I'll make sure of it . . . OK, sir. Have a wonderful day."

Renquest pulled the phone away from his ear, turned to face Dodge, and placed the receiver in its cradle. "He hung up on me."

"Maybe it was something you said," Dodge replied. "What were you talking about?"

"You."

"That'll do it."

Renquest sat down in the high-backed brown leather chair parked behind his desk. Dodge removed several files from the chair, stacked them on the floor beside him, and sat down.

"So, what the hell happened at the prison yesterday? You were supposed to talk to Grayson and get information. Instead, you pissed off everyone in the state."

"They brought this on themselves. I told the marshals not to involve Grayson. He is a manipulative asshole and only cares about one thing: himself. Now we have to dance every step of this entire shitty waltz."

"Well, whatever you plan to do, I suggest you do it fast. The suits don't give a crap about your and Grayson's history. They sure don't give a crap about your job or future."

"Like I said, it's just a step in the dance now."

Dodge knew Renquest didn't care for the unwanted attention the meeting with Grayson had brought to the case, so he decided against mentioning his meeting with the two marshals that morning. No need to add gas to a fire.

Renquest leaned back in his chair. The wood joints strained under the weight. "I suppose we are in it now."

Dodge said he would try to not bring any added attention to the case, but it was a promise he might not be able to keep. He was just paying lip service out of respect for their partnership. It was time to change the subject.

"You find anything on who lived in that apartment?"

Renquest picked up a file from the stack on his desk, opened it, and pulled out a yellow sticky note. He nodded his head, so his black-rimmed reading glasses perched on top of his head slid down to his nose. He looked up from above the frame of his glasses.

"The landlord, Victor Laramie, didn't want to help at first. He tried to withhold the name of the person renting the apartment. He mumbled some bullshit about privacy laws and Big Brother knowing too much about his business already."

"You managed to set him straight, I assume?"

"I encouraged him to assist in the investigation."

"And what, convinced him to be a dutiful citizen?"

"I reminded him of the hidden room in the apartment that was likely not approved by the building inspector. I also mentioned I would contact the Office of Building Code Enforcement and report my findings. Suggested code enforcement might send a whole hoard of inspectors to go through each apartment in the building. If they found a violation, he might have to pay for motel rooms until they make proper repairs. I reminded him the cost of this would fall on him, not the city or county."

"Nice."

"It was all complete horseshit. The city only has two inspectors, and one of them is on short-term disability leave. It would be months before they would even look at the building and would probably just ignore it anyway."

"But I am guessing he didn't know that or wasn't willing to risk it?"

"One person's name saves the hassle of dozens of angry tenants. It's a cost-benefit analysis."

Dodge had dealt with plenty of landlords over the years and realized the rule was "Take a stand until it costs money." Then it's everyone for themselves.

"What is the name of the tenant the landlord gave you?" Dodge asked.

"Leonard Miller. He's also the maintenance man of sorts for two properties owned by the landlord. The one with the creepy closet room and another I need to locate an address for. We have little on Miller. A few arrests for flashing and a peeping conviction. He seems like the kind of person who would have a spank room. I'll keep digging until I find something."

"When was the last time Victor saw Mr. Miller?"

"Hadn't seen him in at least a month," Renquest said.

"He wasn't worried when he didn't get the rent check?"

"That's the funny thing. The rent was paid up for six months. In cash."

Dodge shook his head. "Greed, man. A person disappears for a year, and as long as the landlord gets his money, no one will bother looking for them."

"Tell me about it," Renquest said. "I remember finding a guy mummified in his bed. The son had been cashing his disability checks and paying the rent for almost two years."

Dodge thought about what Renquest had just said. "Are there any other properties Mr. Miller is linked to?"

Renquest leafed through the file. "Give me a second." His eyes studied the open file in front of him. "Ah, yes, there is. Seven hundred block of Saint Mary's Avenue. The landlord has Miller listed as a tenant on both properties."

"So, he is the primary occupant on two different apartments owned by the same landlord?"

"That's what the computer spit out."

"I know the first building is largely Section Eight housing. I wonder if the St. Mary's address is as well?"

"Why does that matter?" Renquest asked.

"Some slumlords run a scam on the government and rent multiple apartments to the same tenant in different buildings, giving them two apartments for which they get the guaranteed government subsidy check. The leasee lives in the first apartment, and the second apartment is then rented out for cash at full market value. Inspectors for the Housing Authority are overworked and spread thin, and landlords can get away with the fraud for years before being caught," Dodge said.

Renquest shrugged. "Nice scam. I planned on sending a couple of uniforms to sit on it for a few hours tonight."

Dodge waved the idea off. He didn't want uniforms with marked squad cars alerting everyone in the neighborhood the building was being watched.

"Don't send marked units."

"You think he might be at the other property?" Renquest asked.

"Miller has to know we locked his place down by now. If he can't return, he will go someplace safe."

Renquest tossed his readers on the desk. "A lot of these guys keep little rooms in the buildings they work. They serve as a place to sleep if they have to work late or be at the building early in the morning to let city utility workers in for inspections."

"My thoughts exactly. There is zero evidence, and a black and white could set Miller running."

"You want this one?"

"I think it is worth a try. If Miller is there, I can get a description and license plate. You can run Miller's identifiers through the Department of Motor Vehicles and the FBI system to see what that turns up."

"You want officers to make a routine pass in case you need any help?"

Shaking his head again, Dodge said, "I have some things to

do and plan to head there later tonight, after dinner."

"Sounds good, but be careful. There is no telling what we are dealing with yet. Might be a freezer full of human heads at that place."

"Thanks for the nightmares," Dodge said, turning to leave.

"I heard about Kelly today," Renquest said. Dodge stopped. "I'm sorry. Sometimes you can't save everyone. Even harder the second time." Dodge said nothing. "I know you will want to snoop around on this. As your partner, I advise against getting involved. As your friend, let me know if you need anything."

"Thanks."

"But be careful. I know those detectives. If they smell blood in the water, they will start a feeding frenzy."

Dodge nodded. He left Renquest's office and headed toward the stairs. He needed to go to the office to bring Chief Johnson up to speed and catch up on some paperwork. The judge's daughter's case and Kelly would have to wait until later tonight.

CHAPTER 9

THE AFTERNOON SUN SHONE straight down the east-west street Café le Chez sat on. It warmed the air enough that patrons could use the outdoor seating that lined much of the sidewalks of downtown Main Street. The restaurant and bar district stretched for about five city blocks, from east to west, with Café le Chez in the heart of town. Before they labeled it a historic district, it underwent many renovations over the years. Much the same as other towns across America, the suburban boom of the 1950s pushed families to the edge of town to newly developed neighborhoods. Each neighborhood was a self-sufficient pod with gas stations, parks, and drugstores. As people fled downtown, the businesses followed. It was a matter of simple economics, and businesses had to follow customers. This left the city center with "For Rent" signs adorning storefronts and broken windows for blocks.

But Café le Chez was one restaurant that stayed in business. It had catered to drunks and prostitutes during the seventies and eighties. The food was satisfying and cheap. In the nineties, twenty-somethings moved in, prizing walkability to downtown bars and restaurants over yards that required landscaping. Café le Chez served specialty beer and appetizers at a higher price. Regular folks moved back to the inner city, and so did other businesses. Simple economics. Go where the people are. As the neighborhood's socioeconomic status increased, old sin businesses rebranded as breweries and wine and cheese bars. There were more quaint eateries, a theater, and art stores that featured local artists. And Café le Chez sat right smack in the middle of it. Just like always.

The café was a popular gathering place for the art community and those who enjoyed French pastries as opposed to American fare for breakfast. Anna came for the coffee. She imagined the café as part of a bustling street in downtown Paris. While she had never been to Paris, she watched most of the travel shows and vowed to make the journey one day. But for the moment, she was at Café le Chez, and the coffee was excellent.

Anna sat facing the east to block the sun from shining in her eyes and provide some cover for anyone approaching her head-on. Anna looked at her watch and noticed he was running a little late. She knew what time he went to work and what time he usually left. Even if he had been working outside the office, it was customary for him to return an hour before going home for the day. She had paid incredibly close attention to the coffee truck that sat next to the curb a block to the east of Café le Chez. Twice a day, he would stop and get coffee, once in the morning and again around three o'clock in the afternoon. She guessed the last visit was for his midday pick-me-up. At least, that is what Kelly had once told her.

Anna looked at her watch again. It was closer to four o'clock than three, yet he had still not come out for his coffee. Maybe he had made coffee in the office today? Perhaps he left the building using the alley and she had just missed him? She thought about getting up and walking closer toward the government building. She decided to wait for ten more minutes. If Dodge didn't show in that time, a closer look would reveal if his truck was still parked in the garage. The wait was short.

She saw him walk out the front door at ten to four and toward the coffee truck. He disappeared out of sight behind the truck and reappeared after a few seconds. Anna didn't see a cup of coffee in his hand. He was walking in her direction now. The change in routine caught Anna off guard, causing her to sit up straight. Any closer and she would have to choose to either leave or stay. Dodge crossed the street about half a block from Café le

Chez. They were now on the same side of the street. If leaving was the choice, now would be the time. She didn't move, hoping he would not notice her sitting at the table. He was nearly at the entrance to the cafe when he made eye contact. *Damn it.*

"Hello, Anna!"

"Hi," Anna said. "I see you come here for the coffee too?"

"No. I normally hit the coffee truck up outside my office," Dodge said as he pointed down the street behind him. "But today, he was out of the potent stuff, so I had to walk down here."

"Is that where you work?" Anna asked.

Dodge nodded, and a moment of awkward silence followed until he broke the silence.

"Thanks for giving me that key to Kelly's place."

"Oh, no problem. I didn't need it anymore," Anna said. "Did you go over there?"

"I did."

"Did you find anything?"

"The place had been turned over like someone was looking for something. But I had never been inside Kelly's place before that day, so I don't know what I was supposed to look for." Anna said nothing. "I left the key above the door in case I wanted to go back and check it out. It is the middle of the month, and I don't think the landlord will try to rent the place until the beginning of next month."

"What will the police do with all of her stuff?"

"If no one claims the property, the landlord will sell it or keep it for staging empty units for show." Anna nodded. "Well, I need to get my fix and get back to the office."

Anna stood. "I was wondering if you would have time to talk later?"

"I have something I need to do later on," he said. "But I have some questions I need to ask you. To help fill in the blanks."

Anna smiled. "OK."

Dodge pulled a business card out of his pocket and wrote his personal cell number on the back. "Here is my number. Call or text around eight tonight. I should be done by then. We can get some dinner and talk."

"Sounds good."

"All right then. I'll pick a place and let you know when."

Anna sat back down as Dodge went into the café to order his coffee. He reappeared a few minutes later and waved to her as he headed back toward his office. Her heart was racing. She could feel the pounding in her chest, and her face felt flush and warm. She liked him. She finished her coffee and caught a cab heading out of downtown toward her apartment. There was a need to look perfect tonight. And she knew how to achieve it. Anna tapped on the glass separating her from the driver. She told him a new address. Then the cab driver made a U-turn and headed in the opposite direction.

Staring out the window, Anna watched the building fly past. Taller buildings gave way to shorter ones the farther the cab traveled from the city center. A few blocks later, the driver pulled over outside Kelly's apartment building. Anna handed the man a twenty then went into the building and jumped up to retrieve the key from where Dodge had said he hid it last night. She glanced left, then right. She went inside and closed the door.

CHAPTER 10

BY THE TIME DODGE MADE IT to the address Renquest had given him as Leonard Miller's second apartment, the sun was below the horizon, and it was raining. The plan had been to check on Leonard Miller's second apartment after dinner, but a last-minute meeting with a substance abuse treatment provider had brought him within four blocks of the address.

Might as well stop now, he thought. It was difficult to see the stenciled numbers against the brown brick façade when there were numbers. Residents of this neighborhood didn't care if cops could find the correct building. Police showed up for arrests or homicides, and even then, it was last on the priority list. It was evident community policing wasn't part of the city's plan for this neighborhood.

He could barely make out the cross street on the small green rectangular sign marked as Wilson Street, seven hundred block. City planners always placed odd numbers on the south side. He began counting as he drove past each building, stopping in front of what should have been 705 Saint Mary's Avenue. A white panel van with no windows obscured his view of the front of the building. He continued past, pulling into a space opposite 709 to watch for any movement in or out of the building. He sat for a half an hour until he was sure it was safe to get a closer look. Dealers often posted lookouts on rooftops and in empty apartments to watch for police. While he wasn't in a marked car, he knew his truck stood out, making him an easy mark.

The idea of Renquest sending a couple of uniforms to watch

his back popped into his head, but he decided since this was a recon mission, the officers would hinder more than help him. He unholstered his weapon and eased the slide back just far enough to see the shiny edge of a silver casing resting in the chamber. Then he grabbed his flashlight from the glove box and headed across the street toward the building marked 705. Dodge scanned the surrounding buildings for moving curtains and flickering lights. There was no movement in the windows facing the street. He moved closer to the building, keeping cars between him and the open half-lit sidewalk, stopping short of the white panel van that had blocked his view earlier.

Dodge understood that lurking around and looking like a cop, or worse, a snitch, would certainly be noticed by the residents of the complex. The building would lock down. If the suspect was inside, he might get nervous and run. Once he was in the wind, it might be impossible to locate him again. The time was right. He rose from behind the van just as his phone vibrated in his jacket pocket. The vibration caught him off guard, causing him to pause. He shielded the screen as he pulled the phone from his pocket so the ambient light wouldn't give him away. It was a message from Anna.

Are we still on? Anna.

He first wanted to get a quick survey of the building, then he would text her back. He placed the phone back in his pocket and stepped out from behind the van again. No lights were on in the lower windows on either side of the front steps. There was a faint glow emanating from a third-floor window, but it appeared to be coming from an adjacent room. He made his way up to the front door and inspected the nameplates and intercom box. The faceplate was missing, and all the wires were cut—most likely by drug addicts stealing copper to support their habit. The nameplate had apartment numbers 1A, 1B, 1C, 2A, 2B, and 2C, continuing on until it ended on 4C. No names. Dodge guessed the building had four floors with three apartments on each one. Peering through years of dirt and grime covering the glass of the front door, he could make out a staircase and a hallway on the left. He assumed the layout of the other floors was similar.

As he moved back down the stairs, he spotted a narrow set of stairs under the window to the first-floor apartment to his left. He knew that many of these old buildings had basement entrances that led to boiler rooms, maintenance areas, and water control rooms. The light from his flashlight bounced off the railing and into the dark opening. He could see a metal security door with a small square glass at eye level.

His phone buzzed again. It was another message from Anna.

If I don't hear from you, I'll assume that you are not coming and make other plans.

He thought for a minute and stared at his phone. After a quick look to check his six, he responded to Anna's text. *Meet in an hour at O'Connell's. Dodge.*

Doing the math, he calculated it should take him no longer than fifteen minutes to get to the restaurant. Another five minutes to find a parking spot and five to wash up in the restroom before meeting Anna. Twenty-five minutes. That gave him a little over thirty minutes to check out the building. He needed to get a sense of the neighborhood. Dodge paid close attention to which apartment's lights were on and the ones with blacked-out windows. Then, he made a list of the cars on the street and recorded the license plates. He might have Renquest run the tags through the state bureau of motor vehicle's computer system later in the week. Maybe they'd get lucky and get a hit on Leonard Miller's car. It was worth a shot.

He took a few quick pictures of the building, the staircase, and the basement entrance then walked back to his truck. Once he was inside the warm cab, he began copying license plate numbers from the fifteen or so cars parked on the street, listing the vehicles according to which side of the street they were parked on, as most people prefer to park on the same side as the building they live in. He made a quick sketch of the area to aid local police if things went south later that night. When finished, he looked at his watch. Ten minutes to spare. He texted Anna that he was on his way. Dodge started his truck and pulled out into the street. He made a left on Vine Street, heading back toward downtown.

Traffic was light for a midweek evening, making the drive to the restaurant about fifteen minutes long, just as he had guessed. On a busy traffic day, the same venture could take thirty minutes. In hindsight, he didn't recall a night over the past couple of years where he had had a faster commute. He wondered if the cooler evening temperatures and damp air made people stay at home, or if something else happened. Random luck was a myth. He always imagined that people created their own fate through actions and were rewarded by karma. He had not saved a life or done anything special today, so why the light traffic? Dodge turned on the radio to the local news channel while circling the block, looking for a place to park.

The weatherman came on first and said it had been raining since five o'clock, but there was no risk of flooding. Cool temperatures with higher than average humidity. After tapering off later, it would be clear and dry. The traffic report was next. An accident on the bypass was doubtful to ruin anyone's plans for dinner in the downtown district. The traffic guy said all the other roads were clear, calling an official end to the evening rush hour.

He spotted an empty parking spot across the street and made a U-turn, just a half-block walk to the restaurant. He was late, but the brief walk wouldn't make any difference. Within a few minutes, Dodge stepped inside the pub and scanned the entryway for Anna. He spotted her at the far end of the bar in a seat with unobstructed views of the entire restaurant. Her back was against a wall, facing the front door and the kitchen entrance. She chose well. Anna spotted him at the same time and motioned to him. He made his way through the crowd by the bar and sat next to her.

Her hair was a slightly different color. The shade was more brunette with streaks of blond culminating at the tips. She was wearing a blue dress that made her eyes resemble the color of the Caribbean Sea. Everything matched. Her dress. Her eyes. Her nails. And even her shoes were blue. She looked beautiful.

There was something about her that made him feel relaxed and comfortable. He also couldn't deny his attraction to her at that moment.

"How long have you been waiting?"

"Not too long."

She had a glass of wine resting on a cocktail napkin to prevent condensation from the glass pooling on the bar. Using a cocktail napkin in place of a coaster meant the pub had a busy weekend and needed a shipment of coasters with the weekly alcohol delivery. Dodge also noticed a second napkin sitting on the front edge of the bar. He figured she was on her second glass of wine, as napkins are replaced between drinks. A second glass told him she had been waiting for not more than half an hour. She had arrived early.

"Hope I am not late. I had something to finish up before I left the office."

"I got here early. I just sat listening to the jukebox. Until the band started setting up." Anna looked over her right shoulder and nodded toward the stage. "It may get a little loud in here."

"You didn't have anything else to do tonight?" he asked.

"Nothing I couldn't put off until tomorrow."

The band began tuning up their instruments and checking the microphones for sound. There were sounds of drums and cymbals being smacked. The guitarist tuned his Les Paul by thrashing the same string over and over until reaching the right key. The lead singer for the band barked "Check, check. One, two" into the microphone, testing for feedback. The place was getting loud, forcing Dodge to lean closer to Anna when he spoke.

"How about a change of scenery?"

"That might be a good idea," Anna said.

"I know a Mexican place that should still be open. Best tacos in town!"

Anna leaned in, placing her mouth just inches from his ear. Her warm breath tickled the side of his neck, causing a shiver.

"Is it good?"

"It's quiet. I think you will like it. Well, I like it anyway."

Anna looked at him, placed her hand on his leg, just up from his knee, and looked him in the eyes. "It's OK."

"What's OK?"

Her hand moved up his leg. "If you like it, I am sure I'll like it, too."

Dodge rose and slid his chair up to the bar. He removed Anna's jacket from the back of her chair, placing it over her shoulders. She pulled it tight in the front, leaving the arms of the coat dangling at her sides. Ever a gallant date, he took from his wallet two crisp twenty-dollar bills and placed them on the counter. He finished his drink, setting the empty glass on top of the bills, and followed Anna out to the sidewalk. It had stopped raining, but the storm left something in the air. It smelled of the ocean. He loved that about the east coast of Virginia.

"Where did you park?" Anna asked.

"Down the street, about half a block."

A valet approached them and spoke with a heavy accent. "You got ticket?"

The valet was a young Hispanic boy, likely from southern Mexico or one of the Central American countries that bordered Mexico. He was short, maybe five-feet-five inches, and skinny as a rail. The kid looked like he hadn't eaten a full meal in days.

"No, I parked myself tonight."

"I get for you. Keys, please."

"It's OK. We can walk. Besides, I wouldn't want you to get into any trouble."

"No trouble. Slow tonight." He held out his hand for Dodge's keys. "Besides, the pretty lady shouldn't walk. Should be picked up like a queen."

Noticing a blush on Anna's face, Dodge he dropped his keys in the valet's outstretched hand. "Are you sure you won't get into any trouble?"

"No trouble. I go get the car for the pretty lady."

It only took the kid about three minutes to retrieve the truck. The speedy service, combined with his lanky appearance, earned the valet an additional ten dollars on top of the regular tip before the couple headed east toward the waterfront.

He pulled into the parking lot and stopped at the Mexican food truck he told Anna about. The owner was closing shop and had cleared off all the picnic tables customers used to eat at after ordering. Dodge waved at the man and got out of the truck. The owner reset one of the picnic tables with a napkin dispenser and some plastic silverware, then took the couple's order: five tacos, three carne asada for him and two vegetarian for Anna, along with two sodas. The two sat at one of the cement picnic tables waiting for their food. Dodge spread his jacket across the bench seat so Anna would have a dry place to sit. Soon, the truck owner brought their meals. After finishing the tacos, the pair tossed the empty cardboard containers into a trash receptacle, thanked the owner, and headed into the park. There was a chill in the air he found comfortable after the muggy days of summer.

"What did you think about the food?"

"I'll admit, I was a little nervous when I saw the food truck, but I have to say it was one of the better tacos I have ever had," Anna said.

Anna wrapped her arm through Dodge's at the elbow, pulling in tight. He responded by flexing his bicep, drawing her in closer.

"I don't know what it is about the park, but it always relaxes me," he said.

Anna looked up at him. "I always avoid the park at night. It's too quiet and creepy for me."

"Nothing is further from the truth."

Dodge had always enjoyed the city's parks, be it at night or during the day. He believed the investment in parks by municipalities returned dividends that were immeasurable in monetary terms. It fostered a sense of community pride and gave people an oasis in an asphalt jungle. It was a place where families living in high-rise apartment buildings came for picnics. Kids felt actual grass under their feet. Fathers taught future MLB stars how to throw and catch a baseball. But his work reminded him of the darker side. Just behind the next row of bushes or sliding side door of a windowless panel van was a potential threat. It was the reason he sat with his back to the wall in restaurants.

Anna's hip brushed his weapon as she continued to pull in closer. "Says the guy who always carries a gun."

"The department requires me to carry my weapon because of my position on the task force. I am always on call," he said, scanning the tree line. "Besides, makes you feel better, doesn't it?"

"It's not the gun. It's the company," she said.

"I hate to break it to you, but the company is only safe because of the gun. Truth is, I can't fight for shit."

"I don't believe that for a second. You are more than just a gun and badge. You are a hero. I can't imagine many people as dedicated to their job as you. I can't imagine any that are better at it than you."

Kelly had said that exact thing many times. At that moment, in that dress, Anna reminded him of her.

As the couple rounded a long turn in the path, the waterfront came into view. The water was calm. The slight sound of waves slapping the sea wall, one after another, put Dodge at ease. They could see small red lights swaying, first left then right, on the masts of sailboats anchored in the harbor.

"You see that out there?" he pointed at the blinking red lights in the harbor. "One day, I'll leave this all behind, sell everything except what I can't live without, and sail away."

"Where will you go?"

The idea to retire on a sailboat occurred to him on a four-day pass from a tour in Afghanistan. While he didn't want the time off, he figured why not relax on a short Mediterranean cruise? He flew to Turkey, but at the port, he found out they canceled the cruise. The tour company offered to return the cost of the package, but Dodge figured he wasted six hours on a plane, so he might as well do something. The tour company also booked sailing lesson trips. Thus began the dream, a dream to retire on the open water, beholden to no one and nothing. He had been saving for a boat since that day fourteen years ago.

"Everywhere and nowhere," he said.

"You don't have a destination in mind? Say, like, Belize?"

"That would defeat the purpose. I can park my boat in any harbor. Take a dinghy to shore for food and booze. Anywhere warm works for me."

"But you would have no home base? No place to come back to."

"Home base is where you make it. For me, it will be an island port. Drop anchor, drink rum, and fish."

The excitement surged through him. He was getting closer to his dream. Anna shivered. The shawl didn't offer much protection from the brisk air blowing in off the bay. Dodge slipped off his jacket and draped it over her shoulders. She re-engaged her arm, interlocking it, and pulled close.

"Let's get you home before you catch a cold," he said.

"And before the creepers come out!"

It was getting late, so they turned and walked back toward his truck. By the time they reached the parking lot, the roach coach had left, along with most everyone else who had been at the park. He opened the door and helped her into the vehicle. After finishing a cigarette, he hopped in, started the truck, and turned left out of the parking lot toward his house.

—⁓—

The bright red numbers on the alarm clock read 12:25 a.m. Dodge was lying in bed, smoking a cigarette, rehashing the day's events. He pictured the apartment building he had visited before his dinner with Anna. It became a practice early in his career to always run scenarios in his mind before embarking on home visits or searches of a suspect's home. It was something he had become very good at and pushed for its use at the Academy when instructing fresh recruits. The idea was to think before an upcoming home visit. Who was supposed to be home, and what did you plan to discuss? The first scenario was the perfect visit, no problems and everything goes well. Then you dissect it for different potential outcomes. Like picking at a scab until it bleeds. What if the offender wasn't the only person home? How might that affect your safety? The dissection continues until you reach the worst-case scenario, which involves a physical altercation. Only after realizing the worst-case scenario and working through it in reverse order should an agent go ahead.

The first two scenarios he tried to run just didn't work. He didn't know the layout of the basement or how many people who lived in the building had criminal records. The only thing he knew was he needed to enter through the basement door to avoid any tenants. Experience told him suspects used the basement in emergencies. Dodge was well aware he was flouting a number of his own rules. Playing it by ear was a dumb rookie mistake, but until he could lay eyes on the interior of the basement, he had no choice.

Wide awake and restless, he snuffed out his cigarette in the ashtray on the bedside table. Searches always amped him up, and night provided cover. It was harder for other residents to spot him at night and easier to recall details from his earlier visit to the building. He sat up in bed, and Anna moved. He remained motionless until he was sure she was asleep. He had told her he had to leave early in the morning and she could let herself out. The coffee was on the kitchen counter if she wanted a cup before leaving.

He grabbed his pants and a shirt hanging on the hamper and went into the bathroom to get dressed, so as not to wake Anna. After finishing in the bathroom, he turned the light off, grabbed his duty weapon from the top drawer of the side table, then headed out the front door. Through his rearview mirror, he saw the bright red glow of taillights reflecting off the window's glass as he pushed the brake pedal to put the truck in gear. The light faded as the vehicle pulled away from the curb toward downtown.

CHAPTER 11

THE RAIN WAS FALLING STEADILY, but not enough for the truck's wipers to work correctly. The blades vibrated on every return trip, resulting in a squeaking noise. Aware the noise could be heard outside his vehicle, Dodge shut the wipers off until the glass was wet enough to stop the vibration. He slowed the truck to a crawl one-half block from the building and shut off the headlights. He allowed his eyes time to adjust to the lighting conditions, as only a few of the streetlights were working.

Before deciding to move closer on foot, he watched the structures for half an hour. Using the same technique as last time, he stayed low and moved deliberately, using the cars lining the street for cover. He made it to the basement stairs in short order. A quick glance at the surrounding buildings reassured him no one took notice. Dodge peeked through the dirty, soot-stained square glass window, but he had trouble seeing through the years of grime and neglect. What appeared a negative was positive. It meant *he* couldn't be seen.

He pulled the lock pick set out of his back pocket and inserted a pick into the lock mechanism but stopped before jiggling the first tumbler. With his left hand, he turned the doorknob. No need to break in when the door is unlocked. *Time for a welfare check to make sure anyone inside is not hurt or injured.* The handle caught for a split second, and the bolt released from its housing in the doorjamb. Dodge placed the pick set back in his jacket pocket and unholstered his weapon, his left hand not relinquishing control of the door handle in case someone tried to jerk it open from the other side. The door had an inside swing, allowing for his weight as an advantage. If anyone tried to push the door closed, he could push through using his shoulder. His body weight would force the door through anyone standing on the other side. Mass plus momentum, that was how he won a fight.

The door opened. The hinges creaked from years of rust buildup. There was no resistance from the other side, and he relaxed his posture to let his muscles rest before entering. The hallway was dark and smelled of old clothes and urine. He could see a flicker of light shining against the wall at the end of the hall. There, the hall T-boned another hall extending left to right. This wasn't the layout he expected. Based on his observation of the floor above, the hall should have been straight, with rooms to the left and right sides. Dodge shook his head. He had been distracted and broke his most important rule: be prepared. A decision had to be made. Should he call Renquest for backup or continue alone? Entry was made and having searched hundreds of basements as a parole agent, he knew he would have no cell signal as soon as he entered. The thick brick walls and poor electrical wiring prevented wireless signals from entering or leaving the basement, and going back outside to call for backup increased the chances of drawing attention to himself. He had come this far. Best to just get it over with, which meant breaking another rule: use backup when in doubt.

Dodge reached for the flashlight on the left side of his duty belt, opposite his holster, using his left hand. He pressed the button at the rear of the flashlight twice to bypass the extra-bright beam and stop on the low beam. Why announce his presence sooner than necessary? He came to a door on his left and tried the handle. Locked. He moved forward slow and steady, his eyes scanning from right to front to left and back again. He slowed to check the handle on a door to his right. Locked.

About ten feet from the end of the hall, he could feel the woo-woo hairs on the back of his neck stand up. He continued on, breaking another rule: always listen to the woo-woo hairs. If another agent in his office was taking the risks he was taking, there would be a conversation followed by immediate safety retraining. *But this is a do as I say, not as I do moment,* he told himself.

Five feet. He killed the light. Three feet. He kept his Glock tucked close to his chest as he hugged the left wall, enabling a line of sight to the right with minimal exposure. A closed door with no windows. No threat. Dodge tilted his body until he had a complete view of the hall to the left, exposing only a small part of his face. The maneuver allowed him to bring his weapon to eye level with front sight on anything that moved. He inhaled deeply before heading down the left corridor. A light emanated from a room at the end. Once he was just outside the door to the room, he rushed in, banking on the element of surprise. His weapon swept from left to right, searching for a target.

He yelled, "Clear!"

It was instinctive. No one was around to hear it. He stood in a dirty, roach-infested makeshift sleeping quarter. Against one wall stood a cot with a bare mattress laying askew. Empty food containers and crumpled paper covered the floor. The room resembled the apartment with the tiny room built into the closet. But it was what he noticed on the wall above the bed that drew his attention. A collage of pictures, just like the one found in the hidden room earlier in the week. He scanned the wall for any familiar faces, stopping on each image momentarily before moving to the next. His heart raced from the adrenaline pumping through his veins. He got tunnel vision and was experiencing auditory exclusion, both symptoms of an advanced excited state. That is probably why he didn't hear the footsteps behind him.

A sharp pain radiated from the back of his neck. The pictures on the wall went out of focus. Darkness closed in from his peripherals. As his knees buckled, he tried to turn to face whatever had attacked him. He spun like the Tilt-A-Whirl ride at the county fair. A small ray of light was all he could perceive, the glimpse of a bright silver reflection that shone like a star, then he hit the ground. Darkness engulfed him.

When his eyes opened, he could feel hands touching his arms and legs. Voices echoed in his ears, but he couldn't make out what they were saying. The light was back, flashing in his eyes, but not like the silver star he saw earlier. This light was a rapid flash followed by blurred images of unfamiliar faces. Dodge tried to sit up, but someone pushed him down. He struggled to get a sense of what was happening to him. He closed his eyes and held them shut while he counted out loud to ten. When he got to ten, his breathing had slowed, and he opened his eyes. There was still no recognition of the faces huddled around him. Then a familiar voice echoed in his ears.

"Dodge. Can you hear me? Dodge?" the voice asked. "Get off him. Let's give him some room to breathe." He recognized the voice. It was Renquest.

"What are you doing here?" He sat upright.

"We got a call from a woman in the building across the street. She said she saw a man run from the basement after breaking in," Renquest said. "I knew you were going to watch this place tonight, so I sent over a cruiser to check it out."

Dodge tried to shake off the cobwebs in his head. "Can someone help me up? It smells like piss down here."

Renquest and an EMT lifted him to his feet. He stumbled before the two men could stabilize him again.

"Let's go out to the ambulance and get that bump on your head checked out," Renquest said.

After the ambulance crew took his blood pressure and provided an ice pack for his head, Dodge walked back to the building's front, where Renquest was supervising the scene.

"What time is it?"

"Just about three in the morning," Renquest said. "What time did you get here?"

His fingers rubbed the knot that sprouted on the back of his head. "After 1:00 a.m."

"Do you remember anything?"

"Not really. I remember standing in the room you found me in. I was looking at the pictures plastered on the wall and ceiling. The next thing I know, I am on the ground, and you are there."

"That's all you remember?"

"Pretty much," Dodge said. "Other than stars."

"Stars?"

"Yeah. Like in the cartoons, when someone gets knocked out. I saw stars. Well, one anyway. I always thought that was just a comedy gig."

"But you never saw who hit you?"

Dodge shook his head.

Renquest signaled for an officer to drive Dodge to the station for debriefing. Both men were aware that an after-action report was needed, and his statement was part of that process.

"When I am finished, can someone bring me back to my truck?"

"I'll have an officer drop it off. I don't want you driving just yet. Better to make sure there isn't any permanent damage before you get behind the wheel again," Renquest said.

Dodge reluctantly agreed and went with the officer to the station.

———

The man stood in the hallway to the right of the glass door. The entrance was off-center to make room for the mailboxes that lined the wall opposite the stairs, which provided him a place to watch without being seen. This building was tenant-free, as the owners were remodeling the interior to attract a more stable clientele that was able to pay the rent on time. He had read an article about how residents were forced to leave, a result of asbestos and lead paint. Both are known carcinogens and require specialty crews with lots of equipment to remove dangerous substances. The timing made it an excellent place to watch the apartment building across the street. He could come at night after the crews left and watch undisturbed. He knew his target came twice a week to check on the sump pumps in the basement. It made a great place to stage an ambush. Much easier than at his apartment. And that was what Fisch did.

It was clean and quick. He covered the body in lime and wrapped it in plastic to keep the rodents away. He rolled the body up in a rug and dragged it to the room containing the phone line junction boxes. No one had landlines anymore, and the building wasn't wired for internet. No one would go into that room. Initially, he had only needed to hide the body for a few days, but things changed, and getting away long enough at night to retrieve the corpse proved harder than he thought. Tonight was the first time his schedule allowed for a return visit without interruptions.

The man did what he always did and parked a few blocks away, using the alley to traverse the short distance to the building under construction. Once at the back of the building, he approached the entrance in the dark. Then, he just had to wait until the windows in the building across the street went dark. Only then could he cross the road and enter the basement, which he made sure was unlocked on his last visit. A quick trip inside to grab the corpse and toss him in the dumpster behind the building under construction. A few minutes to cover the body with construction debris and old furniture, and he would be in the clear. Nobody would find the body. It would get buried deep in a landfill, covered with twenty feet of garbage in a few days.

But this night had not gone to plan. While waiting for the lights to go out in the building across the street, he noticed a truck slow to a crawl, stopping in front of him. The driver focused on the same building he was watching. The truck parked a few spots down the road, but the driver didn't get out of the vehicle. The darkness made it impossible to see what the driver was doing in the truck. Maybe he wanted to buy drugs. Or perhaps pick up a prostitute. It could have been a million different things. Only it wasn't a million things. It was one thing.

When the man in the truck exited his vehicle and trudged across the street, Fisch recognized him. It was Paul Dodge. *What the hell is he doing here?* The dead guy had no paper trail to this building. He had checked. He knew the landlord was scamming the Section 8 housing system and didn't think he would tell the cops anything for fear of going to jail or, worse, losing his landlord status with HUD. But it was the only explanation he could come up with. The landlord must have talked. None of that mattered anymore. The situation changed from static to dynamic, and adaptation was needed. Fisch watched him kneel behind a panel van. Then, the parole agent pulled out his phone. A bead of sweat formed on Fisch's forehead. Was he calling police for backup? A raid would lead to the discovery of the dead man. They would break in every door in the basement, checking every corner and cubby hole. It would be a matter of time before some dumbass patrol cop stumbled over the rolled-up rug in the telephone junction box room, changing everything.

But Dodge didn't call the police; he never dialed a number. He put the phone back in his pocket and hurried to the stairway leading to the basement. For a moment, Dodge looked right at him. He knew there was no way he could see him from across the street. But the thought he had been made stuck in his head. Then, Dodge disappeared into the building. The man slipped out the back door the same way he had entered, used the alleys to circle behind the building across the street, and entered it through the back. He stood at the end of a long hallway, behind a door with only a small square of glass to see through. A flashlight beam bounced off the wall at the end of the hall to the right.

After a few seconds, Fisch saw the meddling agent appear and turn his flashlight in his direction. Accordingly, Fisch moved away from the window. He unsnapped his holster and gripped the SIG Sauer with his right hand. If Dodge came this way, shooting him would be the only option. After the light disappeared from the window, he looked back out. He was moving toward the room at the other end of the hall. He waited until his target was in the room before walking toward the end of the hall. Fisch was close enough to hear him talking.

There was no cell reception in the old building's basement, so he wasn't making a phone call. Through a reflection in a small mirror on the room's back wall, Fisch could see Dodge standing with his back to the door. He appeared mesmerized by the pictures hung on all the walls and ceilings. Now was the time. He wouldn't hear it coming.

One smack to the back of the head, at the point the neck meets the skull with a blackjack, was all it took. Dodge spun and reached for his belt but came up short. The man looked down, realizing his badge was still hooked to his belt. In the past, he put the badge in his pocket in case he came across another cop. The move provided a way to identify himself and explain his presence. He wondered if he had gotten a glimpse of it.

No way he could see anything but stars, he thought. Fisch left him lying on the floor and retrieved the body from its hiding place. After entering the alley, he decided the risk of driving his car around to the alley was too high. Lifting the rug onto his shoulder, he crossed the street using the alley. He used his momentum to toss the body up and over the side of the dumpster without stopping. Then Fisch gathered trash and construction debris from the ground and threw them on top of the body.

Fisch took one last survey of the area before running down the alley toward his car. He stopped when a patrol car cruised past. It headed in the direction he had just come from, the same direction where he had left the unconscious parole agent. Once the vehicle was out of sight, he walked the final half-block to his car, started the engine, pulled out onto the street, and headed toward downtown. The sound of sirens echoed in the distance. Dodge must have woken up and called for assistance. It didn't matter. The disposed body meant he was in the clear. He just had a few more things to do before it would all be over. He felt himself relax as the buildings passed by his window. The streetlights caused a soothing pulsating flash of light each time he passed under one. He was almost finished.

CHAPTER 12

THE MORNING SUN FLICKERED between the leaves on the trees, making a dappled pattern on the bed. The bright flashes of light caused Anna to open her eyes, squinting until they adapted to the change in brightness. Her right arm reached across the bed to the spot where Dodge had been when she had fallen asleep. Anna felt only the fresh sheet covering the mattress. She sat up and stared at the empty space. She looked around the room, but he wasn't in the bathroom or bedroom.

"Dodge," she called out. Nothing.

Anna climbed out of bed and put on a T-shirt tossed over the back of a chair. She brushed her teeth, washed her face, then combed the tangles from her hair. A brief snoop in the medicine cabinet uncovered an over-the-counter inflammation reducer and an old razor. She closed the medicine cabinet and headed to the living area. She caught the aromatic smell of fresh-brewed coffee as soon as she stepped into the room. Dodge had prepared the coffee machine and set the timer for 8:00 a.m. before their activities last night. Then, she remembered him telling her he had to go to work in the morning and probably would be gone before she awoke. She must have been half asleep when he told her, which was why the conversation slipped her mind.

After pouring herself a cup of coffee, Anna walked the perimeter of the living room, reading each award, plaque, and certificate hung on the walls or sitting on a shelf. There were pictures of Dodge with senators, congressmen, and what Anna could only assume was a high-ranking military officer. Although she wasn't familiar with the military's chain of command, she was sure a star on the collar was the highest rank. There were challenge coins scattered throughout the living room. Half the coins had "U.S. Air Force" written on them, others the "Department of Corrections." Still, others had country names, like Afghanistan and Thailand, stamped around the edges. She picked one up. It was heavy and had an eagle painted on one side. The words "to serve and protect USAF Security Detachment" were printed on the other side.

Putting the coin back on the table, she sat on the couch to drink her coffee and enjoy the quiet morning when the sunlight shining through the front window bounced off an object in the open closet, causing a glint that caught her eye. Anna placed her coffee on the end table and took the five steps to reach the closet. The closet was open and contained several jackets hanging up in order of light to heavy from right to left. A pair of winter boots sat on the floor and a basket with gloves and stocking hats was on the top shelf. Next to the basket was a brown wooden box. The box was the size of a shoebox and had a glossy sheen. Out of instinct, Anna glanced over her shoulder to see if anyone was watching. A guilt mechanism. She pulled the box from the shelf and carried it to the center of the room, where she sat on the floor and placed the wooden box in her lap.

The top of the box swung open longways, like a safe deposit box. Anna helped the lid come to rest, making sure not to overextend the hinges and rendering the top unable to close correctly. The wooden box contained old newspaper clippings and magazine articles. The first couple of clippings included stories concerning sex offenders, with Dodge as an interviewed source. It appeared to Anna that the local media valued his opinion on matters involving sex crimes.

What a horrible world he must live in, she thought. *Every day his job requires him to hear about rape, murder, and child abuse. Why would anyone want to do that job?* A wave of sadness came over her.

After sifting through several clippings, she noticed a piece written roughly ten years ago about Dodge and the rescue of a woman from a serial rapist and murderer. At first glance, it appeared the same as other articles in the box, but her eyes focused on a name. She needed a last name and read more to see if it was mentioned. The name was Gosling, Kelly Ann Gosling. Anna wasn't sure what Kelly's last name was but had heard her talking to someone on the phone once and she had said the name Kelly Ann. Last names were a risk in their business. Anna continued to read.

June 22, 2008: Local woman recovered from the clutches of her captor. Kelly Ann Gosling, 24, formerly of Fort Wayne, Indiana, was located, bound, and battered inside the home of a local parolee, Grayson Heller. Gosling had been reported missing by her roommate over two weeks ago, but police were at a loss for suspects and had very few leads in the disappearance.

Anna took another sip from her coffee.

Enter local Parole Agent Paul Dodge. Dodge is a five-year veteran of the Department of Corrections and supervises offenders on parole convicted of sexually based crimes. He begins every day with coffee and a cigarette, then delves into the seedy world of sex offender crimes, including the trail of physical and emotional destruction left in their wake. It was a routine home visit to Heller's residence. He had been a model parolee up to this point. During the routine inspection of the home, which takes place during every home visit, the parole agent noticed a lock securing a bedroom door and questioned Heller about it.

Anna looked up from the article at the pictures hanging on the wall, trying to place any of them to the article she was reading.

During questioning, Heller became combative. A struggle ensued. During the fight, the two men fell to the floor, where Heller pulled a knife from his boot and thrust it into Dodge's stomach.

Anna's hand was instinctively drawn to the spot on her body where the article stated Dodge had been stabbed.

The agent fired a single round from his department-issued Glock 9mm, hitting Heller in the leg. Heller fled the scene. Dodge called for assistance then broke the lock off the bedroom door. Inside, he found Kelly Ann Gosling. She was alive. She had been beaten and was malnourished.

Anna placed her hand over her mouth, shocked by what she was reading.

The Department of Corrections and local police conducted a two-day manhunt for Heller, who was eventually found in an abandoned apartment building less than a mile from his home. Heller, leg infected from the 9mm round lodged in it, was unconscious and taken in for medical care then to jail. A jury convicted him of rape, attempted murder, and kidnapping. Dodge was awarded the Medal of Valor for his actions in saving Gosling.

Anna placed the article in the box and stared across the room, a blank expression on her face. Kelly had never told her how the two had met. She struggled to understand what she had just read, even if it made sense in the abstract. Runaway teen turned prostitute, which damn near got her killed. It was a tale that was often told among the women on the street and was why Anna wanted out.

The sound of a car stopping out front startled her. She looked out the window and saw Dodge climbing out of a police car. She hurried to place the clippings back into the box and set the box back on the shelf, then ran toward the front door. The door opened it before she could make it to the entryway. His clothes were dirty and full of wrinkles. His hair was matted, and he held an ice pack to the back of his head. Dodge sat on the couch, and Anna got a glass of water from the tap.

"What happened?" Anna asked. "Are you OK?"

He nodded, causing him to wince. "I got knocked on the head."

"Where? Who hit you?"

"I don't know." He could sense the anxiety in Anna's voice. She was worried.

"What did the police say?" Anna asked.

"They are looking into it. The problem is I don't remember anything. It happened so fast. I didn't get a look at who it was.

But it must have something to do with the new case I am working."

"Kelly's case?"

Dodge touched the back of his head, causing it to throb all the way to the spot the brain meets the spine. It was like someone beating a giant drum inside his skull. He didn't think he had a concussion but refused to go to the hospital. He was angry that he hadn't followed his own rules. He could have been killed, right there on that dirty floor, and there wasn't a thing he could have done to stop it. The story in the paper would detail how careless he had been. The department would disavow his actions as against policy. Department policy required backup or informing his superiors that he was in the field at night. The department would control the story because with him dead, there would be no one else to fight the narrative. He would have gone from local hero to reckless agent in less than twenty-four hours.

Anna searched the kitchen and bathroom for pain medicine. She was scared and mad. She wanted to shake the life out of him. "What were you thinking?" Her voice echoed in his head. "You could have been killed."

He decided answering her might quiet her. "I'm fine."

Dodge leaned back, allowing his body to sink into the couch cushions. His head tilted back until he was staring at the ceiling.

"You are not fine. You should be at the hospital. And I can't find the painkillers!" She slammed the cupboard door in frustration.

He understood her frustration. He had been so stupid and knew what he did was stupid.

"The pain pills are in the small cabinet next to the fridge."

Anna opened the cabinet and moved some bottles from one side to the other. "I don't see them."

"They're in a prescription bottle. Should be toward the back."

She moved a bottle of antacids and random cold tablet sheets to one side. Spotting the only prescription bottle in the cabinet. She grabbed it, popping off the cap. The label stated the contents of the orange bottle were tramadol. The script was over two years old.

"These pills were prescribed over two years ago."

Dodge held out his hand, not concerned about the expiration date on the bottle, only its contents' ability to ease the pounding in his head.

Anna placed two of the pills in his hand with a glass half-filled with water. Dodge shook off the offer of water and popped the pills into his mouth, grinding the tablets between his teeth. He washed it down with a swig of bourbon, then laid back, his head resting on the back cushions of the couch.

Anna sat beside him. She placed a pillow on her lap for his head. She ran her hands through his hair, dragging strands through her fingers. Gently massaging his scalp with her manicured nails, the throbbing in his head eased. His muscles relaxed, which allowed him to think more clearly.

"Seriously, you could have been really hurt," Anna said. Her voice switched from anger to compassion.

"If they wanted me dead, I wouldn't be laying on this couch with a gigantic knot on the back of my head. There would be a hole in it."

"Maybe he got interrupted before he could finish."

"I was out. I don't know for how long. Whoever it was could have chopped me up and carried me out in buckets in that amount of time. No one would have been the wiser."

"Were you the one who called the police?"

A memory flashed into his head. The last thing he remembered was staring at the pictures posted all over the walls. Then nothing. His memory was fuzzy, and he had lost time.

"Renquest was in the ambulance when I woke up. To be honest, I'm not sure if I called him or how he got there. It's all scattered right now."

Dodge sat up, but Anna grabbed his shoulders and pulled him back onto her lap.

"What do you think you are doing?"

He tried to sit up again. His head started spinning, and his ears rang. It was a feeble try, making it about a quarter of the way to an upright position before lying back down, resting his head back in Anna's lap.

"They need my help processing the scene," he said.

"You are not going anywhere. You need to stay on the couch and rest. If you are needed, they can call."

Dodge tried to speak, but Anna cut him off before he could get a word out of his mouth. "You need to rest."

"Maybe I can just rest a few hours," he said, closing his eyes.

"Just relax. I'll stay as long as you want," Anna said.

The ringing in his ears had quieted, and his head had stopped spinning. He fell asleep.

CHAPTER 13

AT THE SAME TIME DODGE RETURNED HOME, the morning sun shone through the window behind the warden's desk, causing the inmate sitting in the chair opposite him to squint. Seat placements in his office were not random. The warden gave specific instructions to ensure the person across from him faced straight into the morning sun. He was old school and liked to conduct disciplinary meetings with staff and inmates first thing in the morning. People were complacent in the morning. There was less of a chance for a physical altercation. The sun to his back sun guaranteed the warden an advantage. A Colt .357 snub-nosed revolver in a holster attached to the underside of the desk didn't hurt his chances either. He could pull the weapon or shoot without removing it from the holster.

The person on the receiving end of any .357 round fired that day was Grayson Heller. The warden wasn't a fan of Grayson and was aware of his manipulative nature. He was a dangerous inmate and had tricked guards on at least two occasions into smuggling items he used for currency on the inside. Grayson often got what he wanted inside the walls because he had a reach extending far outside the walls trapping him. Everyone, including the warden, was aware of that.

"What is it I can help you with, Inmate Heller?"

"It's not what you can do for me this time, Warden. It is what I can do for you."

"Jesus Christ, are you hearing this asshole?" the warden asked the shift commander standing behind Grayson.

"Yes, sir, Warden."

Grayson appeared unaffected by the insult. "I can help get you that job you have been waiting on for years."

The warden's face remained stoic. "What job are you talking about?"

"The head job. The boss. Who else would I be talking about?"

"What the hell are you talking about?"

"Why must we play these games, Warden? It is childish and, frankly, insulting."

"I'm not playing any games here. I don't have a clue what the fuck you are talking about, Inmate Heller."

Grayson nodded and laughed. "If that's how you want to play it, fine with me. We can just pretend I don't have anyone on the outside, or inside, providing me with information."

"Look, let's cut the shit. We both know you want something. I'm not sure what it is, but I'm willing to bet this isn't coming from a place of compassion. So why don't you just tell me what you want and what it will cost me?"

Grayson stopped laughing. "I want you to get Agent Dodge back here. We need to finish a conversation we started the other day."

The warden leaned forward in his chair. "Why in God's name would he come back to talk to you?"

"Because I can help him with his problem."

"You are so full of shit. Do you even hear yourself? What could you possibly offer me?"

"With all due respect, Warden, that is between Paul Dodge and me."

"With no due respect, you don't get to decide what happens in my prison. You either tell me or go the fuck back to your cell."

"OK. OK. No need to get nasty. I have information for him about a federal judge's daughter."

The warden had been briefed on the case but wasn't aware of all the details. He knew it somehow involved a federal judge. He also recognized Dodge would have never disclosed case details to Grayson. Not a juvenile victim's information, to be sure. It was a play by Grayson to insert himself into the investigation and continue his torture of the man who put him in prison. But what bothered the warden was Grayson's knowledge of the daughter. No one outside of the police department would have that information. The warden now had proof someone on the outside supplied him with information. The warden needed to end the interview and call Dodge to tell him Grayson was on to him.

"I know you think you are some big shot back in the pod, but here, you are just another inmate. You don't get to come into my office and dictate terms." Standing, the warden leaned over his desk a few inches from Grayson's face. "Now, you can go back to your cell. Or better yet." He nodded to the shift commander, who walked over to the office door, signaling the correctional officers stationed outside that the meeting was finished. "How about a few days in the hole to help sort out your attitude problem? And I'm not talking about the solitary wing. I'll stick you in the padded cell reserved for the nut jobs. No windows and no communicating with anyone."

The two guards stepped beside Grayson, one on each side, interlocked their forearms under his armpits, and lifted him out of the chair in one well-rehearsed and disciplined move.

"You tell him what I said. He will come. He will come!"

Grayson's feet skimmed the floor as the two guards escorted him toward the basement, toward the solitary cells.

The warden leaned back on the corner of his desk. The watch commander turned to watch until the guards rounded a corner out of sight.

"What do you want to do with him?" the watch commander asked.

"Put him in the hole. Ten days should wipe the smirk off his face."

"How do you want me to write it up?"

"I don't give a good goddamn. Just do it."

"I need a charge to place an inmate in solitary, sir."

The warden slammed the palm of his hand on the desktop,

making a loud crack and knocking over a jar containing pens and other writing utensils.

"Pissing me off. Good enough charge for you?"

"Sure thing, sir, but I think the AG's office may want something a little more official."

The warden picked up a red file lying on his desk. Red files were reserved for investigations dealing with staff and inmate rule violations. It gave him an idea for placing Grayson in the hole. No one argued against the use of the hole for an inmate's safety.

"Place an investigative hold on him for making threats against one of the staff. It should buy me enough time to talk to Dodge and keep anyone else from sneaking in information."

The watch commander nodded. "Yes, sir."

"And, Commander, I want a detailed list of anyone who has contact with him while he is in the hole. No one goes in without signing the log. You understand?"

"I'll see to it personally."

The warden returned to his desk and punched the quick dial number on his phone for his secretary. "I need you to get me Agent Dodge's number."

She asked if he wanted an office or cell number. Both numbers were available in the internal DOC system.

"His personal number. And I need it yesterday."

The warden hit the disconnect button then sat back in his chair. He worried if he was about to make the right play and hoped Dodge would back him. If not, he could have just killed his career. The secretary's voice chirped from the phone's speaker with the numbers he had requested. He dialed the cell number and waited for an answer.

CHAPTER 14

AN AFTERNOON BREEZE SWIRLED the first fallen autumn leaves outside Dodge's brownstone. The sun's power had diminished, a direct correlation to the numbers associated with the months on a calendar. The light dancing across his face made his nerve endings awaken. First shade, then sun. Shade and sun. He moved his hands over his eyes so he could open them without being blinded.

Once able to see across the room without squinting, he determined no sight aftereffects lingered from the concussion, such as double vision or light sensitivity. He mustered his head off the pillow. While he still felt the effects of a headache, he noticed no dizziness or vertigo. He raised himself up to a seated position. The results of the self-medical examination meant very little without the ability to stand and walk without falling. Many times, the effects of a concussion set in once a person was up and moving around. He crawled toward the middle of the room before attempting to stand up. If he fell, he wouldn't injure himself more by smashing his head onto the edge of a coffee table or other objects situated around his living room.

He stood, taking each move in steps, like learning to dance. First rising to his knees, pausing for any side effects. Then to a crouching position, knees bent, hands planted on the ground. Again, nothing struck him as odd. Under the circumstances, he was doing well. One last step. A slow rise to an upright position. Once standing and noticing no adverse effects, he looked for signs of Anna. He remembered she had gone to the pharmacy to pick up some pain meds and expected her to be back before he woke up. Dodge called her name as he stepped into the bedroom, thinking she might be in the bathroom. No answer. Then, he checked the rest of the house. Anna wasn't in the kitchen, bedroom, or out on the stoop. She must have run some personal errands or possibly gone home to shower and change clothes. He noticed a piece of paper on the floor next to the dining room table. It was a note from Anna.

Dodge, I am sorry I wasn't there when you woke up. I remembered I had something I needed to do today. It's nothing too important, just personal issues I had been putting off. I'll stop by later to check on you. I could cook dinner for you tonight if you want. We never did get to talk about Kelly. Anna

Dodge needed to report to his chief and was surprised a call with threats of suspension hadn't already been issued. It wasn't the first time he had broken policy, and history being the best predictor of future behavior, it wouldn't be the last. He also knew a suspension wouldn't happen today. The department wouldn't risk losing a spot on the task force. They wouldn't want to piss off the Feds by suspending their handpicked investigator. One call from a federal judge would strike fear in any state official. Dodge was safe, for now, or at least his job was.

Chief Johnson's phone was answered by the office secretary, Ms. Marble. She was an older lady who had retired from a state teaching job.

"State Parole. How may I help you?"

"Hello, Ms. Marble, is the Chief—"

"Dodge! Where have you been? Chief Johnson has been looking for you all day. He is livid." Her voice boomed at first but muffled as she didn't want to bring attention to herself.

"Is the chief in?"

"He went out to lunch about twenty minutes ago. You had better get in here. I tell you, I haven't ever seen him this mad."

"When do you expect him back?"

"It doesn't matter what I expect. You better be here when Chief Johnson gets back."

"I have to swing by the doctor's office for a follow-up. I'll be in after my appointment."

This was a lie he hoped would buy him a small respite and give Chief Johnson time to calm down. Dodge was working on task force time when he was attacked, so there was little the department could do to him about his disregard for personal safety. This meeting was going to be more of a general ass chewing from one parole agent to another. Sure, there would be threats, but they would be little more than just that, threats.

"Are you OK?" she asked with a tone of empathy.

"I feel good now, but I could use some pills for this headache. Tell the chief I'll be in as soon as I am finished."

"I'll tell him, and, Dodge, be careful from here on out."

His next move was to talk to Renquest and find out if there were any updates on either case. Renquest briefed him on the progress of the judge's case first, as it was the quickest. There was no update. He discussed the attack on Dodge and broke down what they had found, or didn't find, in the basement. No usable fingerprints. No electronic devices. No witnesses. *Sounded about right*, he thought. Dodge began to entertain the idea that the lead about the basement room, the one he was attacked in, was a setup. Renquest told him to report to the station for an informal meeting with the senior task force officer. Task force leadership took attacks on their own seriously and wanted to find out if his assault was linked to the judge's case. He said he couldn't delay his scolding from Chief Johnson much longer and would report for the meeting with the task force leadership later in the afternoon. He hung up the phone and stopped to get a cup of coffee before finishing the trip to the parole office.

The last glow of the day's sun had faded to dusk. The meeting with Chief Johnson dragged on longer than he had hoped. The first ten minutes he spent yelling. The rest of the meeting went as expected. There would be no suspension today. They agreed the two-day headache was punishment enough. It was suggested any work after dark include a partner or backup from local PD. Chief Johnson left him zero wiggle room on the issue, and Dodge agreed to the terms before going to meet Detective Renquest.

Detective Renquest sat behind his desk, typing case notes on his computer when Dodge arrived. The office was less cluttered than usual. Renquest had a habit of removing files from the file cabinet and leaving them on his desk when finished. The pile had taken on a life of its own, expanding to about five times its original size since the last time he had been to the office.

"You need to have one of the rookies come clean this mess up," Dodge said.

"Dodge. Glad you could make it. Have a seat," Renquest said. "What the hell were you thinking?"

"I told you I would check out the apartment building, and I did."

"Yes, you did. But you failed to inform me about the second visit you made."

"It was late. I didn't want to bother you. Besides, it would likely have been a rookie. That late at night, they are all juiced up on caffeine and trigger happy. They make more noise than a damn freight train."

Renquest wasn't having any of the argument. "I should have known you would pull something like that. You are damn lucky to be alive."

"So I heard."

"Is that supposed to be funny?"

Dodge wasn't trying to be funny and knew he was wrong. "I couldn't sleep, so I went out. Can we forgo the lecture? I'm not in the mood for another ass chewing. My head is pounding, and tomorrow, I have to drive back to the prison to talk to Grayson Heller again."

"Another ass chewing, huh? I take it your chief talked to you today?"

Dodge nodded. "He did."

"I suppose I'll spare you any further discomfort."

"I appreciate it."

"Why are you talking to Grayson again? I thought your last visit knocked him out of the picture."

"He got the warden to agree to another sit-down with me."

"What do you think he is up to?"

"Who knows? It might be as simple as he enjoys fucking with me."

Renquest's eyes darted down toward another file on his desk then back up. "I was sorry to hear about Kelly. I know you two were close."

Dodge was silent.

"You don't think Grayson had anything to do with Kelly's death, do you?" Renquest said.

The two men stayed in silence for a moment.

Renquest looked at the file in his hand. "Well, if it was me—"

Dodge cut him off. "It isn't."

"True, but as I was saying, if it were me, I wouldn't give him too much. The more he knows, the more he will try to manipulate you. He isn't dumb. If he wants to see you again, he has a plan."

Renquest wasn't wrong. Grayson was a master manipulator, and he was drawing him into a hornet's nest. The last thing he wanted was a *Princess Bride* battle of wits.

"You don't know him the way I do."

"I am aware of his capabilities." Renquest tossed his glasses on the desk. "I am also aware of your past with him. Goddamn it. I was there too, remember?"

A rush of shame came over Dodge. His friend was right. He arrived the moment after shots were fired. Renquest was a patrol sergeant who he often used for backup when conducting field visits. That day, Renquest got held up at a traffic accident and was running late. To that point, Grayson had been a model parolee. Not a single missed appointment or failed urine screening. What was the worst that could happen if he started without backup? What happened was his actions forced Renquest to endure an officer down call. It was a burden he carried with him to this day. He knew Renquest always blamed himself for not arriving on time.

"I only meant I won't underestimate him," Dodge said.

"And I don't expect you will. However, if it were me, I would shake his tree and see what falls out. Then I would turn it all over to those two U.S. Marshals. Let them deal with whatever shitstorm brews up. Grayson has a big hard-on for you, and this could be his way of stroking it."

Dodge stood. "I have spent ten years trying to get that son of a bitch out of my life. This could be my chance to put this entire thing with him behind me."

"I know. So, what can I do to help?"

"Nothing at the moment. Let's see how the visit tomorrow plays out. I need to find out what his endgame is."

Renquest nodded. "Holler when you need me."

"I will. But now, I'm going home to have a drink."

"Dodge."

Turning on his way out, Dodge said, "Yeah?"

"Next time, pick up the damn phone, OK?"

He nodded, an assurance he wouldn't go at it alone again, and walked away. Once in the elevator, he checked his phone. There was a message from Anna.

I borrowed a key to your house when I left. I didn't want to knock on the door and wake you if you were still asleep. When are you going to be home? I got some things from the store and thought I could cook dinner. Anna.

Someone helping themselves to a spare key would normally have upset Dodge. But he wasn't this time. Maybe it was the knock to the head or the way Anna looked at him the other night. He felt Anna needed him in some way. A rescue, maybe. Either way, he would deal with that later. Right now, food sounded good. His thoughts switched to the drive home and the traffic conditions. It should be a smooth trip.

OMW. Be about 15.

On his way home, Dodge couldn't stop thinking about the events surrounding his attack—what he could remember anyway. The idea of seeing stars seemed ridiculous to him the more he thought about it. He googled "Results of a head injury" while stopped at a red light. The search results listed tunnel vision, glimpses of light, auditory exclusion, or temporary hearing loss as side effects of a knock to the head. Dodge remembered the onset of tunnel vision and his attempts to fight it off. He didn't recall hearing anything but attributed that to being in a basement. The attacker said nothing, and to get the drop on him, his attacker had to have been silent. The only thing left was the star he saw. The light wasn't made up of bright colors or a white light intensifying then disappearing as he blacked out. The light was more of a shine, like a metallic object reflecting light rays. But what he couldn't figure out was why the glow took the shape of a star. The image was still fuzzy. Maybe trying to forget about it for the night and revisiting the details again in the morning would help. Pulling into the spot in front of his house, he could see Anna in the dining room through the front window. She looked stunning. Before going inside, Dodge stood outside the window and watched her for a moment.

CHAPTER 15

DODGE WANTED TO LEAVE EARLY to avoid much of the morning traffic. The prison visit would waste most of his day, leaving little time for completing any meaningful work. He showered and threw on a pair of jeans and a T-shirt. No need to dress up for Grayson. He would take a button-up shirt to change into before going to work after he finished at the prison. The meeting should be a quick one.

Anna was sleeping, and he sat on the edge of the bed beside her. He didn't want to wake her. He brushed the hair from her face, leaned over, and kissed her forehead.

Anna opened her eyes and smiled.

"Good morning."

"Good morning," Dodge said. "There is a pot of coffee brewing in the kitchen. Sugar and creamer are on the counter. I laid out a towel if you want to take a shower."

"Thank you."

"Stay as long as you'd like. I should be back before four."

"Where are you going?" Anna sat up in bed and pulled the blanket up to cover her breasts.

"I have to go downstate and interview a prisoner. When I get back, maybe we can grab dinner at the new Chinese place on Main tonight."

"I haven't had good Chinese food in months."

"So it's a date."

Anna placed her hand on his. "It's a date."

He tugged on the blanket. "I'll see you tonight."

The drive to the prison took longer than expected. A wreck on the on-ramp to the freeway had traffic backed up for half a mile. It took police time to clear the scene. Once the vehicles were pulled from the traffic lanes, he made up for the lost time. After driving for ninety minutes, he turned onto the half-mile-long road leading to the front gates of the prison. A quick flash of his ID to the guard operating the gate and he was on prison grounds and parked in the assigned spot for state parole agents next to the main visitors' entry.

Once inside, Dodge bypassed the warden's office, heading straight for the interview rooms, stopping only to maneuver the man traps along the way. He arrived at interview room 105A to find it was empty. The warden had always had a standing order to have inmates in the interview room waiting for his arrival. It was a necessary move, as the meeting was taking place on their turf. The inmate had a home-court advantage. He needed to gain leverage back by starting the interview on his time. Grayson gained the upper hand by stalling until he was ready.

Dodge sat at the square metal table with his back to the door. He heard the gates slam shut, followed by the sound of footsteps drawing closer. He heard three sets. Ankle chains made a distinctive clicking sound when they touched the ground in between steps. A snap, then a short drag. *Click-shh. Click-shh.* So, there were two guards bookending Grayson.

The door to the room opened. *Click-shh, click-shh.* The door closed. Dodge refused to turn and acknowledge Grayson's presence in the room. He continued pretending to read a file open on the table.

"Agent Dodge, I told them you would come and see me."

He ignored the comment.

"Is that the information I requested?"

Dodge said nothing. He sensed tension coming from Grayson. Advantage Dodge.

"Agent Dodge!"

Nothing but silence.

Grayson erupted, "I don't have to take this disrespect! I

have something you need." His voice became louder and more distressed. "You talk to me, or I am going back to my cell."

Dodge tried to hide the fact that he was smiling.

"Fuck this!" Grayson came out of the chair, tripping over his leg irons as he stumbled past the corner of the table and toward the only door in the room.

Grayson was mad and acting out of emotion, not reason. Dodge, realizing Grayson would soon regain his composure, needed to start the interview. Instructions to the guards were to not open the door unless Dodge requested it, a move he hoped would reinforce his control over the inmate's movements, demoralizing him. It was equivalent to a tap out in wrestling.

"Sit down."

A look of defeat replaced anger, and Grayson pulled the chair out and sat.

"Why am I here?" Dodge asked.

"I need to be around people. I need to help the other inmates navigate this complex system of guards and inmates."

The idea of Grayson Heller being a good Samaritan caused Dodge to snicker.

"You think it is funny they have forced me to live in the hole, Agent Dodge? Did you order them to put me there?"

"The hole? What are you talking about?"

"The warden stuck me in the hole after a minor disagreement. He claimed I struck a guard and stuck me down there. He is a damn liar."

"And I care why?"

"I can't be in the hole. I need human interaction and intellectual conversation."

"Have you tried not assaulting guards as a first step?"

"Don't pretend to be ignorant. I didn't assault any guards. It was punishment for asking you to come back. We both understand his motivation. It is to see me dead. He hopes that will put him in the director's chair."

"You are so self-involved," Dodge said. "You still believe people care what you want or think." He immediately realized his mistake. If no one cared, why was he being interviewed? There was no backtracking in an interview, he had to move forward.

Grayson smiled. "And yet, you care enough to drive here just to see me. Face it, Agent Dodge, we intertwine our pasts and our futures. I'll always be a part of your and that whore's life."

Dodge felt the burning in his stomach rise into his chest. He was furious. His first instinct was to wrap his hands around the inmate's throat and squeeze until his eyes rolled back in their sockets. Controlling his emotions was paramount. Grayson had thrown his Hail Mary ball by alluding to Kelly and their past. At that moment, his analytic brain took over. Grayson didn't know Kelly was dead. Dodge had wondered if her death would somehow lead back to Grayson. The fact he didn't gloat said he wasn't involved. He wondered, *If not Grayson, then who?*

Now Dodge could concentrate and find out how much knowledge Grayson had on the marshals' case. He was prepared for this eventuality and reached into his jacket and pulled out a manila envelope, tossing it on the table.

"What's that?" Grayson asked.

"They are pictures from the marshals' crime scene. I hoped you might provide some insight into the suspect's mental state."

Grayson was trying to hide his excitement over the prospect of viewing the material within the manila envelope. It was as if someone flipped a switch. He transformed from manipulator to a slave of his desires. The hook was set, and it was time to reel in the catch.

Grayson reached for the envelope. He emptied its contents, and his eyes scanned for anything that stood out to him.

"What do you see?"

Grayson continued examining the photos, then he stopped.

"What is it?" Dodge asked.

"Your prey is an observer. He is not interested in the kill. Only the hunt."

"How do you know that?"

"The photos are pristine. Your subject took the photos and

displayed them for self-pleasure. Predators often like to play with their prey. Your man does not."

Dodge's neck hairs stood on end. Grayson was predictable if nothing else.

"Tell me something I don't know already, or I am walking." He stood up, pointing toward the door. He slammed his left hand on the pile of pictures and dragged them back to his side of the table. Grayson reached for the photos, grabbing one and holding it up.

"Who is this beauty?"

The blood emptied out of Dodge's face as Grayson picked the one picture that changed everything. The judge's daughter. Law enforcement officers were the only ones who knew about her case. His recognition of her in the picture confirmed Grayson was involved. He just didn't know to what extent. He needed to speak with the judge and the girl. Grayson added an aspect of danger that had alluded Dodge. The threat was real. This wasn't just a peeper if Grayson had a hand in this mess. Snatching the picture from Grayson's hands, he scrambled to gather up the remaining photos from the table. He shoved them into the folder and banged on the door, alerting the guards he was ready to leave. Grayson had taken the bait and revealed his hand.

Dodge sipped from a cup of coffee the secretary provided him as he waited in the warden's office. The warden entered from a side door that led to a conference room.

"How did it go?"

"I think he bought it."

The warden sat at his desk, rocking slightly in his leather high-back chair. He used a key to unlock a drawer and grabbed two highball glasses and a bottle of liquor.

"You took a colossal risk bringing all that information up here and letting him look at it."

"Things are rarely as they seem. Take this envelope here." Dodge pulled the manila envelope out of his jacket. "It contains a bunch of photos."

"But he picked out the girl?"

"He did." The envelope spun as it slid across the warden's desk.

The warden removed a handful of pictures.

"Are these the pictures from your case?"

"The girl was the only picture associated with the crime scene," Dodge said. "The rest are just internet images our tech guy put together for me."

"And when you threatened him, Grayson picked out the only picture that mattered? The only picture that would keep him engaged in the investigation, in you. What made you think he wouldn't recognize the other pictures as fakes?"

The legs of the chair squealed, like nails on a chalkboard, when the parole agent pushed his chair back to stand. His mind worked more freely while on his feet.

"I thought about it a good long while last night. I decided it didn't matter."

"Showing your cards is always a risky proposition. If it goes wrong, you can't put that genie back in the bottle," the warden said.

"True, either Grayson would see the girl's picture, or he wouldn't. If he didn't, his angle involved only me. If he did, then he is involved somehow. We didn't share any of the pictures outside of the police department, marshals' office, and me. Someone from the inside has to be feeding him information."

"So, we have a rat. I can check Grayson's phone and visitor logs."

"You won't find anything. If it is a person on the inside, they are aware of how the system works and won't get caught confessing on a visiting room phone."

"They are communicating somehow." The warden paused as it hit him. "Cell phone."

Dodge nodded. "How many phones have you found in the past year in searches?"

"I have boxes of them in the admin building's basement. Some are from cell searches, and some are from visitors attempting to sneak them through the metal detectors."

"How many do you think you catch, overall?"

"I would like to tell you we confiscate most during security checks, but that is not true. With that said, what's your plan to uncover the rat?"

"You need to know what kind of rat you have before you build a trap."

They had decided information would be released on a need-to-know basis only. The plan was to play it close to the vest. Secrets were hard to keep. Everyone in prison had an agenda. The inmates, guards, even the warden, worked angles. For some, it was about survival, as is with guards and inmates. For others, such as the warden, it was political. Dodge was more guarded concerning the latter. He had shared as much information as he was going to share.

"Have you spoken to the girl yet?"

"Not yet. I wasn't sure she could provide any information pertinent to the investigation. No need worrying her."

"How much is the judge aware of?"

"I am assuming all of it. He asked for me."

"Why you?"

"I don't have an answer to that, either. But I will soon. I am going to talk to the daughter after I leave here."

"Good luck. And, remember who her dad is."

The comment drew a smirk. "Thanks. I almost forgot."

Another accident on the interstate ensured darkness awaited him for much of the drive home. After a one-hour delay and using back roads, Dodge arrived at his house and shut off the engine. He would have to meet the judge's daughter tomorrow. While exiting his truck, he realized he forgot to check his phone for messages. He reached into his jacket pocket for his phone. A flicker of light from his front window caught his eye. He didn't expect anyone to be waiting for his return. A set of four stairs led to his front door, and Dodge approached them cautiously. A thin ray of light protruding out from between the door and the jamb caught his attention. The edge of the welcome mat was jammed under the door, preventing it from shutting completely. Stopping halfway up the short set of stairs, he tried to peer through the front window. He didn't see anyone inside but noticed a light coming from inside the bedroom.

CHAPTER 16

DODGE PUSHED THE DOOR OPEN and used his foot to dislodge the welcome mat. The door swung open. He noticed a blood smear on the door handle. The reaction was instinctual—his weapon in his right hand, his flashlight in his left, his two hands meeting in a shooting stance in the center of his chest, the weapon tucked close for maneuvering around tight quarters. The flashlight turned on only when needed, the lack of light used as a concealment technique. His familiarity with his home and the locations of the furniture gave him an advantage. The intruder didn't have that luxury.

He moved to the end of the short entryway hall and stepped into the living and dining room area. His eyes scanned the room. The muzzle of his weapon followed his eyes, right then left then back right, wall to wall and ceiling to floor. Satisfied there was no threat in the front part of the house, he turned his attention to the bedroom. He lowered his weapon to the ready position. First, clear the closet, then the bedroom. Gun raised, he moved toward the closet. Careful not to make a sound. He cleared the closet. Next, he laid his flashlight at the foot of the bed, pointing its beam under it. The light would blind anyone underneath and offer cover for his move to the side to check it for unwanted guests. Nobody was hiding under the bed.

The light was coming from under the bathroom door. Dodge reached for the knob and turned it slowly, making a clicking noise. The element of surprise was no longer his friend. The door opened inward and away from where he positioned himself. The move would be to swing the door open, drop low, and enter fast. Hopefully, the burglar would aim five feet off the ground, center mass for the average person. Any shots fired would hit above his head, allowing him to return fire before his opponent corrected his aim. He took a deep breath, holding it for five seconds before exhaling to calm his nerves. His hands steadied. Another deep breath. Hold and exhale.

The force of the kick slammed the door against the wall. A loud bang exploded as metal and wood crashed together with enough force to knock the towel rack loose, sending it crashing to the floor. The weapons front sight fixated on the target in front of him. His finger moved toward the trigger as he scanned the target for any signs of a weapon. The person was still. No reaction at all. Just a cowering heap of flesh in the fetal position, head tucked under her arms to protect it from any further harm. But he noticed the hair. Dark and shoulder length. He recognized the hands. The nails were groomed, painted bright red. It was Anna.

Anna looked up. Her straight hair was tangled and draped down over her face. Mascara stained her cheeks. Her hands were shaking, and her shirt was torn around the neck.

"Anna, what the hell are you doing here? I almost put a hole in you."

Dodge took her head in his hand and softly cradled it. He tilted her head up and brushed away the hair to show her bloodshot eyes. Anna attempted to look away from him. Her lip was bloody and swollen. Slight bruising on her neck showed the effects of being choked.

"Anna, what happened to you? Are you hurt anywhere else?" He felt guilty for firing questions at her in her current state, but he needed to assess if she had any injuries that required an ER visit.

Anna shook her head.

"Is all the blood on you yours?

Anna nodded.

His first aid training made him more than capable of

tending to any visible wounds. It was the possibility of injuries not visible that gave him pause. Physical and mental. He sat down next to Anna and pulled her close. She rested her head on his shoulder, and he held her tight.

Later, Anna sat on the couch. Her face was washed clean of any signs of dried blood, runny makeup, or tears. Her hair was brushed and pulled back into a ponytail. Dodge was in the kitchen, pouring a cup of coffee after retrieving the medical kit stored in the cabinet below the sink. He added a generous dose of Irish Cream Liquor to Anna's cup. A little alcohol might help calm her nerves. A splash in his didn't seem like a terrible idea either.

Anna held the coffee cup in both hands and sipped the hot beverage. He waited to hear a full account of events. After, Anna's wounds cleaned and bandaged, the medical kit was placed back under the sink.

"I don't want to talk about it. I just want to forget it ever happened," Anna said.

"Anna," he said. "This is not your fault. You didn't do anything wrong."

"It was my fault. I should have known better than to go there. Can't we just forget about it?"

"If you want to let it go, you can. But I can't. That is not how I work," Dodge said. "I need you to tell me what happened to help me understand."

"Promise me you won't call the police. No one will believe a girl like me. Why would they? I'm just another hooker with a bruised face and busted lip. Probably got what I deserved."

"I believe you. Nothing else matters."

"Promise me. Promise you won't get the police involved," Anna pleaded. "I won't cooperate if you do."

Anna was serious. A mixture of fear and determination welled behind her eyes. Dodge knew changing her mind would be next to impossible. Getting her to talk was critical. Once he got the facts, justice was in his hands.

"I promise I won't go to the police. Just start from the

beginning and tell me what happened."

Anna pulled the coffee cup close to her chest, a sign of being guarded. She needed to be handled the same as any other crime victim or battered woman. Walk her through the entire event, helping to fill in the blanks but careful not to lead her into any conclusions. Victims sometimes told the investigator what they thought they wanted to hear. At least, a thousand times he had been in the position he currently found himself in, just not with someone he cared about. Emotions had to be checked at the door.

"Let's start from the beginning. Where did you go yesterday after leaving my apartment?"

"I went straight home to my place," Anna said.

"Did you stop anywhere along the way?"

"No. I drove straight home."

"Were you alone? I mean, was there anyone with you at your place?"

Anna reached out and grabbed Dodge's hand. "I wasn't with anyone else. I swear."

"It's OK. I don't care about any of that." He thought about the next question. "What did you do after first getting home?"

Anna took a deep breath before answering. "I was cleaning up a little. I hadn't had time to clean or do laundry since I was spending so much time over here."

"So, you went to your apartment and cleaned and did laundry. What else did you do?"

"Well, I had some dishes in the sink, and I needed to wash them before they got gross. While I was washing a plate, my phone rang. When I picked it up, my hands were slick from the soapy water, and I dropped the phone in the sink."

"OK. Were you able to get the phone to work again?"

"I reached into the sink and grabbed the phone. I dried it off with a towel and used a hair dryer to dry it out as best as I could. But it wouldn't turn on. That's when I heard my neighbor coming home from work."

"What neighbor?" Dodge asked.

"Billy. He lives across the hall from me."

After letting Anna finish her thought, he still had a few questions to ask. "What is Billy's last name? Do you remember his apartment number?"

"I don't know his last name, but he lives across the hall. It's 1B, I think."

"Did you talk to Billy?"

"Yes."

"What did you talk about?"

"I told him about what happened to my phone, then I asked to borrow his phone."

"Who were you going to call?"

"You. I wanted to let you know my phone wasn't working, and I would see you later that night. I didn't want you to worry."

"OK. What happened when you went to talk to Billy?" Dodge wasn't sure he wanted to know the answer. He could feel his blood pressure rising and hear his heart beating in his ears.

"I barely knew him, only to say hi in the hallway. But he seemed nice, so I figured I could borrow his phone."

"Does Billy know anything about you? Your job or friends?"

"I don't think so. Why?"

"I'm just trying to get as many details as you can remember. Please keep going."

"We went into his apartment because he said he could show me how to fix a wet phone."

"You went into his apartment?" Dodge was baffled by how more people didn't die in the world. People were too trusting. Sometimes they paid the price.

"Well, I mean, I knew who he was. It's not like I had never seen him before."

"I'm not blaming you, OK? I just need to understand what happened at Billy's."

Anna took a deep breath. Her lips trembled. "When we got inside the apartment, Billy locked the door behind him. I didn't think anything about it at first. I lock my door as soon as I am inside, too. Then, he asked why I always looked away when

I passed him in the hallway. I didn't recall ever intentionally avoiding eye contact but apologized in case I had ever upset him. I felt terrible, and as he moved closer, I didn't back away for fear of hurting his feelings again. Next thing I knew, he was right on top of me."

Anna tried to back away but found herself deeper in the apartment and further from the exit. What Billy didn't count on was that Anna was street smart. While her original instincts concerning Billy were wrong, she now understood what was happening. Finding a path of least resistance toward the exit became her goal because being pushed deeper into the apartment wasn't an option. If she couldn't get around Billy, she would have to go straight at him. She decided not to wait and try to catch him off guard. Throw him off balance. She also needed a backup plan, something to draw attention away if the plan didn't work. A small stone coaster sat on an end table next to the couch. The coaster weighed about the same as a coffee mug, heavy enough to hurt if hit with it.

"I lunged at him," she said. Her compact frame slammed against his torso. Her head bounced off his chest, but the impact didn't faze him. Billy grabbed a handful of Anna's hair, while the other hand crashed down across her face. Blood spewed out of her mouth. The hand that struck the massive blow now squeezed her throat, preventing a scream for help. Billy pushed Anna to the couch and used brute force to bend her face first over the arm of the sofa. Anna noticed his grip weaken around her throat as he tried to unbutton his jeans. He didn't notice the coaster concealed in her right hand. Her vocal cords free from the vise-like grip, she shrieked. Anna threw the coaster at the front window facing the sidewalk. The unmistakable sound of breaking glass echoed throughout the apartment. Anyone roaming the sidewalks outside would be alerted by the noise of a window breaking. Billy froze for just a second. Anna reached back, located his eye sockets, and dug her thumbs as deep as possible into the fleshy organs. His grip loosened even more as he screamed in pain. Billy forced her arms down by putting her in a reverse bear hug. She kicked and screamed and used her right heel to scrape down his shin, ending in a hard stomp on the top of his right foot. This move freed her from his grasp.

"I fell backward over the arm of the sofa. When he moved toward me, I kicked him in the balls as hard as I could." She felt his genitals crush into his pelvic bone, causing him to fall to the floor. Anna ran to the front door, turning the handle on the deadbolt to unlock it, freeing her path out of the apartment and onto the sidewalk outside. A cab was parked across the street. Anna yelled at the driver and climbed into the back seat. The driver turned and noticed the blood on her face and asked if she was OK. Panicking and waiting for Billy to emerge from the apartment building's doors to finish the job, Anna screamed at the cab driver to leave. Once on the road, the driver said the hospital was just a few blocks away, but Anna, shaking from the ordeal, gave him Dodge's address. Still scared that Billy might have followed her, Anna hurried through the front door. Once inside, she ran to the bathroom, closed the door, curled up, and cried.

"I want to go to the police station so you can file a complaint against Billy."

Anna shook her head. "I don't want to go to the police. Let's forget this ever happened, and I never see him again, ever!"

Dodge nodded. "Why don't you lay down for a few hours and get some rest? We can talk about it later."

Anna took a sleep aid before curling up on the couch under a throw blanket. Once she was asleep, Dodge sat back in his chair and pulled a throw blanket over his legs. He tried to think about how to handle Anna's situation. He was exhausted. Sleep fell over him within minutes.

CHAPTER 17

DODGE SAT OUTSIDE THE POLICE STATION, debating whether to report what happened to Anna. Loyalty was the most important trait in a person, and Anna had asked him not to talk to the police. He would have wanted the same thing if the roles were reversed. The decision was agonizing. The problem was, a sworn duty as a law enforcement officer bound him to report known crimes. He was convinced Billy committed the same act against other women. Doing nothing would allow him to continue attacking them or, worse, escalate the violence level. Something had to be done. This time he would handle the situation on his own. Matters like this one had ruined careers in the past. There was no point in taking anyone down with him if he was busted.

Careful not to tell Renquest what the information was to be used for, he texted Billy's address for a criminal history workup.

I need a BG. 5522 Kenmore St. 4D. Name: Billy NLN.

A few minutes passed before Dodge's phone vibrated.

Billy Rosen - Possession Marijuana, Unlawful Possession of a Firearm. Need backup?

No, just a lead.

In the judge's case?

No. DOC business.

OK. Holler if you need anything else, and, Dodge, watch your six.

Roger that.

He tossed the phone onto the seat. Billy Rosen had a record for drug possession and weapons violations. Guns were a part of every parole agent's daily life. Assuming everyone had a weapon is what kept you alive. This interaction wouldn't differ from the dozens of home contacts made any other day. He felt the knot on his head as a reminder to plan before going to talk to Billy.

Dodge had no intention of busting through Billy's front door, shouting "Police!," then commencing to kick the shit out of whoever was inside the apartment. Cover from being a law enforcement officer wasn't workable, but concealment was attainable. A cover to prevent his actions from circling back to the department or him. One so strong, no one would question his motives. Then it hit him. The truck tires broke loose, kicking rocks up against the wall as he left the police department parking lot. He turned right and headed toward downtown and the Federal District.

After a quick flip of his badge to the guard at the front gate, an inspection, and a quick scan of the truck bed, the barriers lowered, and he continued into the parking lot reserved for police officers. One more flash of the badge to the Blue Jackets, the nickname for the security staff that manned the entrance and metal detectors, gained him entrance to the lobby. Only U.S. Marshals and Blue Jackets carried firearms in a U.S. courthouse. Blue Jackets were contract security hired by the Marshals Service to provide added screening for visitors. Additional duties included a presence in the courtrooms if a high-profile case was being tried. Most Blue Jackets were retired cops or federal agents seeking extra pay to supplement meager pensions. Dodge assumed many were trying to supplement the part ex-wives took in alimony and child support. The job allowed them to stay in the system without the risk of street work. Everyone checked their weapons before proceeding to the open areas of the building. A good safety policy ensured that the guys on his side were the only ones with guns.

A brief elevator ride to the tenth floor and Dodge was standing outside a courtroom with a sign that read "The

Honorable Judge Rodstein." Inside the courtroom, beyond the large wooden doors, he hoped to find who he needed to execute his plan for Billy Rosen. The courtroom was empty, as there were no criminal hearings scheduled. The interior of the courtroom resembled a grand church. Rows of wooden benches flanked an aisle in the center that ended at the small wooden barrier that separated attendees from court staff. Small tables to the left and right inside the restricted area signified where the defense counsel and prosecutors sat during the proceedings. Every seat in the courtroom faced the front, except for one. Perched high above everyone else in the courtroom was the judge's bench. It exhumed an overwhelming presence, sitting directly below a seal of the U.S. Courts on the wall behind it.

Many people believed the judge's position above everyone allowed the court to gaze down upon the defendant, as a show of power of the state over the accused. In fact, the opposite was true. Sitting in a higher seat forced people to look up at the judge, to recognize the court's authority over the matter before it.

Dodge approached the barrier and saw why he had come. Leaning against the defense table was Deputy U.S. Marshal Fisch and his partner. The partner's name eluded him, but he didn't care that much. He had noticed the partner at the parole office earlier in the week and at the coffee truck as well. Fisch was the alpha, and the partner was of little use.

"Paul Dodge, what can the U.S. Marshals do for you?" Deputy Fisch asked.

Dodge stopped short of the bar. "I need your help."

"And what kind of help are you looking for?"

Using his off hand, Dodge pushed the gate open and stepped past the bar. The two marshals stood, mostly out of habit.

"I need to redeem the favor the marshals owe me."

Fisch and his partner appeared shocked. Dodge guessed it was all an act. The two men knew he would ask for something from them one day.

"That is one set of balls you got. Coming in here and

demanding the U.S. Marshals Service do you a favor. We don't do favors," Fisch said.

The problem he was dealing with was personal, a non-parole agent affair, so he was willing to play the game, to do the dance. He came with nothing and could leave with nothing. The marshals didn't have that luxury. Solving the case as soon as possible was in their best interest, and the marshals' need for him was much greater than the other way around. A fact he could ill afford to have changed.

"Hell, even if you were owed a favor, the amount of information provided doesn't amount to dick. The Marshals Service requested your help, and we can un-request it. So, why don't you get the hell out of my courthouse."

Agent Fisch took a step toward Dodge. The deputy's chest exuded a presence over the parole agent's smaller frame, but he stood his ground. He had faced off against bigger and stronger men than Agent Fisch. Real live killers. Losing a fight didn't bother him in the slightest.

"Worrying about my career is sweet, but I'm doing just fine. I wish the same could be said for yours. If the threat to the judge's daughter isn't resolved soon, you two might have to trade in those suits for Blue Jackets. Now, take a step back, or a career won't be the only thing circling the drain."

A confrontation in the courtroom would be in poor taste, and Fisch took one step back and raised his hands. "Relax, I was only kidding. What is it you need?"

Time to exploit the weakness that had just opened. "For starters, let's stop pretending you don't need me. Stop insulting me and wasting my time."

The second marshal spoke for the first time, "What do you want?"

Dodge pointed at the silver star clipped on the second marshal's belt. "Deputize me."

The two men shared a glance. He knew what was coming.

"Are you out of your damn mind?" Deputy Fisch said. "First, there is a background check, which I am sure you can't clear.

Hell, even if you cleared the background check, what judge would be dumb enough to sign off on a move like this?"

"Not dumb, desperate," Dodge said, looking at the empty desk above and behind them.

"Never going to happen," Deputy Fisch said.

Dodge said nothing. Deputy Fisch asked why he needed a marshals' badge, not how he planned to use it.

"Interstate jurisdiction," Dodge said.

"If a suspect is in another state, give us the information and we will pick the mope up."

"That won't work. This guy is smart. He would sense two Feds a mile away. Besides, if something goes down, I may need to act to seize computers and phones. What I don't need are the rules of evidence and chain of custody getting murky with jurisdictional issues."

The marshals stepped to a far corner of the room to talk out of earshot. The approval was a done deal, but it wouldn't be free. There were no free rides, and being prepared to hear the marshals' demands was something he planned for.

"What's it going to be, fellas?"

"We will get the judge to play ball," Deputy Fisch said.

The smile on Deputy Fisch's face sent shivers down Dodge's spine. Regaining his composure before speaking, he said, "Time is ticking boys," as the two deputies walked toward the door, leading to the judge's chambers. "Oh, and I'll come by to see the judge's daughter. Tell the judge to expect me soon."

Doubt crept in as he plopped his rear up on the table to wait. The odds of the plan working were unknown. He tried going over the details in his mind but couldn't concentrate on specifics. Something was eating at him. It was an uncomfortable feeling. He looked down and noticed he was sitting on the defense table. A little embarrassed, he moved to the table on the opposite side of the room. That was more natural. His concentration returned. The doubts disappeared, and he waited for the two marshals to return with his prize.

The wait was shorter than he expected. Dodge took the elevator to the lobby and exited the building. He got into his truck and headed toward Anna's apartment building. It was time to meet Billy in person.

CHAPTER 18

DODGE PARKED OUTSIDE ANNA'S apartment building and took one last drag off a cigarette before flipping the butt onto the sidewalk. He crossed the narrow street in about five strides and was at the front door within a few seconds. A row of mailboxes was set left of the front door. The postal service had used an old-fashioned label maker to mark the postal boxes, and many of the labels had fallen off. Anna had told him her apartment was on the first floor, right side of the hall. That meant Billy's was across the hall on the left side. There were only three apartments on the first floor—one on the left, one on the right, and one at the end of the hall. Dodge walked directly to the door on the left. He reached for the door knocker for 1B, but before he could pull the small brass U-shaped handle back to knock, the sound of breaking glass from Anna's apartment drew his attention.

The sound echoed through the halls as he knocked on Anna's door. His shoulders square to the frame, he took a stance two feet back, allowing the use of light shining through the peephole to see if someone approached the door. He knocked again. He detected the sound of footsteps inside the apartment. The sound increased in volume the closer to the door the person got. Sunlight still shone through the peephole. His muscles tightened, and his heart rate increased in anticipation of an impending fight. Tunnel vision set in, and sound became a constant echo. Agents were trained on how to fight off the effects of fight or flight. Concentrating on breathing, his fists unclenched, allowing blood to flow back to his hands, the tunnel vision subsided, and the echo in his ears eased. Suddenly, something breached the space between the light source and the peephole. A shadow, then light again. And then, just a shadow.

Dodge's right foot came into contact with the door at the exact spot where the locking mechanism met the jamb, right above the doorknob. The wood around the door handle splintered under the force of the blow. The door continued inward until it met material larger and harder than itself. In this case, the material was bone, one of the hardest bones in the body, the skull. Billy never had a chance. The leading edge of the door pushed through an inch of nose cartilage before coming to rest on his forehead. Billy crumpled to the floor behind the door. Blood spattered from his nose with every breath, and curse words spewed from his mouth. Dodge stepped through the open doorway after looking to see if other tenants noticed the altercation. No one had cared to check on the ruckus, and he closed the door.

"What the fuck?" Billy screamed. "You broke my goddamn nose."

Sliding past Billy, he peered into the apartment. Always check for accomplices. Always assume there are others.

"Who else is here?"

"Fuck you, man! My nose is bleeding."

"You already said that," Dodge said. He threw Billy a towel that had been lying on the floor next to a chair in the entryway. "Now, let's try the question again. Is there anyone else in the apartment?"

Billy's position on the floor allowed Dodge to tower over him. His new deputy marshal badge front and center was right in Billy's line of sight.

"Shit, man, cops aren't supposed to just beat people up. What the fuck? I'm going to report you," Billy said.

"Here are the rules. I ask the questions, and you answer. Do the rules make sense?"

Billy tried to get up, and Dodge pushed him back down.

The goal was to keep Billy on the floor, unable to react with fists or feet. Billy struggled to get up again. Pain compliance was taught at the academy. The human body has several spots that when manipulated would cause immediate pain with little effort, stopping the person from committing further unwanted behavior. He squeezed Billy's nose between his thumb and forefinger to leverage compliance through pain. The cartilage crackled like loose gravel under a shoe. Billy fell back to a sitting position holding his nose, which as a side effect from the pressure, had stopped bleeding.

"All right, man. What do you want?"

"Remember the rules. Now, is there anyone else in the apartment?" Dodge said.

"No, man. Just me."

"Very good. Now, why are you in this apartment? And if you say you live here, I swear to God I'll shoot you, Billy."

"How the fuck do you know my name?"

The response earned Billy another nose twist. "Billy, the rules have been explained. I ask, you answer. I won't repeat the rules again."

Billy nodded.

"I need a verbal response."

"Yes, goddamn it," Billy said. The blood-soaked towel pressed against his face once again.

"Thank you. Whose apartment is this?"

"I don't know her name. Some whore. Why do you care?"

The side of Billy's head where the door had smashed against his skull provided Dodge with another opportunity for pain compliance.

"That isn't very nice," Dodge said.

"No, man, she's a hooker. She fucks for money."

The anger built deep in Dodge's stomach, manifesting as raw energy on the way up and out toward his extremities. His ears grew hot, and his eyes became more focused. The next strike was in the solar plexus. It was a massive blow, knocking the wind out of him. Billy laid on the floor, trying to breathe

"I asked who lives here, not for commentary or opinion."

After a few deep breaths, Billy answered. "Andrea. Her name is Andrea or some shit like that."

"Andrea," Dodge said.

"Her name is Anna."

"Excellent job, Billy. Now that you remember her name, speaking about her with respect should be much easier."

"Whatever, man. What the hell does a marshal care about some hook—" Billy paused and breathed a sigh of relief before he continued. "Why do you care about this Anna chick?"

"That is no concern of yours," Dodge said.

Reaching out a finger, he pointed at Billy's nose. "It hurts when someone pounds on your face, doesn't it? I would like to think once a person has had his face all beaten up, doing that to someone else might not be as pleasurable, knowing how it feels and all."

"What are you talking about, man?" Billy asked.

"Don't start lying again, Billy. We have come so far. Taking a step back in our relationship at this point would be a disappointment."

"I don't know what that bitch told you, but I never laid a hand on her."

The reaction was emotional and primal. Dodge didn't realize what had happened until his weapon was tucked under Billy's chin and pointing through the back of his head. The angle provided the best chance for the bullet to find the sweet spot above the medulla. His index finger moved toward the trigger as his eyes locked with Billy's. Every bone in Dodge's body said to pull the trigger. He was sure this wasn't the first time Billy had beaten on someone weaker. Guys like him always had more victims. But killing Billy wasn't the answer, and he knew it. Billy's eyes were wide. His pupils covered most of their surface, a reaction to the fight-or-flight mechanism. But it was the wet spot between his legs that signaled Billy had gotten the message. He backed his weapon away from under Billy's chin and slid it back in its holster.

"There won't be another warning. Actions have consequences. Do you understand what I am saying?"

"Yeah, man! Please don't fucking kill me!" Billy pleaded.

"If I have to come back here and have this conversation, there won't be a conversation."

Billy nodded and fell back onto the floor, smelling of piss and fear.

"Good," Dodge said. "You have a week to get out, and not just out of this building. I want you out of this town. Hell, let's make it the entire county. I don't want to hear about you even crossing the street in this county. If I do, I'll be forced to finish what was started here. Do you understand?" A tap of the U.S. Marshals badge made sure Billy had noticed and would remember seeing it.

"I'm gone, man. You will never see me again," Billy said.

"One week."

Dodge opened the door and took one last look around for anyone in the building that might have noticed him. He made sure his shiny new silver star was showing for anyone catching a glimpse through their peepholes to see. He lit a cigarette and walked out the front door to the building. It could have gone worse. One thing was for sure, Dodge didn't believe Billy had any intentions of telling anyone what had just happened. But if he did, as a respected parole agent, Dodge would take his chances with a review board. An agent's word against a woman-beating drug dealer, he liked those odds.

After finishing his cigarette in his truck, he drove east on South Street through downtown then turned south on Main Street then made a left on Scott Street. He pulled up to his townhome a little after 1800 hours.

Anna had returned to Dodge's townhome around three in the afternoon. She went downtown for coffee and a sandwich as a late lunch. Dodge had not texted or called yet, which made her worry something might have gone terribly wrong. There was a calmness to his face before he left, but seeing through the mask of false bravado was easy. The thing to remember about a mask was the eyes always showed. Anna noticed the rage in his eyes as she recounted what Billy had done. The thought of what might happen if Dodge found Billy terrified her.

A vehicle pulled into the parking spot out front, and the headlights flashed in the window. Anna could see the cherry from a cigarette glow brighter as the driver took a drag. Everything in her body told her it was him, but she needed to see him. Nothing would make her feel safe until they were together. The sound of the front door creaking as it opened announced he was home. Still, Anna stood waiting in the living room, her heart ready to beat out of her chest. He stepped into the living room and tossed his jacket on the chair. The two stood in silence, staring at each other. The silence was deafening.

"Billy won't be a problem anymore," he said.

"Please tell me you didn't do anything stupid," she said.

"He is fine, mostly. I just slapped him around a little."

"What did he say?"

"I did most of the talking. He is planning to leave town by the end of the week."

"Really, he is leaving? Are you sure you didn't shoot him?" she asked.

"Of course not. I don't shoot people for revenge. A few options were provided, and Billy chose the one that best benefited him," he said.

"Did he say why he did it? I mean to me?" Anna asked.

Dodge took Anna's hand and led her to the couch. She was full of nervous energy, and her hands trembled. He squeezed her hand tighter before speaking.

"Anna, I wish there were a good reason for what happened to you. I wish I had an explanation, but I don't. Evil people exist who do terrible things to other people. Sometimes power is the goal. Other times it is deviant sexual desires that drive people to act. And every now and again, and I believe this is the case with Billy, people are just assholes. He has always been an asshole.

When he was a kid, he was a little asshole. Someday karma may hand out some retribution. Maybe it will even change him for a few months, but people always go back to who they are on the inside. Billy is an asshole who uses women as punching bags because of a shortcoming he is not equipped to deal with."

Anna stared at their hands, cupped together. After a moment of silence, she smiled with a sigh and let go of his hand. She stood, pulling her savior up with her. She threw her arms around his neck and pulled him close, kissing him on the lips before leading him into the bedroom. Dodge flipped the light switch off and closed the door.

CHAPTER 19

THE JUDGE'S HOUSE WAS A STATELY MANOR on the outskirts of the city limits in one of the historic neighborhoods that surrounded the city. When the town was founded over a century and a half ago, the original platted downtown area was close to a mile from its current location and just a handful of buildings made up the city square: a general store, a blacksmith's shop, a saloon, and a hotel, all surrounding a courthouse. As the population grew, more prominent residents built elaborate Victorian mansions to showcase their wealth—a reminder to everyone in town who had the power and money.

In 1895, the area was subjected to one of the worst droughts on record. One summer night, a lightning strike started a fire in the blacksmith's barn. The fire spread to surrounding structures, burning out of control for almost seven hours. Residents later recalled that it was as if the town was in the center of hell. The fire destroyed most of the buildings, shops, and homes in town. Poorer residents, unable to afford to rebuild, left. The old families, the monied families, restored their mansions first. However, city planners moved the center of town a mile to the south to a spot where the railroad had built a depot and water stop. While the new downtown flourished, the old mansions became run-down, falling to the ravages of time and vandals over the decades that followed.

In the 1950s, a group of residents sought to label the old neighborhood a historic district. Grants, loans, and tax breaks were applied to help restore several of the mansions to their former glory. The community changed, but the exclusiveness of the occupiers didn't. The mansions became occupied by new money in a much sought-after zip code.

Deputy Fisch stood at the oversized front door. Daily rounds were part of the judge's detail at 0700. First, he walked the grounds before providing transportation for the judge's daughter to school. His partner reported to the residence at 0800 to transport the judge to the federal courthouse. The two deputies would meet at the courthouse after the judge's daughter, Maggie, was safely at school.

The door opened, and Judge Rodstein appeared in the entryway.

"Good morning, Fisch."

"Good morning, Judge. Here to make the rounds and school transport."

"I'll be glad when this is all over with, Fisch. Frankly, I don't know what this is doing to Maggie. She doesn't seem scared, but she's always good at putting on a false front. When her mom passed, I was the one that needed taking care of. I know she is almost eighteen, but I still worry."

"Maggie is a wonderful kid, Your Honor," Deputy Fisch said.

"It is supposed to be the other way around, you know. I should have been comforting her."

`"I'll check on her after my rounds, sir."

Fisch glanced up at the balcony overlooking the foyer. Maggie stood at the railing, listening to the conversation between the two men. When Fisch made eye contact, she disappeared into the bedroom.

"Thanks, Fisch. She seems to trust you," the judge said and walked into the study, shutting the door behind him.

Fisch waited until he heard the judge talking on the phone before starting up the stairs toward Maggie's room. Before knocking on the door, he made sure the judge had not left the study. Maggie didn't answer, but the door was unlocked. Deputy Fisch pushed the door open, closing and locking it once inside. The floor was covered in clothes, and the bed was unmade. The whole room gave off a rebellious teenager vibe. Maggie must have slipped out before he made it upstairs. As he was about to turn around and leave, Maggie leaped out of the closet. Deputy Fisch's first instinct was to reach for the weapon attached to his side. Twenty years on the job had made for paranoid reflexes.

"What the hell, Maggie?"

"I was just goofing. Geez, relax," she said.

"You can't do shit like that. Aside from almost shooting you in the face, my heart just about stopped," Fisch said, realizing he had yet to release the grip on his weapon. "Get ready. As soon as I finish the walkthrough, we are leaving."

"I was waiting for you."

Fisch was agitated and didn't like to answer to the judge when Maggie was late for school.

"I am here, so get dressed for school. I'll be back in about ten minutes."

Maggie sat, legs crossed, on the edge of the bed. "I called yesterday."

"And I said I would be in court."

"You couldn't call me back?"

"No. While on the subject, what did I say about calling my work phone?"

"I didn't say anything. God, stop being so goddamned paranoid," Maggie said, flailing backward onto her bed, her feet hanging over the edge.

"The marshals can track everything on that phone. Nothing is erased. Every call, text, and photo is saved on a server somewhere just waiting to be audited by the inspector general."

Maggie sat up on the bed and rubbed her legs.

"I lost my phone, so I wanted to call and tell you."

The words echoed in Fisch's head. *I lost my phone.*

"You lost your phone? The phone I gave you? The phone has a record of every call, every text message. Every damn picture. That phone? That's the phone you lost?"

Panicked, Fisch looked around the room, hoping to find the one thing that could ruin him. Maggie liked to mess with his head, and he hoped this was one of those times. A practical joke in which she would reveal the phone after the initial panic, then laugh.

That wasn't the case.

"It's not a big deal. It's here somewhere," Maggie said.

He closed the gap between them. "Now, you listen to me very carefully. We must find that phone. Start by retracing your steps from yesterday and look in every place you spent time. I'll check the house while doing my rounds."

"Why don't you just call it? If the phone rings in the house, we will hear it."

Fisch was chilled to the bone by what she had just said. An entire life was about to be flushed down the toilet, and she didn't seem to care.

"What if the phone rings, and your father answers it? What if someone else finds it or turns the phone into the police as a lost item? You wouldn't want that, would you?"

He could see that Maggie had picked up on the anger in his voice. She tried to back away, but the bed prevented any such retreat. Fisch reached out and placed his large hand on her face, positioning her chin in his palm. He squeezed to bring his forefinger and thumb together, only the bone and muscles of the cheeks prevented the connection.

"If anyone finds that phone, it is all over. I'll go to prison, but I won't go down alone, understand?"

His hand moved her head up and down to mimic affirmation.

"You're hurting me," she pleaded.

"Find the fucking phone, please."

"OK, I promise."

Fisch released the grip on her face. Maggie looked up, and a smirk stretched across her face. Her cheeks were red, and he noticed the marks created by blood rushing to where his fingers had pressed against the cheeks. The marks looked just like fingerprints, big ones. Maggie couldn't be seen in public appearing as if someone had assaulted her, and it would take thirty minutes for the red marks to disappear. Fisch had lost his temper, and she had sway over him once again.

Then while trying to figure out how to explain Maggie's facial bruising, a fleeting thought crossed his mind. If the phone was lost, how did she call him? Panicked, he pulled the phone out of his inside jacket pocket and began pressing buttons until he was staring at the recent call log. His eyes scrolled down the list until finally coming to rest on a number he didn't recognize.

"What phone did you use to call me?" he asked.

"What?"

"If you lost the other phone, what phone did you call from?"

"I borrowed one at school," she said.

Fisch's voice trembled. "You borrowed a phone from someone at school to call me?" The air left his chest. His heart dropped into his stomach.

"Yeah, why? Like I said, I lost mine and borrowed a friend's phone."

"Whose?"

"What?"

"Who was the person you borrowed the phone from?"

"Kevin," she said.

"Kevin? The boy that comes over here to study?"

Fisch knew Kevin Parker, as he was on the cleared list of Maggie's friends that could stay the night if the judge was out of town on business. The judge felt the boy posed no threat to his daughter's virtue as he was gay. Because of his favored status, Kevin and Maggie had become best friends, friends that told each other everything, and that terrified Fisch. He would find out what the Parker boy knew and deal with it later. First, they needed to locate the missing phone.

"I need to do the rounds, or you will be late for school."

Maggie pushed her chest against Fisch's stomach. He tried to back away, only to find his path blocked by a dresser.

"You have five minutes. Besides, it will take a little more

time for these marks to go away," Maggie said, pointing to the red spot on her face.

"You are fucking psycho."

"Are you going to show me how bad I have been?"

Maggie backed away, her left hand gesturing, beckoning him to follow. The right hand popped the buttons on her shirt one at a time, revealing a red lace bra. Her shirt fell to the ground, followed by her bra. He had started something he shouldn't have. Fisch knew it was wrong, but he was in it now. His primal urges took over. There was no controlling it. Besides she had never complained. Hell, she had practically begged for it the first time. He was in too deep to get out easily.

While Deputy Fisch was at the judge's house, the sun peeked through Dodge's bedroom window, and the beams danced across the bed, warming his face. On a typical day, he would have been awake well before the sun rose, but the previous night's activities assured a later night than usual. Anna had used every resource she could muster to repay Dodge for dealing with Billy. The show of appreciation lasted well past midnight with three thank-you moments. Two for her and one for him. A deep sense of relaxation came over his body, resulting in the most restful sleep he had experienced in years.

Anna's head rested on Dodge's chest. Her dark hair draped over his midsection, flowing onto the sheets like a mohair blanket. Not wanting to wake her, he slid a few inches toward the end table and grabbed his phone. When he looked back at Anna, her eyes were open.

"Good morning," she said.

"Good morning."

"What time is it?"

"It's about seven thirty," he said.

Anna sat up, pulling up the sheet to cover her breasts. She picked up the shirt from last night off the floor and noticed a tear in the collar. Dodge opened a drawer to the end table and pulled out a white T-shirt from a pile of folded undershirts and tossed it to her. After putting on the shirt, she went to the bathroom. He could hear the water running and the sound of a toothbrush scraping across teeth. After a few minutes, Anna returned from the bathroom. Her hair was pulled into a ponytail, and she had applied fresh lip gloss.

"Do you have anything planned for today?" he asked.

"No, why?"

"I thought maybe we could head back over to Kelly's apartment. I wanted to take you over there to see if anything was missing. It could help me figure out what really happened to her."

"Don't you have to go to work today?"

"I do have to do a few things at work. It shouldn't take me past noon to finish everything."

There was hesitation in Anna's eyes. "I haven't really thought about going back to her place. It seems weird to be going through all of her stuff now that . . . well, she is gone."

"I know this is hard for you. It is hard for me, too. But I think if you are there, you may remember something important, or see something that is missing."

"What about the police? Won't they get mad if we start poking around her place?"

"They might. That's why we can't get caught."

Anna smiled. "If you really think it might help, I'll go."

Dodge nodded. "I'll give you a call when I am finished at work. You can stay here if you'd like or go home. Just let me know where you are so I know where to pick you up."

Dodge hopped into the shower after a quick shave. Anna joined him. The sex was even better the second time. The water was warm, and their skin was slippery. It was like when two teenagers try something for the first time. There was a lot of fumbling and jockeying for position, but they finally settled into a rhythm. Twenty minutes later, he was dressed and heading out the door for work.

He needed to check in with the sheriff's detective and see if there were any new developments in Kelly's case. The visit also provided him the opportunity to see if they had been to Kelly's apartment yet or planned to search it in the future. His own late-night visit would be simpler if he didn't have to worry about crime scene tape or sealed doors. A closed crime scene didn't alter his intentions either way, but breaking crime scene tape was a felony, and he didn't see any reason to involve Anna in a possible crime. He pulled into the sheriff's station parking lot, parked, walked through the main lobby to the front desk, and asked to speak to Detective Keller or Detective Hanson. When the deputy manning the front desk asked for his name, he flashed his badge and replied, "Dodge."

CHAPTER 20

DEPUTY FISCH DROVE MAGGIE TO SCHOOL after finishing his rounds. On an average day, he would have left once she was safely inside the school walls. Today, the routine changed because of the lost phone. Deputy Fisch circled the block and parked in an empty lot south of the school, where he maintained an unobstructed view of the school's front entrance. Maggie may have told Kevin Parker everything concerning their relationship. If anyone found out what he had done, he would go to federal prison, forced to fight for his life every day. The only thing prison inmates hated worse than a pedophile was a cop.

So far, there were three people aware of his secret. Maggie made one, and the person on the other end of the phone ringing on the seat next to him made two.

"What do you want?" Fisch asked.

"I wanted to say thank you for the gift. Having a phone in prison is the same as a money-printing machine, or in my case, a favors machine," Grayson said.

"The phone isn't for you to look up porn or trade calls for blow jobs. The deal was, I get you a phone, and your friend leaves me alone and shuts her mouth."

"Deputy, I am surprised at your tone. Is there something wrong with that little sidepiece? You should relax. Stress can lead to performance issues, and I am sure she has an insatiable appetite," Grayson said.

The line was silent as Fisch watched Maggie and the Parker

boy exit the school and walk toward the gas station at the end of the block.

"Funny, that's exactly what I heard about inmates and convicted child killers after being placed in gen pop."

Grayson was silent.

"What do you want?" Fisch asked.

"Dodge came to see me, just as I predicted," Grayson said. "I told you if you created the right scenario, he would come. I only wish I could have seen his face when he saw the rooms. You did good. This relationship is really beginning to grow on me."

Fisch, entrenched in watching Maggie and the Parker boy, only caught the last of Grayson's answer. Once the pair faded out of sight behind cars parked along the street between the school and the gas station, Fisch returned his attention to Grayson.

"We don't have a relationship."

"That's not very nice. I expected more from you."

Deputy Fisch shifted his weight from one side to the other, an involuntary reaction to being uncomfortable with his current circumstance. "I suppose you already heard about the dead girl?"

"A lot of girls die. Every day in fact. The news is slow to travel in here. Which one are you talking about, specifically?" Grayson asked.

"You know damn well which one I am talking about. Hell, you probably heard before the cops found out," Fisch said.

"I'll admit, my eyes and ears on the street do an adequate job of keeping me informed about things in the civilized world. But they are not as reliable as if I was there to see and hear it for myself. So, I say again, I don't know to whom you are referring."

Fisch had doubts about Grayson. What he did know was if Grayson was in involved in Kelly Gosling's death in any way, it could mess up his whole plan. If Dodge found out, he would come after Grayson. How long would Grayson hold out before giving him up? Fisch had always planned on dealing with Grayson, but his involvement in a murder outside the prison's walls would force Fisch to move up his timetable. Grayson would have to go. Sooner rather than later. Now was the time to plant the seeds.

"I want you to get this over with. Give him what he wants and destroy the phone." Fisch was aware Grayson would never give up his only communication to the outside world. In fact, he had counted on it. The plan was to have him busted with the phone. Then Fisch would be able to have him killed in a prison yard fight after being placed back in general population as a sanction for concealing contraband. Fisch knew enough guards that would look the other way. Child molesters didn't last long in gen pop.

"All in due time. I need to play with our agent friend a little longer. I get bored easily in here."

Fisch was becoming annoyed with Grayson's self-indulging sense of grandeur. "Excuse the hell out of me if I don't have confidence in your abilities. You are in prison, and he put you in that cage."

"Dodge didn't put me anywhere. The choices were mine that landed me in this place. Just like I'll choose when I leave."

"Yeah, yeah. No one is smarter than you," Fisch quipped. "Save that shit for someone who gives a fuck. Maybe one of your shower buddies."

"Deputy Fisch, I thought we were past the hostilities. Aren't we friends? Since we are partners, what is that pretty thing wearing today? Is it short? Can you see her panties? I can almost smell the lust on her. You really will have to send me a picture. Clothes are optional."

Fisch slammed the phone shut and tossed it on the passenger seat. It bounced off the soft material and hit the dash, falling to the floor under the passenger side dash. He placed the car in gear and pulled away from the curb. Slowly. He stared at Maggie and Kevin Parker as they walked through the school's front doors.

—◦◦◦—

Detective Hanson was away from his office when Dodge had

stopped by the sheriff's office. He was in court for an evidentiary hearing, a murder case in which the suspect gave a full confession then recanted, forcing him to speak with Detective Keller. He didn't care for Keller. It was a first impression thing. He seemed smug and gave off a creeper vibe. Many old-timers in the vice squad did. People could only work with hookers and pimps for so long before the temptation of money or sex compromised their integrity, Dodge guessed. He had had to fight his demons on more than one occasion, but he had done just that. With one exception, Kelly. But that was a long time ago. Their most recent attempt was after she was sober for over a year. He wasn't ashamed of his behavior. His job was to give people second chances. That is what he had been doing with Kelly.

Detective Keller told Dodge that they had a lead on the man seen pushing Kelly the day she died. He had a local address, which was well known to the police. The rap sheet spit out of the National Crime Information Center (NCIC) computer, a database that held arrest records from all over the country, showed twenty felony arrests for drugs and assaults—the earliest incident at age fifteen. Keller wouldn't let him hold the printout, but he saw the FBI number assigned to the suspect. When Keller turned to put the report back in the file, the extra time allowed him to copy the number onto his hand. Once he returned to the office, a few minutes with the NCIC terminal revealed the suspect's name and social security number. With that information, Dodge ran a motor vehicle check and copied his address and vehicle information. The suspect's name was Jonathan Alber. A white male. Forty years of age. Sixty-two inches tall and 220 pounds. He lived on the four hundred block of Mercer Street, which was in the town's industrial area. The industrial area lay between the railroad tracks and the river. It was a rough part of the city, mainly inhabited by drug users and prostitutes. He decided to let the detectives handle this one.

Dodge didn't plan to face the man suspected in Kelly's death. He knew better than to interfere directly in a sheriff's office investigation. That sort of thing was frowned upon and could get him removed from the task force and Maggie Rodstein's case. He wouldn't be able to talk to Grayson anymore, which meant he couldn't find out about his involvement in Kelly's murder. Detectives Keller and Hanson didn't appear interested in putting two and two together. However, shaking the feeling that Grayson Heller was involved proved more difficult. There just wasn't enough evidence to point to him directly.

It was around five in the afternoon when Dodge picked up Anna. They drove straight to Kelly's apartment and parked a block away. He wanted to watch for the detectives or police surveillance before walking into the building. *Better safe than sorry*, he thought. Ten minutes passed. No one looked out of place. Twenty minutes. Then thirty. After thirty-five minutes, he felt no one was watching and it was safe to enter the building. He and Anna walked down the block, traversed the cement stairs leading to the front door, and entered the apartment building.

Once at Kelly's apartment, Dodge reached up to where he had left the key, dead center of the jamb above the door. It wasn't there. He slid his hand to the right six inches. No key. Then he moved his hand to the left, six inches from the center of the jamb. The key was there with the teeth facing to the right. He was right-handed. When he placed the key above the door, the teeth would have been facing left. It was a matter of biology and human engineering. A key held in his right hand would have been pinched between the index finger and thumb, leaving the teeth facing up after being removed from the lock.

Using the key in his left hand, Dodge unlocked the door. He placed the key back above the door using his left hand. The key's teeth pointed to the right and faced the wall. The key was moved by someone left-handed. Human engineering.

The pair headed straight for the bedroom once inside the apartment. He instructed Anna to stand in the middle of the room and stare at the east wall for fifteen seconds, then turn right and stare at the north wall. Another right turn toward the west wall. After fifteen seconds, a right turn and the south wall. Anna did as she was told, and when finished, Dodge asked what she saw. Anna said the room looked the same as it always did. Other than it was a mess.

"Is anything missing? A picture on the wall or a photo of Kelly with someone else?"

Anna said she didn't know what to look for because she never spent more than a few minutes in the bedroom to borrow clothes. Dodge told her it was fine and had been worth a try. Anna walked out of the bedroom into the living room.

While Anna checked the other areas of the house, he sat on the edge of the bed and took in the whole of the room. What was he missing? Someone had been there since he had been there last. The key's location above the door proved that. But who had been there? He knew it wasn't the detectives. What were they looking for? He stared at the half-open closet in front of him. Something didn't seem right. He had looked through the closet the last time. He was sure he closed it when he left. Leave everything as it was. That was the rule. Leaving the door open was sloppy. He wasn't sloppy. Distracted, but not sloppy. He slid his butt to the edge of the bed, then leaned forward and stared into the partially opened closet. He couldn't see it, but the woo-woo hairs on the back of his neck tingled. His subconscious was picking up something there, but his eyes and the logical part of his brain were not ready to see it yet. Just then, Anna yelled from the living room.

The sound of Anna's scream forced him to shoot from the edge of the bed, covering the distance to the living room in a few seconds. His heart rate sped up. His heartbeat pounded in his ears. Anna wasn't in the living room. Then he heard a noise coming from the kitchen. Another three steps, and he was standing in the doorway to the kitchen. In front of him was Anna. She was still, white as a ghost. She was staring at the floor in front of her, gripping a six-inch stainless-steel kitchen knife.

Dodge remained calm. He wasn't sure she knew he was standing behind her, and he didn't want to end up on the business end of a kitchen knife. No matter how small.

"Anna?"

She said nothing.

He repeated her name. "Anna."

She spun around, the knife raised in a slashing position from above her shoulder.

Reacting quickly, he threw up his off hand in a defensive position in front of his face and used his other hand to grasp the arm holding the knife, just above her elbow.

The grip on her arm remained tight. He took one step back, bringing Anna's arm down slowly as he did. "Why did you scream?"

"I saw a rat," she said.

He then stepped in and gently took the knife from her hand. Her left hand. "It's OK. It probably got in from one of the neighbor's apartments. Rats know when no one is home for a while. They are opportunists. They move in when you move out. Survival of the fittest."

Anna looked back at the floor and back up at him. "You must think I am a fool. Screaming like a child at the sight of a rat."

"Just the opposite, really. When I was in Afghanistan, there were rats the size of small dogs. They would come into the base from the desert. The food scraps brought them in. The whole place was a never-ending smorgasbord of half-eaten MREs and trash. I swear one rat was so big, it set off a landmine buried to protect the base's rear from a sneak attack at night. That thing must have weighed ten pounds to set the mine off. The tower guards started firing shots blindly across the minefield. They must have wasted a thousand rounds of ammunition. All for a rat."

Anna smiled.

Dodge nodded. "Let's get out of here."

"You didn't find anything?" Anna asked.

"Nope. Probably ought to let the detectives handle it from here. I just needed to see something for myself," he said, turning to the door. "Why don't you go wait in the truck? I want to wipe down anything we touched in case the detectives decide to search and print the place."

Anna nodded, taking the keys to his truck, she opened the door and left the apartment. He heard her footsteps fade as she moved further away from the apartment. He listened as the front door to the building opened, then closed. A whoosh of air rushed into the apartment as the pressure equalized in the building. Returning his attention to the countertop, he noticed there was no knife holder on it. There wasn't even a coffeepot. The counter was clutter-free and wiped clean enough to eat dinner on. He opened a small drawer. It contained spoons and forks and knives, but nothing as big as the knife he held in his hand. He closed the drawer and opened another drawer. It contained spatulas, wooden spoons, and an empty plastic knife sheath. Dodge took the knife and slipped its blade into the sheath. A perfect fit. Then he placed the knife in the drawer after wiping the handle and closed it. Next, he retraced his steps back to the bedroom, wiping any surface he had touched.

He took one more look to ease his mind as he stood in the entrance to the closet and peered into the darkness. All the clothes hung neatly on hangers, each outfit facing in the same direction. Color-coordinated by season, he imagined. He closed the door and took one more look around the room. He just couldn't put his finger on what was bothering him. He closed the front door and locked it with the key. Then he placed the key back on the top door trim with his right hand. Its teeth pointing left and out. "Human engineering," he said to no one. He made the short walk to his truck and Anna. Again, he decided to let the detectives handle this part. His focus would be on Grayson Heller. But doubt crept into his psyche about his involvement. It just didn't have the Grayson flair to it. And why would he care about having someone on the outside search Kelly's apartment? What could be so crucial after ten years?

Anna said, "All good?" as he hopped into the driver's seat.

"Yep," he replied as he pulled out into the street. "I'll drop you off at your place. I have some work to do on another case tonight."

Anna stared then nodded. He thought he sensed disappointment in her eyes, but he needed to work and think and plan. He couldn't do that while distracted. She got out of his truck in front of her building just as the sun set below the buildings.

"Will I see you later?" Anna asked.

"I'll call you." Dodge knew it appeared as a blow-off, but he didn't mean it that way.

Anna closed the door. He watched her in the mirror as he pulled away and headed toward home.

CHAPTER 21

DETECTIVE RENQUEST WALKED down the alley toward the uniformed officers hovering over a white sheet. He could feel the chill in the morning air and the smell of rotting food spewing over the sides of the dumpsters lined up against the alley walls. The smell was so bad, he could almost taste it. An odd mixture of decaying organic material and death. He hated these calls. Children were always the hardest cases to work. The pressure to solve the case quickly became political as grieving parents made for good headlines on the evening news. Not to mention a life snuffed out before driving a car or going to prom. Senseless violence. As a detective, Renquest could only deal with the aftermath. The cases involving child victims haunted him the most.

The coroner and crime scene team had beaten him to the scene. Renquest could see a pair of feet protruding out from the sheet covering the victim. The cloth was void of bloodstains, and there didn't appear to be any blood on the ground surrounding the body. Renquest conducted a routine scan of the area for anything out of place or anyone watching with unusual interest. Nothing and no one appeared out of place except for the victim.

"What do we have?" Renquest asked the coroner.

"Male, approximate age sixteen years old."

"Cause of death?"

"I won't know for sure until I get the body back to the lab, but preliminary indications point to strangulation." The coroner pulled the sheet down, uncovering the head and chest areas, and pointed to bruising on both sides of the neck. "From the bruising pattern, I would say it was an adult male or a female."

"Any other visible wounds?"

"Not so far, but I'll know more when I get him on the slab."

The coroner stood next to Detective Renquest and pulled the sheet back over the body.

"There is something odd, Detective."

"Other than what appears to be a well-dressed kid lying dead in an alley?" Renquest's attempt at humor landed flat. The coroner just stared at him for a moment before continuing.

"His underwear is missing."

"What do you mean *missing*? Like he wasn't wearing any, or they were removed?"

The coroner knelt beside the body, pulling the sheet up, exposing the boy's lower torso.

"No. The underwear was removed and the pants replaced postmortem."

"OK, I'll bite. How do you know that?" Renquest asked.

The coroner pointed at the victim's waistline, to where the pants met the abdomen in the front. "If you look here, you can see the jeans waistband in the front is folded over. This likely happened when the pants were pulled up. The attacker wasn't able to hold the body off the ground while redressing the vic. Either because he, or she, was too weak to lift the body off the ground or the attacker was in a hurry."

"Pants can't have a folded waistband?"

"Of course, they can. It usually happens when the wearer is overweight, and the extra skin forces the waistband to fold over in the front or back of the pants." The coroner pointed to Detective Renquest's waistband, showing an example of the creased waistband scenario he had just described. The move embarrassed Renquest, and he tugged at his jacket to cover his hefty waistline. The coroner smiled and turned back to the body. "And I'll bet that when I get the body on the slab, we will find road material in the back of his pants and anal area."

"From when the pants dragged on the pavement to be pulled up," Renquest stated.

"That's right. But that is not what sold me on the redressing."

"What did?"

"Look here at the zipper area."

Renquest knelt beside the body and examined the area of the pants where the zipper was. He noticed the top button was undone, and the zipper was about halfway up. But something had stopped the zipper from reaching the top.

"Is that skin?"

"Foreskin to be exact," replied the coroner. "If you look, you see that there is no blood on the front of the pants."

"Meaning the skin was caught in the zipper postmortem."

The coroner nodded. "Likely up to an hour after death."

Renquest stood up, and the coroner replaced the sheet over the body. Renquest wasn't sure why someone would want to stage the scene as a sexual assault, but he knew someone who might shed some light on the motives. He waved over a uniformed officer.

"You have a phone on you?"

"Yes, sir."

"Good. Call headquarters and tell the watch commander that Detective Renquest requests Dodge to come to the scene."

"You lose your phone, Detective?"

"Nope."

Renquest had his phone in his pocket, but he didn't want to be the one to call. The two men had an unwritten rule that whoever called the other into a case involving a dead body, the caller had to do the family notification, and Renquest didn't like child death notifications. It was shady as hell, but he was sure his partner had pulled the same trick many times.

Renquest turned back to the coroner and instructed him not to touch or move the body until Dodge arrived and took the scene.

"Sure thing, Detective."

Renquest took one last look around the scene. He peered

into the dumpsters. Hoping to find the missing underwear and careful not to disturb anything, he knew the CSI crew would do an in-depth dumpster diving campaign later that day. He checked the rooftops for any cameras that might have been recording the alley the previous night. Many businesses placed cameras in the back to monitor the rear entrances that are often left unlocked because of the high staff traffic. He saw nothing that would show a crime had taken place in the alley, except for the body. The entire scene made him uncomfortable. Renquest was glad it would soon be Dodge's problem. He leaned up against a brick wall that formed the back of a convenience store and sipped his coffee, waiting for him to arrive.

———

Dodge was preparing to ask for a parolee's phone for inspection when his phone rang. He looked at the number and recognized the prefix. He answered. The voice on the other end was the watch commander for the local police department.

"This is Dodge," he said. "Thanks for calling, sir. Tell Detective Renquest I'll be there as soon as I can."

Disconnecting the call, he returned his attention to the parolee sitting across the desk from him.

"Sorry about that. Where were we?"

"I asked about me being able to buy a personal laptop."

"Ah, that's right. Well, I think the issue is down the road a bit. Let's concentrate on more reachable shorter-term goals."

"Like what?"

"How about devising a safety plan for your computer use at the job center?"

Safety plans were a tool used to hold sex offenders accountable for their decisions. The plan covered an activity the offender wanted to take part in and set rules and responsibilities. For internet usage, the offender would make the rules for using the internet and what responses they might have if, say, an inappropriate pop-up flashed on the screen. It was essential to let the offender recognize the rules, and the agent's job was to guide them in the right direction.

"Can I go home and write down some rules and bring them to the next appointment?"

"That is exactly what I planned to suggest. Our next appointment will be two weeks from today at ten o'clock."

Dodge handed the offender an appointment card and reminded him to sign out at the reception desk on his way out. So as not to forget what had transpired over the last half hour, he set to typing up his notes of the meeting. He then emailed Chief Johnson about the call out, grabbed his jacket and weapon, and headed to the crime scene. Dodge stopped at a coffee shop along the way before arriving at the alley where the boy's body was found earlier that morning. Detective Renquest was directing a crime scene forensics team on where to search for evidence. He turned to see his partner holding out a white Styrofoam cup. Steam was still venting from the holes in the lid.

"So, what do we have here?" Dodge asked.

"We have what appears to be a dead teen. The medical examiner put the time of death sometime last night between midnight and zero-three hundred."

Glancing at his watch, Dodge asked, "Any idea of who he is?"

Renquest signaled to the medical examiner to remove the sheet from the body.

"No ID, no wallet," Renquest said. The medical examiner folded the sheet three times on top of itself, stopping just above the waistline. "Not unusual for a teen to not carry a wallet. But I would expect to find a school ID or coffee shop loyalty card with his name on it."

"So, this isn't a robbery."

"What makes you think that?"

The body was splayed out on the cold, hard asphalt, but Dodge was quick to notice the telltale signs of a front on strangulation. Bruise marks that narrow in the center of the neck and fan out like wings toward the ears. Pressure from the thumbs positioned over the trachea caused air restriction to the lungs. The other four fingers on each hand wrapped around the neck and formed the fan shape, as the attacker tried to touch his thumbs and fingers through the neck.

"Frontal strangulation is personal. Not too often associated with a robbery," Dodge said.

"I agree," the medical examiner answered. "But as I told the detective, I'll have more answers once I get the body downtown to the lab."

"Anything else?" Dodge asked. "Like a sexual component linking him to the case?"

The medical examiner looked at the detective, who nodded his head.

Renquest said, "Show him. That's why we called him."

The medical examiner folded the sheet over one more time, revealing the victim's torso. Dodge leaned in to examine the body but realized he had forgotten his protective gloves. Renquest pulled a glove out of his jacket pocket and handed it to him.

"Where is his underwear?"

"We were hoping you could shed some light on that." Renquest threw a side glance at the medical examiner. "See anything else?"

Standing up and taking two steps back, Dodge sought a broader picture of the scene. After circling the body several times, kneeling, then standing up again, he found himself next to Renquest.

"The suspect undressed the body somewhere else, moved postmortem, and redressed at the scene. Signs of movement under the body show manipulation after being placed here. The zipper has flesh caught in it, which would have been too painful to leave while alive. No clotting of the wound indicates it happened postmortem."

"You don't miss a thing, do you?"

The medical examiner looked at Dodge, who nodded his permission to cover the body. He looked at the roof lines surrounding the alley. No cameras. There were five dumpsters in the alley, including the one next to the body.

"I have already looked," Renquest said.

"Looked for what?"

"For cameras and dumpsites. There are no cameras in the alley, and I have CSI coming to dig through the dumpsters for anything the killer may have disposed of."

"I doubt they will find anything," Dodge said. "There is no way the subject left evidence in a dumpster next to the body. No one surprised him, assuming the body was dressed here. Maybe he knew the routine of the restaurant employees and the delivery trucks? I doubt any working girls use this alley for business. It smells like a damn sewer. Even the lowliest street girl has standards."

A quick glance of his surroundings, assured Dodge he had taken everything in.

"I agree, but we will check every dumpster and every gutter."

Renquest's phone rang. He stepped away from the group for more privacy. When he returned, he stared at the sheet on the ground. The blank expression on his faced echoed what the phone call had entailed. It was that of someone who discovered the identity of a child murder victim. Knowing the name of a vic was a massive break in the case, but when an officer found the identity of a child victim, it became real. It's no longer just a victim. It is someone's son or daughter. If an officer had children the same age with similar characteristics, it hit home even harder.

"What is his name?" Dodge asked.

"Parents reported their son missing this morning. The boy went out to study with a friend at the library but never returned home. The report said he was wearing brown corduroy pants and a blue T-shirt."

All three men looked down at the brown corduroy cuff of the pants leg protruding from under the white sheet.

"The vic's name is Kevin Parker. He was a junior at Central High," Renquest said.

"OK, we know who. That leaves the how and why." A feeling of guilt creeped over Dodge as the adrenaline kicked in from knowing the boy's name. It was a huge break.

Having what he thought he needed from the scene, he turned and began walking away.

"I think this one will fall into your court," Renquest yelled after him.

He stopped and without turning said, "Look, Renquest. A body with missing underwear does not a sex crime make. Call me if you put two and two together with a sexual component."

Before he could take a step, Renquest hit him with the other part of the phone call he had just received.

"The person Kevin Parker was planning to meet at the library was Maggie Rodstein. I am sure you remember her."

Dodge wanted to keep walking, to pretend he had not heard what Renquest said, but he had. There was nothing he could do about it.

"Are you sure? I mean, are you sure that is who our vic was meeting at the library?"

"Shit just got interesting, didn't it?"

"I would describe it another way."

"How would you describe it?"

"*Fubar.*"

A haze fell over Dodge as he walked back to his truck. What did this recent development mean? The cases were separate, but working one without considering the outcome against the other was now impossible. It made things more complicated. And he needed to know more before his next move. A wrong step would jeopardize both cases. He needed to gather more information on Kevin Parker.

"Where are you going?" Renquest shouted.

"To learn as much as I can about the Parker boy," Dodge shouted as he turned the corner toward his truck. His engine started, and the radio blared yacht rock as he pulled into traffic, heading toward Central High.

CHAPTER 22

A FEW STUDENTS LINGERED in the halls as Dodge arrived at Central High School. He wanted to talk to the principal during a lunch break when most of the student population left campus to hit the local fast-food restaurants and convenience stores located around the school. He sat in the small wooden chairs that lined the wall next to the principal's door, thinking back to his time as a student. He had not been the best student to roam the halls, but he had not been the worst either.

"Agent Dodge, Principal Lowe will see you now," the secretary said.

Dodge nodded and stood. The principal greeted him with a handshake, and they sat across the desk from one another. It was a strange feeling to be on the receiving side of the table. The feeling was one he didn't care for, and he quickly broke the ice.

"So, whatever happened to Principal Nilovek?" Dodge recalled, having liked Nilovek and remembered a fair and compassionate educator.

"Principal Nilovek retired about seven years ago. Up and moved to Florida," Principal Lowe answered. "Nothing but sunshine and warm water for him now."

"You took over as principal after he retired?"

"The job was given to me interim for one year. The position has to be approved by the school board, and the teacher's union fought against me."

"Why would the union not want you to be principal?"

"I started as an assistant principal toward the end of Nilovek's tenure. He was grooming me to take over once he retired. However, I was an outsider and never attended or taught at Central. Naturally, the union wanted to fill the position with one of the rank and file. The first year was an audition to win the staff's trust. But I am sure you are not here to talk about my rise to the pinnacle of a moderately sized inner-city school. So, what can I do for you, Agent Dodge?"

"I am here to talk to one, well, two of your students," Dodge said.

"Most of our students are respectful kids who come from excellent families. I can't imagine any of them involved in anything that required a police response."

"Parole," Dodge said.

"I'm sorry?"

"You said the police department. I am a parole agent with the Department of Corrections."

At that moment he decided to hold back he was part of a task force with the police department that worked sex crimes. Just the mention of sex abuse to a school official led to attorneys getting involved. Investigations stopped before they ever got going. Close to the vest was the best way to play it.

"Well, I can't imagine why any of my students would need to talk to a parole officer. May I ask what this is about?"

"I am just following up on a lead involving a current case," Dodge said, hoping to move the conversation forward.

The principal appeared satisfied. "Who are the two students?" he asked.

Dodge pulled out a small notepad from his inner jacket pocket. He opened the notepad and rifled through a few pages before stopping. There was nothing on the page, and he knew the names of the two students but didn't want to appear too anxious. The delay made the situation seem less urgent. *I know enough to come here, but not enough to have memorized the names.*

"Let's see here . . . Oh, there we are. Maggie Rodstein and Kevin Parker."

The principal stared at him as if he should know who the two students were. Dodge maintained a blank expression. After a few seconds, the principal asked his secretary to bring in the day's attendance reports.

"The morning attendance reports can be accessed already?"

"I receive them for every period."

Principal Lowe must have seen the look of confusion on Dodge's face because he explained the tech-heavy attendance program and how it worked. Five years ago, the school received a grant from the federal government to help safeguard schools against violence. Lowe had an idea he had been working on for several years. He wanted to use the school IDs to keep real-time attendance. First, they replaced student IDs with ones that incorporated radio frequency chips. Next, he had all the classroom doors fitted with RF readers. As the students passed through the classroom door, the reader registered their attendance in the class.

The secretary brought in the first-period attendance reports and handed them to Principal Lowe.

"The attendance report shows Maggie is out sick today. So is Kevin. That is unusual," Principal Lowe said.

There was now an urgency to get what he came for because once the family received a notification, word would spread quickly. Everyone would have heard in an hour. The school would clamp down on information, and he will be left with unanswered questions.

"What is so unusual about those two particular students being absent on the same day?"

"Both students were working on a perfect attendance award for the quarter."

"People get sick," Dodge said. "It isn't uncommon for students to fake a cold or cough to get a free day from school."

"The school has an online learning curriculum that absent students can take advantage of to offset any sick days. If they complete a few simple exercises, it restores their attendance record. The program has shown real promise in keeping kids engaged and slowing skip days," Principal Lowe said with pride oozing from his pores.

"Maybe they just haven't completed the work yet."

The principal shook his head, disapprovingly. "No, these two are very close. Those two out at the same time just seems a little too coincidental."

Principal Lowe set the attendance report on his desk and explained Maggie and Kevin's relationship. The two started attending the school at the same time and lived just a few blocks apart. They were in many of the same classes and walked the halls during breaks and attend sporting events together. In all aspects, they seemed like an average high school couple. But something told the veteran parole agent there was something Principal Lowe wasn't telling him.

The phone in Dodge's pocket vibrated. It was a message from Detective Renquest saying he had just finished notifying Kevin Parker's family of his death. They were on the way to the coroner's office to ID the body. He only had a half hour before the entire town was aware of what happened last night.

"Were the two dating?"

"Heavens no. While the best of friends, Kevin's interests lay in a different persuasion than young Maggie."

Dodge knew what he meant without having to ask questions. Kevin was gay, and Principal Lowe couldn't reveal that information, as it was a breach of student privacy.

"Do you have addresses for Maggie and Kevin? I need to speak to them or their parents." Although he knew both addresses, he felt it would seem suspicious if he didn't ask after showing so much interest in the two students. The principal wrote the information on an index card and passed it across the desk. Dodge asked the principal to keep their conversation private until he heard from him or the police. Principal Lowe agreed. The men shook hands again.

Before Dodge reached the door, Principal Lowe blurted out one more question. "Is there anything I need to know, Agent Dodge? I would like to get in front of any rumors before they become a problem."

Stopping in his tracks but not looking back, Dodge said, "I'll be in touch. Thank you again for your time."

CHAPTER 23

THE MOMENT DODGE CLEARED the school parking lot, he placed a call to Renquest. He needed to buy enough time to get to the judge's house before Maggie learned about Kevin Parker. Dodge worried that when she found out what had happened to the Parker boy, the marshals and her father might circle the wagons to protect her. He needed to nail down a few details before access to her was cut off. Did Maggie and Kevin Parker hang out last night, and was anyone else present? Did Kevin have a cell phone? When did the two split up? Where was he going after they separated? Much more information was needed, and Maggie was the last person to see Kevin Parker alive besides the killer.

A call to Renquest filled him in on the meeting with Principal Lowe. He explained the friendship between Maggie and Kevin and asked if Kevin Parker's parents had finished the identification. Renquest said the ID was complete, and the parents were now meeting with a priest at a chapel in the coroner's office complex. The family's impromptu meeting with the priest bought Dodge more time, but there was still cause to hurry. Although against regulations, he used the vehicle's emergency lights to help maneuver through traffic and navigate intersections. It only took ten minutes to reach the judge's neighborhood after leaving the school.

As Dodge pulled into the semicircular driveway, he noticed a black Ford sedan with tinted windows parked at the house. The vehicle was a standard-issue Ford Crown Victoria, right down to the blackout rims. The car had U.S. Government plates, and he assumed it belonged to the U.S. Marshals Office. That meant Deputy Fisch was at the residence. He knew that Fisch being at the house likely made talking to Maggie Rodstein more difficult.

The door opened before Dodge could even knock. Deputy Fisch stood in the doorway like an impassable barricade.

"Dodge, I was expecting you today," Deputy Fisch said.

"How's that?"

"How's what?" he answered.

"How is it you expected me today?"

"Locals found that boy from Maggie's school dead in an alley this morning. I figured the police would contact you for help. Eventually, you would put two and two together and come here to interview Maggie."

That boy. *A strange choice of words*, Dodge thought. Fisch would have known Kevin Parker. The kid was best friends with Maggie and visited the house many times, according to the principal. He would have been on any list of approved visitors.

"Try to talk to Maggie? Is there a reason I wouldn't be able to? And while I am asking questions, how did you find out about the Parker boy so quick?"

Deputy Fisch paused, and Dodge assumed Fisch wouldn't give up his source inside the police department.

"This is the U.S. Marshals Service, not some hillbilly sheriff's department. The marshals monitor all police radio traffic."

Dodge had just caught Fisch in a lie. Police policy mandated that once a victim is identified as a juvenile, radio traffic moves to a closed frequency. Fisch, nor the U.S. Marshals, can listen for the victim's name. A slip of the tongue by Fisch confirmed the leaks in the investigation came from the same source at the police department. He would have Renquest handle that issue later. The focus now was on Maggie.

"I need to speak to her as soon as possible. The two were friends, and Maggie may have information that can help us find out what happened."

"The two were close," Fisch said. "Maggie is distraught and won't be talking to you or anyone else today. If you would like to leave a card, I'll make sure the judge gets it. I'll call when Maggie is ready to talk."

"So, she knows the Parker boy is dead."

"I told Maggie this morning. As I said, she was upset and needed to rest. The judge gave her a Valium, and she is sleeping. It will be hours before she wakes up."

A noise came from the other side of the door, and Dodge attempted to shift to get a better view. Fisch moved his colossal frame, trying to block the unwanted visitor from viewing what was behind him in the house.

"Now, if you will excuse me, I have rounds to make. The judge will be in contact when he determines Maggie is ready to give a statement."

Dodge, seeing his chances to talk to Maggie disappearing, retrieved a business card from his jacket pocket. He shoved the card out toward the closing door, forcing the door to catch his hand, jarring the card free and forcing it to fall just outside the doorway. He pulled his hand back, grasping it, faking an injury. Fisch reopened the door and bent over to pick up the business card. Using the dropped card distraction, Dodge could see into the foyer. He made out the silhouette of a man comparable in size to Judge Rodstein.

"Excuse me, Judge," Dodge yelled.

"Is that you, Dodge?"

Realizing the error, Fisch stood up. A smile creeped across Dodge's face at having bested Fisch with a Three Stooges move. There was no time to relish the moment. He needed to get the judge to allow Maggie to be interviewed. The judge approached the front door and looked at Deputy Fisch standing at attention, holding the front door open with his rear end.

"Finish your rounds, Fisch. I'll be fine."

Fisch gave the judge a look of protest. The judge reassured Fisch he was fine, and Fisch walked outside to the side of the house.

"Agent Dodge. I would like to say I don't know why you are here, but I am all too aware of what happened this morning. Maggie is a mess. I don't think it would be good for her to talk to anyone right now."

Fathers protect their daughters, and Dodge needed to be careful not to close off the judge by backing him into a corner. *It would be better to try another route*, he thought.

"I am sure she is, Your Honor, and I understand. Perhaps I could ask you a few questions about Kevin Parker?"

The judge invited his guest into the spacious house, leading him through a door on the right next to the entryway. "I am not sure what, if any, help I can give you, but I'll try. What those parents must be going through right now is unimaginable. Maggie and I plan to visit them once they have had a chance to, well, come to terms with the immense tragedy that has beset their family."

"They will appreciate that, Your Honor."

The judge walked over to a large wooden globe sitting in the corner of the study. The globe was the size of a regular office chair and had wheels for easy moving. The map covering the surface appeared to be early sixteenth or seventeenth century. Dodge used to have an interest in old maps and spent hours on the weekends searching map sites on the internet. On the globe design, he noticed Florida was more box-shaped and shorter than is shown on modern maps. The misshape of Florida was a trait of maps earlier than the 1700s, when Florida's coast had yet to be mapped in more detail.

Separating the top of the globe at the equator, the judge opened the top, and the globes' actual purpose became clear. It was a bar containing the typical liquors for making martinis and a bottle of bourbon in the middle. The judge pulled the bourbon from its resting place. He poured one glass, then a second. He handed one to Dodge and took a sip as he sat in a high-backed reading chair.

"What would you like to know, Agent Dodge?"

Caution was best used here. He didn't want to tip his

hand to any connections between the Parker boy and the case involving Maggie. As of now, there was no evidence linking the two cases, but instinct told Dodge it was there. He just needed more information.

"How well did you know Kevin?"

"He used to come over a couple of times a week. Kevin and Maggie would study, go to the mall, and sometimes he would spend the night."

The judge's answer had given him an opening to probe deeper into the relationship between Kevin Parker and Maggie.

"You didn't have a problem with a boy staying overnight with your daughter?"

"Not at all. The two grew up together. Besides, Maggie wasn't Kevin's type."

Dodge paused harder, hoping the judge could sense his hesitation and not make him ask. When the judge didn't answer, he asked the question.

"What was Kevin's type?"

The judge was now the silent one, and as lead investigator on the case, he needed confirmation concerning Kevin's sexual preference.

After a moment, the judge answered, "Boys."

The answer to his first genuine question earned him a sip of bourbon.

"You said he used to come over a lot. Did something happen?"

"I am not sure. When I asked Maggie about it, she said Kevin was just busy with school and glee club. I just figured he had a boyfriend and was spending less time with Maggie and more with whoever he was dating."

"When was the last time you saw Kevin?"

"He was over a few days ago. When I came home from work, he and Maggie were studying in this very room. In fact, he was sitting in that chair," he said, pointing to the chair Dodge sat in.

The thought of someone dead having occupied the very seat he sat in sent chills through his body. But that answered Dodge's second question. Now, for the third question.

"Can you think of anyone who would want to harm him?"

"Not at all. Kevin was a wonderful kid and lived just a few blocks from here."

"Was he ever known to be into drugs or other activities that could have placed him at risk of violence?"

"I cannot imagine Kevin doing drugs. If he was, Maggie didn't know, or she would've told me."

"Teenagers have secrets," Dodge said.

"Not those two. They told each other everything. To be honest, if I wanted to know something about Maggie at school, all I had to do was ask Kevin."

The interview had gone well, and he had gotten the answers he wanted from the judge. The rest of his questions were for Maggie.

"Sir, when do you think I can talk to Maggie?"

"Do you think she knows something? I mean, about what happened to Kevin?"

"I don't know yet. But Kevin's parents said they were to meet last night at the library. Maggie might have been the last person to have seen him alive."

"Well, that clarifies why she was so distraught over the news. I know they were best friends, but she lost it. I had to administer a sedative to calm her down. She won't be down until this evening."

Dodge reached into his inside jacket pocket, pulled out another business card, and handed it to the judge.

"Can you call me when she is ready to talk?"

The judge took the card and placed it in his shirt pocket.

"I'll let you know, Agent Dodge. Now, I have to get to the courthouse."

Dodge stood, finishing the last of the bourbon in his glass and placing the empty glass on the table next to the door as he left the room. He glanced up from the entryway toward the top of the stairs. Standing there, peering out over the open foyer was Maggie Rodstein. She watched his every move. He pulled the last remaining business card from his jacket pocket and placed it on the small circular table by the front door. He then looked back up at Maggie and walked out, closing the door behind him.

Upon getting into his car, he waited for a few minutes to see if Maggie came out or peered through the window by where he left the business card. Nothing. He hoped she would take the card and call, but he never put too much faith in other people. The case would be worked with or without young Maggie's help.

CHAPTER 24

AFTER LEAVING THE JUDGE'S HOUSE, Dodge and Detective Renquest needed to go over the facts of the Kevin Parker case and anything collected on Maggie Rodstein's case. Dodge also needed to fill Renquest in on his trips to see Grayson and how that tangent was shaking out.

The two men met at a diner near the police station and ate lunch before discussing work. Dodge was adamant the cases were linked somehow, but Renquest needed convincing. Dodge laid out his findings, pointing to the fact Maggie Rodstein was the last person to see Kevin Parker alive. He gave the details of the meeting with Grayson but admitted that nothing linked him to either of the cases. Although aware of the tenuous relationship between the parties in each case, his gut instinct told him the cases were connected, even if only circumstantially. Finding the connection was now essential to solving both cases.

After an hour of eating and discussing facts and theories, the men left the diner. Renquest headed back to the office to check the lab results from the Parker autopsy. The medical examiner had called during lunch to confirm the cause of death: homicide by strangulation. Dodge planned to stop by Anna's apartment before going home to comb through the files, pictures, and statements gathered over the past week. He hoped the evidence would bridge Maggie's case with Kevin Parker's death. The one thing the parole agent knew was that Maggie Rodstein was the key to solving both cases.

The sun had disappeared behind the city's taller buildings

moments before Dodge arrived home. He opened the blinds to let the fading light bestow a calming aura in the room. The light only lasted half an hour before the timer on the desk lamp clicked, forcing artificial light to take over where the natural light once reigned.

He began scouring over the photos and statements from Maggie's case, looking for anything he may have missed. He compared the face under the sheet earlier that morning to those that lined the wall of the hidden room containing the photo of Maggie. Kevin Parker wasn't on either of the creeper's walls, which ruled out the cases being related through the first crime scene. Grayson wasn't involved in the Parker boy's death.

Dodge was going over the evidence one more time when the corner of an envelope buried under a pile of unopened mail caught his eye. The return address showed it was from a law firm downtown. He often received legal papers concerning inmates' lawsuits but had had none filed against him for three years. Pulling the letter from the bottom of the pile caused the top half to collapse. Papers poured like a waterfall to the floor. Dodge looked at the mess scattered across his dining room floor and cursed. Looking at the envelope, he recognized the law firm's name and tore the end of the envelope open. It was a copy of Kelly's last will and testament. She had left all her possessions to him. He didn't have time to deal with lawyers, and it was too late to call. He would contact the attorneys listed on the document tomorrow or maybe the next day. The urgency to respond was low. Kelly wasn't going anywhere, and he was sure her possessions amounted to a closet full of clothes and maybe a hundred bucks in a savings account somewhere.

Before turning his attention back to the piles of case materials strewn across his desk, Dodge poured another drink. Then he felt the unmistakable vibration of a cell phone ringing in his pocket. He had set the device to vibrate while at the Parker crime scene earlier in the day and never returned to its original ring setting. After pulling the phone from his front pocket, he looked and didn't recognize the number. Usually, he'd let an unknown call go to voicemail, but he needed a break, so he answered. The voice on the other line sounded panicked and stricken with fear. The caller was Maggie Rodstein.

Driving to meet with her, Dodge thought about Maggie and the fear in her voice. If she knew who killed Kevin Parker, she wasn't safe. He had told Maggie to inform Deputy Fisch if her life was in danger. It was his job to protect her, after all. Dodge told her he trusted his contacts, but she became more panicked and rambled on about how the police would just cover everything up. What she said made little sense, but there was another problem. Maggie was a teenager, and the law stated she wasn't to be questioned without a parent present. There were strict laws involving juvenile interviews and witnesses. He needed to talk to her to find out what she knew about Kevin Parker's murder and the link between the two cases. And he needed to question her without Judge Rodstein or the U.S. Marshals breathing down his neck or sculpting answers for her.

They decided to meet at a place that provided privacy and was open to the public: the city library. It was late enough that people would be scarce, but the building would be well lit and had reading rooms for privacy. Dodge entered through the front door and headed to the periodical section on the third floor. He walked down the center aisle, looking left then right as he passed rows of magazines and journals. The library had changed since he had last roamed its aisles, and he was having trouble finding the reading rooms. They were not where he remembered.

At the far end of the center aisle, there were six tables with chairs pushed in. The tables were covered with magazines and newspapers students had read throughout the day, ready for the night librarian to return them to the proper racks. Directly behind the row of tables were four rooms with cubical desks facing the back wall. The desk arrangement forced users to face away from the door to avoid distractions and concentrate on studying. Dodge preferred to face the door. *Old habits die hard*, he thought.

Only one room had a light on. The closer he came to the

door, the more he could make out a person inside the room. A hooded sweatshirt covered the head, but he could make out strands of long blonde hair protruding from under the gray hoodie. The girl was sitting on the floor, staring at a cell phone. As Dodge reached for the door handle, the girl looked up and jumped to her feet, startled. She must have realized the only exit was now blocked. She was cornered and scared.

Dodge raised his hands in a gesture to show her he wasn't a threat. He then reached into his jacket pocket and produced a leather wallet containing a Corrections ID and held it out so she could see the picture in the upper left-hand corner. The ID must have been convincing because the girl opened the door and sat at the lone desk.

The door opened inward, and Dodge took a position opposite the door swing. It was the best position to maintain control over the door and offered an excellent vantage point of the aisle leading to the four rooms. The setup wasn't perfect, but it was damn close. He wanted Maggie facing the window. He didn't know who Maggie thought was after her, but he was confident the look in her eyes would alert him if the person came within visual range.

Maggie spoke first. "You were the man talking to my dad today, aren't you?"

"Yes. My name is Paul Dodge, but call me Dodge. Everyone does," he said.

He gave Maggie time to ask another question. She said nothing.

"I see you got the card I left for you. Was it the card from the table, or did your father give it to you?"

"It was the one from the table," she said. "Why did you leave it there and not just give the card to my dad?"

"Sometimes people want to talk, but they don't want other people to know." Dodge smiled and continued. "Sometimes other people want to protect someone and don't help in an investigation. But I think you are neither of those things."

Maggie said nothing.

"My job is to investigate crimes that involve children."

"Like Kevin?" Maggie asked.

"Yes," Dodge said.

Maggie looked down at the floor. A single tear rolled down her cheek before she tucked the emotion back into a place deep inside and looked back up at him.

"So, you are a cop?"

"I am a parole agent. I work for the Department of Corrections. However, I consult with the police department on certain types of cases."

"Like what happened to Kevin," she said again.

Dodge thought hard before answering, not wanting to reveal anything about the Parker boy's case and remembering Maggie was just a child.

"I work cases the police ask for my help on. Many cases involve the death of a child. Your friend Kevin was a teenager, so here I am."

He had hoped the answer would satisfy Maggie's curiosity and move on to why they were meeting in a college library at night. He decided to be direct and ask before she could respond with another question concerning Kevin Parker.

"What can you tell me about Kevin Parker? That is why you called me today, right?"

Maggie paused. The experienced investigator in him could tell she was having second thoughts about the meeting. He needed answers, and he needed them now.

"Do you know why Kevin Parker is dead?" he asked.

Maggie shook her head no.

"That's good, Maggie. Now, do you know who hurt him?"

Maggie nodded her head in the affirmative.

"Can you tell me who hurt Kevin?"

Maggie didn't move and just stared at the floor. It was at that moment, he realized he might have rushed into the meat of his questions, scaring her off, and needed to backtrack.

"Maggie," Dodge said. "Tell me about the other day. The last day you spent with Kevin."

Maggie talked about how she and Kevin had been hanging out after school. "I was waiting for my ride. When my detail arrived, Kevin walked home, and that was the last time I saw him."

"Who picked you up from school?" Dodge asked.

"John . . . uh, I mean Deputy Fisch. He always picks me up after school."

It seemed weird to him that someone under protection would call a handler by their first name, but he didn't allow the detail to distract him. He could return to this point if needed. He wanted Maggie to continue talking.

"Does Kevin always walk home? Is it normal for no one to come and pick him up?"

"Yeah, he almost always walks, unless it is raining or freezing outside."

"Did you speak to him again?"

"No, we had nothing planned."

"Kevin's parents claimed the two of you had plans to meet at the library to study. Why would they think that?"

Maggie looked at Dodge and shrugged her shoulders.

"You said earlier you know who hurt Kevin. Can you tell me who that was? I can protect you if you are scared."

"He will kill me if he finds out I told you anything. Coming here was a mistake!"

Dodge shifted a little to his left to block the door if Maggie tried to leave. He didn't want her to feel trapped but also didn't want her to go until he knew what she knew.

"I came to meet you, so tell me what you know. It will feel better to get it off your chest."

"You don't understand. He is very dangerous, and I won't say anything else. If he finds out, I'll be next. Or my dad."

Maggie stood up and reached into the pouch of her sweatshirt, pulling out a cell phone. She handed the phone to Dodge and said everything was on it. He asked whose phone it was, but she didn't answer. Maggie then brushed past him and opened the door, disappearing into the rows of bookshelves.

Dodge looked at the cell phone and back in the direction in which Maggie had ran. He wasn't sure what he would find on the device, but he knew whatever it was it had frightened Maggie Rodstein enough to call him. The phone's GPS was disabled, and a few touches of buttons turned off the data signal to ensure no one could access the phone remotely. He placed the phone in his pocket and left the library study room. He needed to see what was on that phone. But he also needed to be careful not to compromise any evidence the phone might contain.

CHAPTER 25

RETURNING HOME, DODGE BACKED up the data on the cell phone Maggie gave him to a virtual machine. The computer had no outside internet connections, and he encrypted the data out of an abundance of caution. He placed the device in a Faraday bag so outside actors couldn't hack or manipulate it. The bag also blocked any GPS signal the phone might send or receive. The device was placed in a desk drawer and locked for safekeeping. In the morning, he would take the phone to the office for a thorough forensic analysis. Call logs, contacts, and text messages were an excellent place to investigate Maggie's claims. Things would start rolling tomorrow. He shut off the light and went to bed.

At his office the next morning, Dodge removed the phone from the Faraday bag and connected it to his computer to retrieve any photos, texts, and call logs saved to the device. A friend had written a program for him, allowing him to examine mobile devices without having to power up the device and risk compromising digital evidence.

Dodge used the program sparingly, as the department shunned the practice. This issue had been a point of contention between himself and the department for years. He believed the rules followed the law and court rulings, which in this case favored the state. The department, under new softer leadership, had a group of attorneys who misinterpreted decisions handed down by judges and favored the offenders. None of this mattered in this case, as the owner of the phone willingly handed it over, so he had every right to examine it for evidence.

The program took about ten minutes to boot up and finish its work retrieving the data saved on the phone. While waiting, Dodge stepped out of his office to grab a cup of coffee from the break room and stopped at another agent's desk to talk about office gripes and upcoming safety training. By the time he had returned, the program had finished. He sat at his desk and began browsing through the text messages now viewable on the laptop computer. There appeared to be thousands of texts sent and received, all from one number. Dodge used 411 to search the phone number on the Internet, but the number wasn't traceable. He then used investigative software to locate the owner to see if it tied into any other cases in the system. Nothing.

The phone contained thousands of phone calls and texts to a single untraceable number. The only identifier for the number was it was saved under DJF. Dodge assumed DJF were the initials of the owner of the number. He examined the rest of the phone data for additional evidence, starting with the pictures. The phone had stored about one hundred individual images to internal memory and a removable SD drive. Almost all the photos made the veteran agent cringe, as most of the pictures showed Maggie Rodstein in varying stages of undress. The images appeared to have been taken by Maggie and sent to the unidentified person at the other number. Whoever the unknown phone number belonged to, the two were more than just friends. The pictures and text messages revealed an intimate relationship between them, one that had a sexual component. Dodge couldn't imagine how horrifying it must have been to let a stranger see the phone's contents. The thought reassured him on the merits of Maggie's story.

One message referred to meeting after school and attached to the text was a racy picture of Maggie in a red lace bra and thong. The response was a smiley face emoji. Dodge continued to read message after message until he couldn't look anymore. He kept repeating the initials DJF, DJF, DJF in his head. *Who the hell is DJF?* Then it hit him like a freight train. If he was correct, he needed to let his chief know what he was thinking and Renquest, too. He knew to cover his ass when he was in doubt.

He stood and peered through the window and across the bullpen. Chief Johnson was at his desk. When he looked up, Dodge waved him to his office.

"What do you need?" Chief Johnson said.

"Come in and close the door."

"Where are you at in the judge's daughter case?"

"Funny you should ask that. You know the case the locals asked me to consult on with the dead teenager downtown?"

"Dodge, you need to learn no is an acceptable answer. There is a job to do here, and I need you working *our* cases."

Shrugging off the comment, Dodge continued. "The Parker boy in the alley was friends with Maggie Rodstein."

"How good of friends?"

"She was the last one to see him alive," Dodge said.

Finding the two cases were related meant Maggie Rodstein's case was more significant than just some average street pervert with a picture on the wall. Now a dead kid was thrown into the mix? Watchers don't murder. They watch from afar and don't harm innocent children.

Chief Johnson was still skeptical. "Are you sure about this?"

"I mean, Maggie and Kevin Parker grew up together and lived not too far from each other."

"So did three of my ex-wives. That don't make us friends."

"Add all that to Maggie being the last one to see the Parker boy before he died. This is not a coincidence."

Chief Johnson sat down across the desk from his subordinate. He threw back his head and let out a loud groan.

"Have you confirmed any of this?"

"I spoke to her last night."

"The girl?" Chief Johnson asked.

"Yeah."

"What do the marshals think about this?"

Dodge didn't answer.

"The marshals don't know, do they? Jesus Christ, Dodge!

You can't withhold this kind of information from the agency attached to protect her."

He shook his head in disbelief. Then, Chief Johnson saw the phone hooked up to Dodge's computer.

"Where did that come from?" Chief Johnson pointed at the cell phone.

"Maggie gave the phone to me last night."

"The judge's daughter gave you her cell phone?"

"Yes, she called me last night, and we met at the City College Library."

"Alone! What the hell were you thinking? All she has to do is make a complaint, and you are in deep shit." The veins on chief Johnson's bald head pulsated. The throbbing veins looked like little blue worms crawling under the skin.

"What is she going to accuse me of?" Dodge asked.

"Anything she wants to. Hell, it doesn't have to be true. It just needs to be enough to garner an audience at HQ." Chief Johnson appeared very concerned. Dodge wasn't sure if the concern was for him or Chief Johnson, but it didn't matter. What was done was done.

"Meeting her at the library was the only way she would talk to me, and the marshals blocked all of my attempts to interview her."

"What about her dad, the judge? Did you even try to talk to him?" Chief Johnson asked.

"I did. The judge said some shit about Maggie being too upset to talk."

The look on Chief Johnson's face showed he was still angry with one of his parole agent's taking a meeting with a minor, but he was still listening. It was time to lay out his theory.

"Look, we can review my mistakes later. I need to show you what I found. You need to tell me if I'm am heading in the right direction or way off base," Dodge said.

Chief Johnson protested the change in topic but agreed to hear Dodge's thoughts on both cases. "What do you have?"

Dodge spent the next several minutes explaining the text

messages and photos on the phone. He detailed the processes, attempts to trace the phone number, and why those attempts were unsuccessful. Then he said who he thought the phone number Maggie Rodstein had texted over and over belonged to.

"Are you fucking serious?"

It could have gone better.

"It all makes sense," Dodge said. "Why would Maggie need a burner phone? Why would she be so scared of the person who gave her the phone to use?"

He waited for an answer, but Chief Johnson just sat there. Not moving. Not even blinking.

"Think about it . . . DJF." Dodge allowed his chief to put it together on his own. When he didn't respond, Dodge provided him the answer. "Deputy John Fisch."

"Are you insane? Your theory is that a U.S. Marshal is banging a federal judge's daughter who he is charged with protecting. Why would he do that? Why risk his pension and freedom for some young tail?"

What Chief Johnson just said was not lost on Dodge. He could only come up with one solution. "Because Fisch is a predator. It is inside of him, just below the surface. Festering. Waiting for the perfect moment to rise to the top and explode. It just is, Chief."

The room fell silent. Dodge had sold the story as best he could. If unable to get the man in front of him to believe, he would have a much harder time convincing others that a U.S. Marshal was a sexual predator.

Finally, Chief Johnson spoke up. "Well, ain't this a shit show. What are you going to do?"

A five-hundred-pound weight had been lifted off Dodge's shoulders. With Chief Johnson behind him, the theory now had some credibility.

"Well, now I have to bring Renquest on board."

"Do you think he will believe you?" Chief Johnson asked.

"I have known Renquest for years. Getting him to believe isn't the hard part. Getting him to back me is the challenge. The brass won't like this, and it's not just this case. Fisch will now be our number one suspect for the Parker boy's murder."

The men spoke for a few more minutes. Dodge agreed to call as soon as Renquest was on board. When that happened, the three of them could come up with a plan to trap Deputy Fisch without getting themselves or Maggie Rodstein hurt. The plan had to be concise and straightforward. Low on moving parts, but they needed it yesterday.

—⁓—

Detective Renquest walked into the kitchen of his modest two-bedroom home located just inside the city limits. He preferred not to live in the city's heart, where he spent most of his adult life as a cop. The stench of the job stuck to him. After coming home, the solitude washed most of the smell away. His dog stood at his side, staring, asking for its master to let the weight of the day melt away with a few modest strokes of his fur.

Renquest removed his tie by loosening the knot and slipping the noose over his head and tossed his jacket on the recliner. Next, he kicked off each shoe, one landed by the chair and the other upside down under the table. Finally, he opened the refrigerator door and grabbed a cold bottle of beer. The dog continued to watch every move, waiting for his turn. Renquest moved into the living room and sat down in a recliner, easing back just enough to lift the leg rest. The dog proceeded to the side of the chair with Renquest's empty hand.

"Hey there, Custus. How was your day today?"

The dog leaned into its master's hand as Renquest stroked the dog's head. Custus struggled to get closer, but the chair blocked his path.

"Come on, boy," Renquest said, patting his lap.

The dog obliged and snuggled into place on his master's lap. Renquest felt the phone in his shirt pocket vibrate. The dog looked up at its owner. The call was from Dodge, and he wanted to meet at a diner across town. Renquest tried to blow off the invitation, saying he was busy, but his partner said the matter was too important to wait. The two men needed to meet tonight.

"Make sure no one follows you," Dodge said.

By the time Detective Renquest arrived at the diner, it was almost 7:00 p.m. Dodge sat facing the door and had a cup of coffee. Upon seeing Renquest, he signaled for the waitress to bring another cup of coffee for his partner. Renquest looked around at the other patrons. Everyone appeared to be locals out after work or families sitting down to a late dinner.

"So, why did I drive to this shitty diner at the end of a long day?"

"Back when I first started this job, I used to come here during late-night fieldwork in the Valley. Back then, the Valley was one of the few places sex offenders could live. County sex offender restrictions kept them out of most of the decent neighborhoods."

"Ah, the good old days," Renquest said.

"I used to stop here, grab a burger, and go over my field notes, looking for anything I might have missed during the home visits. The routine would save another trip back here the next morning if I needed to follow up on something out of the ordinary."

"Nothing concerning this job is ordinary. What I wouldn't give for an old-fashioned murder. A spouse catches the other spouse in bed with someone else and shoots them right there and waits for the police."

"Things have gotten more complicated lately," Dodge said.

"I have five more years to retirement. Then, I am never leaving the house again."

The waitress came and turned over the coffee mug in front of Renquest and filled the cup to the top. Renquest had to take a drink before adding cream and sugar.

"Anything else, sweetie," the waitress asked.

"Not now," Renquest answered. "Maybe in ten or fifteen minutes."

"Just let me know when you are ready, hun," the waitress said.

"You won't sleep tonight with all that sugar," Dodge said.

"I don't sleep," Renquest said. "Why are we here, Dodge?"

Dodge looked around the diner, examining each patron, then out the window into the parking lot. Satisfied they were not being watched, he reached into a jacket pocket and pulled out a cell phone in a clear baggie, tossing it on the paper placemat in front of Renquest.

"What is this?"

"That is the reason we are meeting in this shitty diner," Dodge said.

Renquest picked up the bag and noticed it wasn't an evidence bag, which meant no chain of custody issues. This phone would never be evidence. He removed the phone from the bag for closer examination.

"It's a cell phone and a prepay to boot," Renquest said.

"Turn the phone on and look at the text messages and photos."

Renquest spent the next several minutes scanning through the contents of the phone. Once finished, he placed the phone back on the table.

"So, the owner received a lot of messages from a DJF about hooking up. Why do I care?"

"That phone belonged to Maggie Rodstein," Dodge said.

Renquest went silent. Dodge watched as Renquest stared at the phone.

"Do you know what Deputy Fisch's first name is?"

Renquest laughed. "I always thought it was asshole."

"Deputy Fisch's name is John. John Fisch."

"Yeah, so . . ." Renquest stopped in midsentence. His mind was working, trying to put everything together. Then his eyes narrowed to a piercing stare. Blood flowed to his ears and nose, causing his skin to turn red, and the veins in his forehead pulsated like worms squirming under the skin. "That son of a bitch was banging the girl," Renquest said.

"Yeah," Dodge said.

"Are you sure about this? If we accuse a Deputy U.S. Marshal of sex with an underage girl, we better have all the facts straight."

Dodge nodded. "I'm sure. Now we just need to prove it. Oh, and one more thing. I am sure Fisch killed the Parker boy, too."

Renquest placed his coffee on the table. "How did you link the Parker case to Fisch and the girl?"

Over the next fifteen minutes, he told Renquest about his conversations with the principal at the school and Maggie and even Fisch himself. All the interviews had one thing in common: Maggie and Kevin Parker were best friends and told each other everything.

"Did Maggie tell Kevin Parker about the relationship?"

"I didn't have time to ask about the rape. Let's call it what it is. Badges don't get a pass," Dodge said.

Over the past decade, states passed laws that made it a felony for persons in positions of power to have sexual relations with wards under their care.

Renquest stuck his hands out to calm his partner. "I agree, Dodge." Renquest paused in the middle of the thought. "Let me ask you something. Did you make sure this device wouldn't be traced? I turned it on, and that is a Faraday bag."

"I want Deputy Fisch to trace the phone."

"If Fisch finds out Maggie doesn't have the phone, he will kill her. How do you plan to protect her? Does the judge know?"

"I can't risk putting Maggie or her father in danger. For now, it is best if we keep this between my chief and us."

"Chief Johnson is backing your play?"

"For the time being. We just have to formulate a plan."

The two men ordered food while working on the rough outlines of a plan to trap Deputy Marshal Fisch. Dodge began by reviewing what he felt was wrong with the first crime scene.

"The scene was too clean."

"Did you see that place? It was amateur hour, man."

"Not the hidden room. It was immaculate," Dodge said. "Did the bedding go to the lab for DNA testing?"

"Yes, but the lab is running behind. It may take a few more weeks. I can call and try to put a rush on it?"

Looking up between bites of his cheeseburger, Dodge told Renquest not to bother. He knew all DNA evidence had been wiped clean because the first crime scene was staged for the task force. The two men talked about the basement where Dodge had been attacked. Dodge felt Fisch had been watching him since the beginning of the investigation, logging his moves and steering the investigation in the direction he wanted, toward Leonard Miller. No one knew Dodge was going to that building, yet he remembered seeing suspicious cars running both times he was at the location. Why would the attacker leave him alive? No one would have found his body for days, even weeks, with a few precautions. The attack, and leaving Dodge alive, was another move to lead investigators away from the actual target. A dead parole agent would have had every law enforcement agency in the state on alert. Fisch didn't want that. He just wanted everyone out on the streets looking for Leonard Miller.

"What about that pervert at the state prison?" Renquest asked. "Why bring him into this? It seems like a risky move."

Renquest listened as his partner explained why Grayson was the ultimate patsy. Everyone knew the history between Dodge and Grayson. Dodge gave speeches on the events of that night at least twice a year. Many of the things he learned from the experience he used to teach fresh recruits at the Corrections Academy about what not to do. Deputy Fisch knew Grayson would distract Dodge, causing him to get tunnel vision and fixate on his nemesis. If Grayson became a problem, Fisch would likely have him taken out in the shower by another inmate for a nominal fee or the promise of extra privileges. No one would care that Grayson was dead, and most in the prison would secretly applaud his murder. The case would be closed, and Fisch would be in the clear.

A few hours passed before Renquest decided to go home to feed Custus and get much-needed sleep before tomorrow's shift. He stood up at the table and placed a fifty-dollar bill on the table, enough to cover both meals and the tip. He then looked down at his partner.

"What is it?" Dodge asked.

"I just don't understand why Fisch killed the boy. Sex with a teenager is one thing, but murder? I just don't get it."

"I don't know. Maybe it was jealousy. Maybe it was self-preservation. But whatever it was, it's done now, and we need to keep Fisch from making another victim of Maggie Rodstein."

Renquest shook his head and walked out into the chilly night air. He had an uneasy feeling about what was about to happen. His mind raced as he drove home for the second time that day. He trusted Dodge, but trying to take down a U.S. Marshal was a risk. He wasn't sure how much to tell his superiors at headquarters. His current thought was as little as possible. He arrived home and went inside his house. He fed Custus and finished the beer he had opened earlier. Then he went to bed, but he slept little.

CHAPTER 26

DETECTIVES HANSON AND KELLER had been monitoring the phones, hoping to get a line on Jonathan Alber. They had canvassed the neighborhood he lived in. No one had seen him for a couple of days. Neighbors said it wasn't uncommon for him to disappear for a week after he earned some money. He had a drug habit. A habit that involved binges after big paydays. One neighbor said the only two things he cared about was hookers and blow. Not necessarily in that order. Always at the same time. Now that they had an idea about his tendencies after a score, they narrowed down the search to the areas of town where they knew cocaine was sold and where prostitutes worked their trade. Detective Keller made calls to his usual prostitute informants, telling them to keep an eye out for a wanted man. He let them know a good tip would be worth one get out of jail free card. The bait usually worked. It was hard for prostitutes to earn money if they were in lockup. No money meant trouble from their pimps, generally in the form of a black eye or busted lip. A reprisal that cost them cash in a job where appearance was everything. Detective Hanson did the same with his street contacts. Mainly drug dealers and addicts. Not as reliable of a bunch, but they had come through for him before.

The phone at the front desk rang. The sergeant handling the citizen helpline answered and listened to the caller on the other end. After a minute, the officer transferred the call to Detective Keller's desk phone.

"I think we have something here," the desk sergeant said.

"Did you patch him through to my phone?" Keller asked.

"Should be there now."

Detective Keller picked up the receiver and pushed the flashing red button. The woman's voice came over the headset. She was yelling in a foreign language, and Keller thought it sounded like Chinese.

"Ma'am, I need you to slow down and speak English."

The woman continued to yell. Not at him but at someone else in the room with her.

"Ma'am. Can you tell me what your name is?"

The woman answered, "Julie. Julie Wong."

"Well, Julie, can you tell me why you called?"

"This man. He come in high all the time. He want freaky stuff from girls. I tell him no. Then he start tearing up the place."

"Is the man still there?"

"He unconscious. One of my girls hit him on head with bottle," Julie said.

"He is still there?"

"Yes . . . yes, he still here. Sleeping like baby. He the man you looking for."

"Julie, we have an officer en route. If he wakes up, try and keep him there."

"He no pay. He not going anywhere."

Detective Keller hung up and motioned to Detective Hanson. "Time to go. I think we've got him."

By the time the detectives arrived at Julie's Massage and Relaxation Clinic, well known as a front for prostitution, the patrol officer had the man in handcuffs and seated in the back of his patrol car.

Detective Keller walked over to the car and peered into the back window. "It's Jonathan Alber," he said, turning to Detective Hanson.

"Take him downtown, and put him in interview room two," Detective Hanson told the patrol officer. "I don't want him talking to anyone else. Stand outside the room and don't let anyone enter unless it is Detective Keller or me. Understand?"

"Roger that," the patrol officer said as he got into his car and turned onto the street, heading in the direction of the station.

Detective Keller went inside to talk to Julie Wong. He found out the man they had in custody had visited the sex shop regularly for several months. He liked one of the girls that contracted out to Wong's business. She was the only one he asked for when he patronized the establishment. Julie Wong didn't know the girl's real name, and she wasn't there that night. She had called earlier, saying she wouldn't need a room that day. Julie Wong was sure the girl was a prostitute on the street during the night and came to Julie's shop when she needed extra money or the temperature dropped to freezing outside. She said that most of the girls there were there for the same reason.

Detective Keller handed Julie Wong a business card with a phone number on the back. He told her to call him the next time someone from Vice came snooping around her place, and he would handle it. She smiled, and he walked back outside to Detective Hanson, who was finishing up interviewing some of the girls working at the shop that night.

"Let's get to the station. I don't want him to call a lawyer before we get to talk to him."

Detective Hanson nodded, and the two piled into the black Crown Vic and headed back to the station.

Across town, at the same time Detectives Keller and Hanson were getting ready to question Jonathan Alber about Kelly Gosling's death, Dodge was putting the final touches on his plan to catch Deputy Fisch. He had visited Maggie Rodstein's home and had remembered to draw a map after leaving, detailing the obvious entry and exit points to the home, including where Maggie's room was located on the second floor. If he needed to get her out of the house, he felt confident he could do that safely. Dodge had visited the school earlier that week. Not much had changed since he was a student, including the basic layout of the building. He knew if there was a threat to one of its students, the building would go into lockdown. No one in. No one out. Local police would provide a safety barrier for anyone trying to gain access during the lockdown. Police protocol stated no one was to be granted entry. That also meant U.S. Marshals. Maggie Rodstein would be safe if she were inside and Fisch tried to abduct her on school grounds. That left him one more person to keep safe. Grayson Heller. And the thought of helping Grayson soured his stomach.

Grayson was involved with Fisch, but Dodge saw Grayson's involvement as an attempt at a personal vendetta against him. He didn't believe Grayson had anything to do with the repulsive acts committed by Deputy Fisch regarding Maggie Rodstein, nor did he think Grayson was involved in Kevin Parker's murder. Dodge had not been able to make any connection between the two. The only people Grayson Heller had contact with involved in the case were Fisch and himself, and his last visit to the prison revealed the connection between Maggie Rodstein and Grayson. He picked her picture out of a group of twenty or so photos. It was the only picture that got a second glance from him. He knew what Maggie Rodstein looked like. He could have only obtained that information from Fisch.

Nothing was reported in the press about the case, and the facts were held tight by the task force and U.S. Marshals' office. Deputy Fisch's one visit to Grayson in prison was enough to pass along information, or a cell phone, to Grayson through another inmate. Dodge's money was on a cell phone. That was how Fisch communicated with Grayson. The prison needed to find the phone and separate Grayson from any contact with other inmates and the outside world. Even his lawyer. For his own safety. Dodge had said it many times. Grayson Heller was a survivor. He would always do what best increased his chances of living a long and full life. In fact, he had said that exact thing to Fisch several days ago. He now feared those words placed Grayson's life in danger. The human side of him said, "Who cares?" The moral side, which took an oath to protect people from harm, said something different. In the end, it wasn't even a choice. He would do all he could to keep Grayson safe. Doing something and liking it were two different things. He could live with one, but not the other.

—◦◦◦—

Detectives Keller and Hanson sat in the briefing room, staring at the computer monitor, which showed a live feed of the interrogation room. The man's large hands were cuffed through a metal hoop welded to the table. He had to bend over at the waist to even scratch his nose. He had been in the room for an hour now. The patrol officer provided him with a cup of coffee, which he finished in two large gulps. The two detectives looked at each other.

"You suppose he has to go to the bathroom yet?" Detective Hanson said.

"It has been just over an hour. He should be ripe for the picking by now," Detective Keller said.

Detective Keller stood. "You start the questioning by introducing yourself. Make sure you tell him you work in the Homicide Division. I want him to know how deep the shit is he is in."

"OK," said Detective Hanson.

"Then I'll come in and introduce myself as Vice. If we can get him to believe he may have a way out of a murder wrap, he may be willing to give up his boss," Detective Keller said as he began to reach for the door handle to the interrogation room.

"Are we sure he is working for someone?" Detective Hanson said. "I mean, he could have had a beef with the hooker. We know he used prostitutes. Hell, the lady at the massage parlor told us he had a favorite. Maybe this broad was his favorite. Maybe his pillow talk got too detailed, so he had to knock her off?"

Detective Keller turned back to face Detective Keller, staring blankly at him. "This guy is a contract killer. He doesn't go freelance. No money, no kill. He has a boss, and he got paid for this job. We just need to get him to give that up. If he thinks he can get around a murder wrap, he might talk. Now, get in there and make him believe we have him for the murder of the Gosling girl."

Keller was finished talking, and Hanson knew the look on his partner's face meant the discussion was over. Keller used his key card to unlock the door, and Hanson entered the interrogation room. Keller turned to watch on the computer monitor with the volume just high enough to hear without allowing other officers walking past the room to eavesdrop. He would wait ten minutes before the planned interruption. *That should be enough time for Alber to begin to sweat*, he thought. His addiction would betray him as he came down from the high he was experiencing. The detective knew he would want to get out of that room and get his next fix.

Detective Hanson placed the tape recorder on the table. He hit the small record button on the left of the device. The recorder was a digital model, and it didn't require a tape at all. It stored all its data on built-in memory banks. Each bank could hold up to four hours of data. Neither detective thought they would need even one complete memory bank. Detective Hanson started the interview by mentioning his name and Alber's name, followed by the date and time.

Detective Keller noticed the suspect's eyes glance up when Hanson mentioned he was from the homicide unit. The word *homicide* struck a chord, invoking a reaction in the suspect who rubbed his hands and shifted his weight in the chair. He was uncomfortable. Keller observed the pair's interactions. He wanted to see how Hanson worked the suspect. A kind of professional curiosity. They had him, and a few more minutes wouldn't hurt anything. Hanson mentioned the bus accident downtown. The bald man didn't look up. Hanson then asked if he knew Kelly Gosling. The rattling of the restrained man's chains on the metal table was the only response. Hanson asked Alber where he was that morning. Only more silence.

Keller decided he had waited long enough. He opened the door and entered the interview room.

"My name is Detective Keller. I work with the Vice Unit." He paused for any reaction. He saw none. "As you have probably guessed, you are here concerning the murder of a young woman the other day. She was pushed in front of a bus at a downtown intersection."

Bloodshot eyes, pupils dilated from the effects of opiates, looked up at the detectives. "I don't know nothing about no bus accident."

Keller walked behind Alber and placed a hand on his shoulder. "See, we know that is not true. You were there. We have a video that was posted online clearly showing you in the crowd after the accident. We also have written witness statements identifying you as the man that pushed the woman in front of the bus."

"They are lying."

"The only one lying is you." Keller motioned Hanson to lay out the still photos of the crime scene taken from social media. "You see, there you are, plain as day. So why don't we try this again?" Keller said. "I know you are a businessman. You don't do revenge. You work for money, just like Detective Hanson and me here. What we want to know is who paid you for this contract?"

As he sat up straight in his chair, the chains of his restraints pulled taut against the steel ring binding him to the table. "What's in it for me?"

"If you tell us who paid you, we can talk to the prosecutor to see if he will drop the murder charge against you. Maybe a reckless endangerment charge. Your lawyer can argue you were trying to help her. Maybe she pulled away from your grasp and fell into the path of the bus?" Keller said. "We will also drop the trespass and destruction of property charges from tonight at the massage parlor. You may only do five to ten if convicted. That is way better than the needle."

"I want the deal in writing," the bald man said.

"Absolutely. Just as soon as you tell me the name of your partner."

Keller and Hanson watched as Alber seemed to be in some sort of trance. Staring at the floor, then glancing around the room as if looking for someone who wasn't there. It was about five minutes before he agreed to tell the detectives his partner's name.

"I don't know her real name. She goes by Andrea at the whorehouse."

"Andrea, what?" Hanson asked.

"Like I said, I don't know her real name. It's not like we were going to get married. She was a lay is all."

"That's funny because the woman who owns the massage parlor said you always asked for the same girl when you came in," Detective Keller said.

"She was a good lay."

"Do you know what corner she works on the street?" Keller asked.

"I only dealt with her at the massage parlor."

"Can you describe her to us?" Hanson asked.

"She is a hooker."

"If you want the deal, you will need to be more specific," Keller said.

The detectives spent the next fifteen minutes getting a physical description of the woman who hired the contract killer to push Kelly Gosling in front of a city bus. She was around five-feet-seven inches tall, weighed about 135 pounds, and had black hair but would sometimes dye it blond. He also said she used to be friends with the victim. They worked the streets together but met in rehab. Alber didn't know where Andrea lived and had never picked her up on the road before. The information gave the two detectives a starting point.

When they were finished with the interview, Hanson took the prisoner to the holding cell, where he would wait to be arraigned the next day on one count of murder. Keller began looking at the computerized files of arrests in the past five years for anyone named Andrea having a prostitution or drug charge. He found two. One arrest involved a local politician and a hooker that turned out to be a transvestite prostitute. When the politician found out his date had a penis, he beat the hell out of her. The prostitute, in this case, was a victim, and the charges against her were dropped. *Fucking trannies,* he thought.

The second one looked more promising. A young girl named Andrea was arrested for prostitution about three years ago. She was sentenced to two years, but the judge suspended all of her time if she agreed to complete inpatient treatment. She was placed on probation and released directly to the treatment facility. If he wanted to know more, he would have to contact local probation. Probation services should still have a file and photo of the girl.

When Hanson returned from the booking area, the two detectives decided to call it a night. They would meet up tomorrow for coffee before heading to local probation to try and identify Andrea. Keller was going to call Dodge and provide him with an update but decided to wait until they met with probation. If that lead turned out to be a dead end, there was no need to talk to him yet. The two men went their separate ways for the rest of the night.

CHAPTER 27

DODGE POURED A FRESH CUP OF COFFEE and sat at his desk. The cup was his fourth of the day, and he could feel the effects of the caffeine surging through his veins. He had spent the night finalizing a plan to take down Deputy Fisch. His plan needed to be precise without placing Maggie or her father in danger. It would be nice if *he* didn't get shot. Dodge had called Chief Johnson and Renquest to meet him and go over the details to get any concerns and logistics ironed out. Each of the three men had an important role to play.

The plan began with a call to the warden in charge of where Grayson was serving his time. The goal was to use Grayson to trap Fisch. The two men couldn't be allowed to communicate during the operation. Grayson was the easiest because his position was static. It never changed.

"I know, Warden," Chief Johnson said. "This is the only way we can get it done."

Renquest and Dodge listened as he told the warden about the plan. Not too much, only his part. They all thought it was better to keep the operation compartmentalized.

"I will, and you do the same. Thanks again, Warden."

Chief Johnson hung up the phone, and a smirk stretched across his face. The first piece was complete.

"Is he going to cooperate?" Dodge asked.

"He is."

"Can we trust him?" Renquest asked.

"I have known the warden for ten years. The one thing you

can count on from the Warden is he will do what's best for the warden."

Dodge nodded.

"Now, to figure out what the warden wants in return," Renquest said.

"The warden wants to be the Secretary of DOC," Chief Johnson said.

"How does that help us?" Renquest asked.

Dodge answered this time. "If this plays out right and proper, the warden will be in that chair sooner rather than later. Taking down a dirty Fed and burying Grayson under the prison would be a political win for the governor. Who appoints the secretary?"

"The governor," Renquest said.

"The governor would promote him for election propaganda," Chief Johnson added.

Renquest agreed with the plan and his role. But he had one question burning in the back of his mind. "What if the plan fails?"

The two men looked at Renquest.

"Let's make sure it doesn't," Dodge said.

The three men sat in Dodge's office for the next few hours and worked out the remaining details. Renquest asked why they were even worried about Grayson since he was in prison. The warden controlled his movements and communications with the outside world. Grayson could be placed in solitary. He was just another stooge of Deputy Fisch. Someone who provided a distraction and led the investigation away from the real target.

Dodge told the two men about his visit with Grayson. He described Grayson's reaction after showing him the crime scene photos.

"So, he didn't look at the pictures you gave him. What does that mean?" Renquest asked.

"Grayson is a hebephile in prison for over a decade," Chief Johnson answered.

"English, please," Renquest said.

"It means he shouldn't have been able to control himself. He would have popped a chubby right at the table with me sitting across from him. I would have left and never came back. Ending his game," Dodge said.

Dodge went on to describe how he and the warden had a guard he trusted hide a cell signal detector during his rounds. The sensor found cell phone signals coming from the area of Grayson's cell. The discovery wasn't enough to charge Grayson, but it was more than enough to clear the block, dismantle each cell, and strip-search each prisoner for contraband.

"Who gave him the phone?" Renquest asked.

"Chief Johnson had the warden run every employee on the block under suspicion for smuggling contraband into the facility against contact with Grayson."

"What did you find?"

"Not a single guard under suspicion had any contact with Grayson."

"So, how did he get the phone?"

"I had the Warden dig a little deeper into past cellmates of Grayson's over the last six months, and he found something. A former inmate shared a wall with Grayson for almost a year. Then six months ago, the cellmate moved to a minimum-security facility. The warden suspected nothing."

"Don't inmates move all the time? I mean, for treatment and other reasons," Renquest asked.

Chief Johnson chimed in, "Inmates do move a lot, but the warden is keen to the move and signs the final paperwork. This time, everything was handled at headquarters. All hush-hush."

Dodge said, "And after some digging in the inmate's visitation log, we found a name."

Renquest threw his hands up in disgust. "Deputy U.S. Marshal Fisch."

"Turns out, this inmate was an old informant for Fisch, and he used that as cover for going to speak to him. Fisch smuggled the phone to the inmate with instructions to give it to Grayson. Once Fisch knew the phone was in Grayson's hands, he put in to transfer the inmate. The reasoning was that he was at risk because of his past with the marshals."

"How do you know all of this?"

"We have the inmate in protective custody. The staff faked a medical emergency and placed him in solitary. He receives no outside or inside communications. After a few hours alone in a padded cell, he spilled everything to investigators. He gave up everyone involved."

"Why don't we just arrest Fisch? We have plenty to hold him on," Renquest said.

"Not enough yet," Chief Johnson said.

"Chief is right," Dodge answered. "We need more to slap the cuffs on a deputy U.S. Marshal."

"But we need to do it quickly because if the Feds catch wind of anything, they will circle the wagons to minimize damage," Chief Johnson said.

"OK, what's next?" Renquest asked.

"Now, I set up a meeting with Fisch and set the plan in motion."

Renquest gazed back at Dodge in bewilderment. "Are you serious?"

"We have to get him moving. The more he panics, the more likely he will make a mistake."

"What about the girl? What if he tries to grab her?"

"He might, but I can have the school locked down. He won't be able to get Maggie once chains go on the door."

"They canceled school for the rest of the week," Renquest said.

The air flew from Dodge's lungs, and his heart skip a beat. "What?"

"The Parker boy's death. The school thought it best if they canceled classes until next week. They are providing counselors for any student who wants to talk. We are providing a minor detail at the school to help with traffic and security."

The news caught him by surprise. He hadn't considered the school would cancel classes. Half of his plan hinged on the idea that Maggie Rodstein would be safely locked in school with armed guards and a thousand other students as witnesses. The development wasn't good. He needed to find Maggie and put her somewhere safe.

"I need you to go to the station and wait for me," Dodge said to Renquest.

"What are you going to do?" Renquest asked.

"I am going to get Maggie and bring her to you. You just be ready when I get there. If Fisch is following me, the handoff will have to be quick and flawless. But first, I am going to meet with Fisch at the federal courthouse. When I am sure he has taken the bait, I'll go to Judge Rodstein's house and grab Maggie."

"Roger that."

"Chief, you will stay here and monitor the warden's progress with the search. Contact me as soon as they have Grayson in custody and the phone is secure."

"Copy that."

The three men stood. All of them had concerns about the viability of the plan, but none spoke up. It was a comprehensive plan with a lot of moving parts. A number of things could go wrong. A compromised guard might tell Grayson about the search. Dodge might not find Maggie Rodstein before Fisch got to her, or Fisch could panic and take hostages. The possibilities were endless, but it was the best plan he could muster. Personally, he gave it one chance in three. Those were not high odds, but he had to play the hand dealt to him. If all else failed, bluff.

His phone vibrated in his pocket. The number on the screen was Anna's, but he had no time for her right now. He slid the red phone icon to the right and sent the call to voicemail, then placed the phone back in his pocket. His phone vibrated again. He pressed the button on the side of his phone to stop it from shaking. It was likely the notification Anna had left him a voicemail. He would call her later, after Maggie was safe and Fisch was in handcuffs or dead.

CHAPTER 28

DODGE SAT IN THE SMALL RECEPTION AREA, waiting to see Deputy Fisch. The receptionist, who sat behind a two-inch-thick plexiglass window, waved him over. She swapped his ID for a visitor pass hung around his neck. The receptionist buzzed the door to his right and said Deputy Fisch's office was the third door on the left. Using the distance between each door, he calculated that the offices must be two to three times the size of his own. Four doors on the left-hand wall placed Fisch's next to last.

Fisch was in the middle of typing an email when Dodge appeared at his door. He continued typing, only lifting a hand to wave him into his office. Dodge took a seat in a large brown leather chair across from Fisch. The chair was a high-backed style with arms raised three inches too high to be comfortable, pinning his arms to his sides. He noticed there was no longer easy access to his firearm. He wondered if it was by design.

"What can I do for you, Agent Dodge?"

"I wanted to let you know that we have made some progress on the Parker boy's murder," he said.

"What was his name? Kalen?"

"Kevin. Kevin Parker," Dodge said.

"That's right. Kevin Parker."

"As you know, I have been assisting local PD investigating the Parker boy's murder. The task force believes the Parker case is linked to Maggie Rodstein's case."

Fisch looked up from the computer and removed his reading

glasses. His full attention was on Dodge.

"What makes you believe the two cases are linked?"

"We know that Maggie and Kevin were best friends. We are aware Maggie was the last person to see Kevin Parker alive," Dodge said.

"Besides his killer," Fisch said.

"Of course, besides the person who killed him."

"If that's all you have, that's damn thin, and you better have more if you plan to make a federal judge's daughter a suspect in a murder," Fisch said.

"Look, I don't think Maggie killed Kevin Parker. The cause of death was strangulation. She is not strong enough to pin Kevin to the ground and choke him. Also, it appears the killer moved the body or undressed it at the scene for some purpose."

"You mean like some kind of sex thing?"

Dodge didn't want to show his hand but needed to throw a curveball and mix things up. He bet Fisch didn't have a thing for adolescent boys and wanted to test his reaction. "We aren't sure yet. The rape kit is not back from the lab. But it wouldn't surprise me if it came back positive for forced sexual contact."

Fisch said nothing. No reaction. Dodge expected a tell, as machismo will rear its head when a straight man's sexuality is challenged.

"Some things we withheld from the official reports. The brass thought it would give us an advantage playing this tight to the vest."

"What did you find?"

A reaction was needed. It was all or nothing. He would have to show his cards. No response, and the plan may fail. He reached into his pocket, pulling out a plastic bag containing a cell phone. He placed it on Fisch's desk and watched his face and hands for a tell. Fisch's eyes focused on the phone. Nothing. Then, Fisch's right hand moved away from the plastic bag. Not much, a half-inch or less. It was a psychological response. He recognized the phone. Instinctively, his mind wanted to create distance from the item. Dodge had him.

"Have you been able to jailbreak the phone?" Fisch asked.

"No, we don't have the software or manpower to break the password. That is why I am here."

Dodge detected a slight glimpse of surprise in Fisch's eyes.

"What do you want me to do?"

Hook, line, and sinker. "Well, while the state has budget restraints and personnel issues, I figured the U.S. Marshals would have the money and resources to jailbreak the phone. Whatever is on that phone could break both cases wide open. What do you think?"

Fisch reached over and picked up the bag containing the cell phone. He held the bag up at eye level and laid it back on the desk in front of him.

"I'll see what our tech guys can do."

"Call me as soon as you find anything," Dodge said as he stood to leave.

"You will be my first call," Fisch said as he walked him to the door. "And thank you, Agent Dodge. Maybe after today, we can put all this to bed."

"I hope so. I would like to give Kevin Parker's family some good news for a change. I'll give you a call later today. We can meet up and coordinate how we want to handle whatever you are able to turn up on that phone."

Dodge left the office through the same door he had entered. He took the elevator to the ground floor and the stairs to the parking garage below the building. Once in his truck, he made a call to the parole IT department.

"This is Dodge. Did you pick up the phone's signature?"

A voice replied, "Sure did. The phone powered on as soon as you left the office. I enabled GPS tracking. The phone is inside the building."

"Good. Let Detective Renquest know when he leaves the building and keep me up to date on his whereabouts."

"No problem. I sent a link to your email with a username and password. Once you log in, you should be able to follow the signal in real time."

"That's great. Thanks again."

Dodge lit a cigarette. His plan was working. He just needed to stop by his house to pick up a burner phone, the one he used to access his fake social media accounts. Using a VPN and Wi-Fi calling on his burner phone to mask his identity and make it appear he, or his device to be more precise, was in another city or state. Basically, anywhere but where he was when actually making the call. The signal could be traced, but it would take time. More time than he planned to be on the call. Then a short drive to Maggie's house to meet with the judge and deliver Maggie Rodstein to Renquest, where her safety would be assured until they had Fisch in custody.

On the drive, something nagged at him. He thought Fisch would have moved on the phone. Dodge gave him the evidence that could put him in prison for fifty years, and he sat on it? Leaving it in the one place sure to bury him? Maybe everything he believed was wrong. Maybe Fisch wasn't the killer he thought he was. He would find out soon enough, for he was pulling into Maggie Rodstein's neighborhood.

CHAPTER 29

THE WARDEN STOOD in the Pod Command Center with an enormous man in green coveralls. He had on a bulletproof vest with knee and elbow pads like a roofer or floor installer might wear. In his right hand was a radio. His left held a helmet with a plexiglass shield. He stood at attention beside the warden, watching the closed-circuit television monitors that lined the walls.

"My team is ready, sir. We locked the pod down and are ready to breach. All we need is the go from you."

The warden nodded his head, and the enormous man in the green uniform spoke into his walkie talkie.

"It's a go. *Breach! Breach!*"

Five teams comprised of five guards each burst through the pod doors. One group at each end on both sides. The fifth team headed straight for Grayson's cell. The men began yelling instructions at the inmates as they made their way through the pods.

"Turn around! Get on the ground!"

Team Five was in the cell and had Grayson cuffed and pulled in less than thirty seconds from initial entry. He didn't even have time to put on his pants. He lay on the floor in his underwear, vulnerable and shaken. The extraction and search were also a show for the other inmates. Strategic use of force is a signal. If they messed up, someone would come to get them. No hesitation. They had been warned. A CERT team officer had Grayson's cheek pinned to the dirty, cold cement floor.

The warden looked around the cell, then at Grayson. "You sit tight. I'll be with you in a minute." He watched the search team in its efforts to find Grayson's cell phone. "Keep searching until you find it. It has to be here somewhere."

The leader of the search team nodded to his men to continue the search, pulling apart everything, even the bedding, and pillows.

The warden looked down at Grayson, who by this time had gone limp, a sign he had given up any struggle to get free, and instructed the guards to move him to medical to check for injuries. He was careful to follow protocol at every step. No need to open a civil rights lawsuit.

"When the nurses have cleared him in medical, search his person. Don't let him out of your sight for one second. Do you hear me, Sergeant?"

"Yes, sir," the muscular guard yelled as he picked up Grayson by his arm, lifting him to his feet in one fluid motion.

After the guard and Grayson were out of sight, the leader of the search team approached the warden.

"Sir, we have not located the phone or any other contraband."

"Keep looking! I want this cell stripped down to the bare floor. Everything gets X-rayed."

"Roger that."

"Oh, and, Sergeant, make sure staff conduct a *full search* of his person."

"Yes, sir."

The sergeant left and followed the guards and Grayson to the medical wing. The warden stepped into the cell. The bedding was on the floor, and Grayson's personal items were in boxes, each item noted and initialed for the record. No cell phone. The warden wondered if the phone was handed off to another inmate before the search. Had his plan been leaked? Was it hidden in any of a thousand nooks and crannies in a hundred rooms throughout the prison? They needed to find the phone and update Dodge before the outside world found out what was happening inside the prison walls. News of the raid would leak when the other pods found out Grayson was the target. Prisons leaked information like the Titanic took on water. Inside the walls, information was power, and the good guys would lose that power sooner rather than later.

———◊◊◊———

While Grayson was being examined by prison medical personnel, Dodge turned onto the street Maggie Rodstein lived on. He took out his phone and accessed the internet to check and see if Deputy Fisch was still at the courthouse with the wiped phone he had been given him as bait. A little green circle blinked on and off, centered on a map. A small text balloon hovered over the blinking circle, identifying the location with the federal courthouse's street address. Something was wrong. He could feel it in his bones. The woo-woo hairs on the back of his neck were standing straight up. As if an electrical charge surged through his body, causing his polarization to change from positive to negative or negative to positive. A lump formed in his throat as he approached the Rodstein's drive and made the turn and headed toward the house.

He knew instantly something was wrong by the time he was halfway to the front door. He stopped the car thirty feet short of the walkway that led to the front portico. Dodge exited his truck, gun in his right hand, making his way to the historic home's front corner. Staying clear of the front windows and any number of shooting lines, he could make out from the upstairs window. He made his way from the east corner of the home to the first large window facing the driveway. The window was to the judge's personal study, the same room Dodge had stood in less than a week ago and had a drink while meeting with Judge Rodstein for the first time. He raised his weapon to the ready position. Chest high. Muzzle aimed toward the street. A deep breath. In, then out. In and out. Then, he tilted his head to the right, just enough to see half of the room but expose only a small part of his body as a target. He knew instantly Fisch wasn't waiting inside.

In the doorway to the study lay the judge. His body half in the study and half in the foyer. Dodge quickly made his way to the front door, which was standing open. He could see the judge sprawled out on the floor. Half of his head was missing, but that was a figure of speech. The skull wasn't missing; it was scattered in chunks and spattered all over the floor and entryway to the study. It looked as if the judge had come out of the room to greet whoever opened the door. Fisch, undoubtedly, as he had a key to the front door as part of his protection plan for Maggie. The bullet wound entered through the front of the head, meaning the judge was facing his shooter. If he had answered the door when shot, his body would have fallen farther into the foyer. No, the judge was shot as soon as he stepped out of the study. From three feet away, maximum.

Two fingers to the side of the judge's neck proved he was dead. He used his phone and called local dispatch to alert them to the grisly scene. After describing what he was wearing, a precautionary measure to ensure he wouldn't get shot when the responding officers arrived, he went about clearing the house. One room at a time. He began with the room upstairs where he saw Maggie Rodstein standing the last time he was there. Dodge made his way up the curved stairs, slow and steady. He hugged the wall to keep the railing from impeding his right-handed gait if Fisch was hiding downstairs and tried to surprise him. Halfway up, he crouched low and waited for half a minute. He was listening for any sounds or movements above or below him. It was quiet. The only noises he heard were his own heartbeat and the wail of sirens far in the distance. At least five minutes out.

Once at the top of the stairs, he ignored the other two doors that were closed toward the end of the hall, instead focusing all his attention on the door he believed to be Maggie's room. Again, he crouched on the handle side of the door and turned the knob. It clicked. He pushed the door open but paused before looking inside. *The shot would come as soon as the door swung open,* he thought.

No shot. No noise at all. Standing up, Dodge spun into the room, weapon up, scanning from right to left. The room was empty. A backpack was open on the bed with a red sweatshirt half stuffed into one compartment, the hood and a sleeve dangling over the side of the bed, one sleeve touching the floor. As he approached the backpack, he noticed Maggie's phone, the one he had seen her with at the library, at the foot of the bed. The screen was shattered, and the case was cracked. He feared for her safety. He also had no way to track her. There was no telling where she was. The sirens were just down the street now. Careful not to touch anything, Dodge made his way down the stairs and to the front door, announcing himself before exiting to meet with the arriving officers.

After leading the two patrolmen into the house to finish clearing the first floor, Dodge walked back to his car to place a call to the DOC IT technician. He knew Fisch had Maggie Rodstein but couldn't figure out how he got out of the building unnoticed. They had put trackers on his government and personal vehicles. Robbie, the IT technician, confirmed the phone had not left the courthouse. He scratched his head, as he assumed Fisch would use one of the two vehicles at his disposal. Signing out a different pool car when the one assigned to you is mechanically sound is a lot of paperwork. It also takes time and leaves a paper trail. Where could Fisch get a car he wouldn't have to sign out?

"Robbie, can you dig up some information on Fisch's partner? Make sure to find any vehicles registered to him."

"Yeah, I can get his name off of the sign-in sheet from when they were here to talk to the chief," Robbie said.

"Good. Call me as soon as you have a description of his personal cars." That was it. He must have borrowed his partner's car.

After ending the call, Dodge made his way back up to the house. Several more officers had arrived while he was on the phone, including a homicide detective and a couple of FBI agents. Two of the officers were sent to knock on the neighbors' doors and see if anyone saw any cars leaving the house in the past hour. One of the FBI agents approached Dodge as the two officers walked down the drive toward the house across the street to carry out his request.

"Agent Dodge, we need to talk to you," the agent said, flashing his badge as if the blue jacket with FBI stenciled in yellow didn't make it clear which alphabet soup agency employed him.

"What are you all doing to find Maggie Rodstein?" Dodge asked.

"Do we know she is missing for sure? Maybe she is with her friends at the mall?"

The cover your ass routine was starting already. "Look, I don't want to tell you how to do your job, but I am going to. There is a half-packed backpack and a smashed cell phone in the girls' room. I don't think she left all the things she had just stuffed into a bag, then stomped her phone before leaving on her own. Oh, and there is a dead federal judge laying in the foyer."

"How do we know she didn't kill her dad, then ran away?" the agent asked.

The frustration Dodge was feeling hit a tipping point. "Are you fucking kidding me? Is that the shit they teach you at Quantico? Personally, I would ask for my money back. The girl was taken by her U.S. Marshal handler. Deputy Fisch was having a relationship with her and is suspected of murdering her best friend. In about five minutes that officer," Dodge pointed to the patrolman talking to the neighbor across the street, "is going to come over and give a description of the vehicle that left with Maggie Rodstein inside. That vehicle is going to match Deputy Fisch's partner's car."

"You seem pretty sure of yourself," the first agent said.

"You seem like a dumbass. Call Detective Renquest at PD headquarters. He will tell you exactly what I just told you." Dodge shook his head. "Now, I am going to find the girl while you guys diddle yourselves and look for someone else to blame for this mess."

The FBI agent grabbed Dodge's arm. "We are not done yet."

Dodge stared at the agent, a look of resolve on his face. "You should let go of my arm unless you want me to snap yours off."

The agent held onto his arm a few seconds longer before releasing him. "As I said, we are not done."

"You can arrest me or shoot me, but I am leaving. And if that girl winds up dead, I'll be at the newspapers and TV stations telling my side of the story. I have a pretty good relationship with several local reporters. How's yours?"

The agent winced. The thought of lousy publicity usually made the Feds stand down. The FBI had never had the stomach for public scrutiny. Loud in their successes and quiet in their failures. To Dodge, it was leverage. He walked back to his car and placed a call to the warden. He needed to know if they had found Grayson's phone yet.

The warden answered on the second ring. He said they had found Grayson's phone. The warden had guessed wrong. Grayson had not hidden it in a cubby hole or nook in the prison walls. Nor did he try to conceal the phone somewhere in his cell. Grayson hid the device the same way inmates had been hiding and smuggling contraband for centuries. The phone was wrapped in a plastic sandwich bag and firmly tucked into his rectum.

The dangling string gave the hiding spot away. Fear of the item getting stuck in his rectum prompted Grayson to tape a line to the phone's back to help pull it out. The guards saw the string dangling from between his legs during the strip search. One punch to the stomach caused a chain reaction of muscle contortions, forcing the phone to evacuate from its hiding spot and drop onto the floor. After catching his breath, Grayson sang like a stool pigeon to save his own skin. The reaction was as natural as breathing to him. Just as Dodge had said, Grayson was a survivor.

"We have the phone, but it's passcode protected, and the

son of a bitch won't give us the code unless he gets a deal."

"No deals," Dodge said. "He will give up the passcode. Just tell him you are going to put him in general population. He won't last a week with the bangers and murderers. He knows that, and he will give up the passcode."

"I'll lock him in solitary until this is over. Grayson won't have contact with anyone unless I approve the visitor."

"Good. Call Chief Johnson and update him on what you have found. Be sure to keep me informed on any confession Grayson gives. I can use that against Fisch if things go more south."

"Will do, Dodge. And good luck."

Next, Dodge dialed Renquest's number, telling him every detail concerning the judge's fate and Maggie being missing. Renquest said he heard about the judge and requested to be kept in the loop as the investigation evolved.

"Don't count on it," Dodge said. "The FBI is there and are probably sealing out the locals as we speak."

"Screw the FBI. They share nothing," Renquest said.

"And they aren't even trying to find the girl."

"So, what do you want to do now?"

"I am going to find Maggie Rodstein."

"Do you have any leads on where he might have taken her? Or if she is even alive?"

"I don't," Dodge said. "But I have his number, and he is expecting me to call to let him know how things are going. I am sure Fisch knows we have found the judge by now. He told me the marshals monitor local police bands on the scanner."

"So, you're just going to call him?" Renquest asked. "That seems more like an audible than a play."

Dodge knew Renquest was right. But it was his only shot. "Just be ready. When I find Fisch, I'll send you the coordinates. Get Chief Johnson and be ready for my call."

"Oh, I almost forgot, those two detectives have been trying to reach you. They got the guy that pushed Kelly in front of the bus," Renquest said.

"Did he say why or who he was working for?"

"Yeah, he gave the name of some hooker. 1 didn't write it down. 1 assumed it was some sort of street beef. 1 can look up their report in the system. They must submit a preliminary report within two hours of the interview. Department policy."

"We can talk about it once we have Maggie Rodstein safe. 1 need to focus on what is in front of me now. Kelly will have to wait."

"Will do. I'll pick up your chief and bring him here. We will be ready when you call."

"Roger that."

Dodge ended the call and put the phone in his jacket pocket when his phone buzzed, signaling it had received a text message.

I know you know, and that is why you have been avoiding me. Please let me explain. 1 wasn't trying to hurt or deceive you. 1 can make it right. 1 promise –Anna

For the second time that day, Dodge felt a knot form in the pit of his stomach. Could Anna be the person who hired Jonathan Alber to kill Kelly? She was friends with Kelly. They could have met in rehab. Truth is he never felt the need to pry about any substance abuse issues Anna may have had in her past. He didn't feel it was his place. Besides, they were not that serious.

As he approached the street his townhome was on, he thought back to that day he and Anna were in Kelly's apartment. Something had been gnawing at his psyche since that day. He tried to picture the apartment in his mind. His memory scanned room by room until reaching the bedroom closet. The shoes were all laid out in a row on the floor. Shirts, slacks, and dresses all hung up in a row. *Dresses,* he thought. Then it hit him. Now he knew what had been tugging at him. He would need to meet with Anna. But only after he had Maggie Rodstein and Fisch behind bars. That had to come first. His personal endeavors would take a back seat for a few hours. He pulled into the space in front of his townhome and went inside to gather supplies.

CHAPTER 30

BEING READY FOR THE FIGHT that came next was all that was on Dodge's mind. A .40 caliber Glock with one topped-off magazine wasn't enough if Fisch decided he wanted to shoot it out. A lot more ammo was needed, along with a backup weapon. He headed for the bedroom closet. In the back wall, behind a row of hanging suits, was a safe. The safe was larger than a safe found in a hotel room, but not full-sized like a stand-alone gun safe. This safe held five handguns with extra magazines and a thousand rounds of ammunition. He removed two spare magazines for the Glock and a small .38 caliber revolver, along with two boxes of ammo for each weapon. Each magazine for the Glock was topped off and shoved in a pocket. Then he placed five rounds into the cylinder for the snub-nosed revolver. The revolver went in a holster around his ankle. For good measure, he grabbed a switchblade knife and pushed the knife into his back pocket.

No sooner than Dodge had closed the safe door, his phone rang. The number coming through flashed *Unavailable* on the caller ID.

He answered, "This is Dodge."

The line was silent.

"Fisch?" Dodge asked.

"I know you are looking for me. I also know you have been to the judge's house."

"Still monitoring that police band radio?" Dodge asked.

"I told you once before, the U.S. Marshals always listen to

the locals on the radio. It is how we stay ahead of the game," Fisch said. "It is also how I know you are looking for Maggie. The locals just can't keep their mouths shut over the radio."

Dodge's skin burned as his face turned flush from anger. "What do you want?"

"Don't play stupid, Dodge. You know what I want."

He needed to buy more time. "Actually, I don't. Why don't you tell me?"

"Don't use psychology on me. It is insulting," Fisch said. "If you want the girl, come and get her. Alone. If I even smell a local, I'll cut her throat and let her bleed out right here on this floor. You remember what that sense of helplessness feels like, don't you?"

"You know I can't do that."

"You come, or she dies."

The faint sounds of whimpering and muffled pleas could be heard in the background. Maggie was still alive.

"OK, just don't hurt her," Dodge said.

"That's good. As long as you do what I ask, the little bitch will be fine."

"But if you want me to come to you, you are going to have to tell me where you are."

Fisch laughed. The laugh sounded sinister, like a cartoon bad guy's laugh. "If you were listening to me, I gave you all you need to find us. The devil is in the details, Dodge. You have one hour. At sixty-one minutes, she dies."

The phone went dead.

Dodge thought for a minute. Where did he have Maggie? Did anything point to their location? "Think," he said to himself. Then it hit him, the place where Fisch whacked him on the head. That is where he had Maggie.

Sitting on the edge of the bed, he thought about how this could go. Fisch surrendering would be the best outcome, but that wasn't likely to happen. If he wanted to surrender, he wouldn't have called and set up a meeting. Fisch would have just turned himself into the marshals. He might have to rely on his weapons skills. Make himself small. Move and shoot. Targets in motion were hard to hit. Being on defense was always a terrible plan, but it was all he had. Dodge grabbed the rest of the gear along with his ballistic vest.

Next, he texted the plan to Renquest and Chief Johnson. If he called them, they would try to talk him out of what he was about to do and remind him of what he already knew. Dodge didn't need convincing. The plan was terrible. He knew that already, and there was no time for banter. He sat in his truck, typed the message, and hit send.

The phone made the obligatory beep notifying him the text reached its recipients. He purposefully left out where he was going but told the men Deputy Fisch had Maggie, and he was instructed to come alone. Chief Johnson and Renquest needed to understand why things had to happen this way. Dodge had assured the men he would send the location when he had Maggie. He convinced himself the pair had plausible deniability this way.

The little orange light lit the letter D on the gear shift, and he headed toward the showdown with Fisch. The trip would take ten to fifteen minutes at this hour, enough time to run two scenarios in his head. It felt good to follow one of his rules again, which calmed his nerves.

—/—

At that exact moment, Maggie sat bound to a chair in the same room where Dodge had lain helpless and unconscious not that long ago. The same pictures were plastered on the walls and ceilings. The same discarded fast-food bags were scattered across the floor. She wasn't aware of her location's relevance, but the irony wasn't lost on Fisch.

He paced back and forth. He was talking to himself and appeared agitated. His limbs flailed as if he was in conversation with someone, only no one was there. His hands were open, then clenched into fists. Other times he shoved his hands into his pants pockets so hard she thought the pockets might rip off.

Deputy Fisch turned and noticed Maggie was watching him. He stopped and stared at her. Chills ran up her spine. His eyes appeared hollow and void of color, reminding Maggie of a doll's glass eyes. She felt as if he was staring right through her, as if she were not real. She saw pain, confusion, and anger in his eyes.

Fisch stood next to her and pulled a long-bladed knife with a serrated edge out of his pocket. The light from the overhead bulb reflected off the stainless-steel blade. Maggie tried to move to put distance between her and her assailant, but the rope and gray tape binding her to the chair held firm. Fisch moved around behind her, wrapping his hand around her hair. As he pulled his fingers through her strands, he squeezed them into a fist and snared a handful, jerking her head back. The pull was hard enough to pull the front two legs of the chair off the floor. Fisch placed the knife blade against the side of Maggie's neck. She could feel the icy steel of the blade pressing against her skin.

"Your savior has a half hour to show up, or he won't like what he finds in this room."

Maggie tried to scream, but Fisch pressed the knife harder against her neck. She found she couldn't make a sound. The air from her lungs was too erratic to engage the vocal cords and produce an audible octave.

"Agent Dodge has a history of saving the girl, and I am counting on that," he said.

Maggie caught her breath. She laughed, first a low, humble laugh, but then a burst of more hysterical laughter came through.

"What do you find so funny?"

"This is your plan?"

"What about my plan do you find funny? The part where you are tied up and die."

"The part I find funny is how a dickless piece of shit like you gets his thrills off taking advantage of a teenager and then killing her dad. It was no wonder you couldn't get it up half the time."

Fisch became enraged. He swung around to face Maggie,

drew back his right arm, and released a massive blow, striking her on the left cheek, knocking the chair out from under her. Her head bounced off the concrete floor like a rubber ball, knocking her unconscious. Blood trickled from an open cut on her cheek and pooled next to her face. Strands of blonde hair soaked red with blood sprawled across the floor.

Fisch watched her body for signs of playing possum. He had seen it more than once in his career. A suspect shot would lie motionless, pretending to be unconscious. When the approaching officer holstered their weapon to check the body for a pulse or signs of breathing, the suspect attacked. Fisch placed the heel of his boot on the fingers of Maggie's right hand. He applied pressure. Light at first, then harder. Not a flinch. Feeling confident she was out, Fisch leaned over and picked her up, sliding the chair legs back under her until the entire package was upright again. He checked the bindings for weaknesses and added a piece of tape over the mouth to make sure she couldn't scream and warn Dodge.

Fisch saw a flash of headlights through the street-level window facing the street. He heard a vehicle door close. Not light, like a car door, but a large SUV or a truck. A heavy door. He continued to wait in silence. The sound of the metal door to the basement opening and closing came next. No attempts were made to hide the approach. If it was Dodge, Fisch knew he was coming. He didn't need to be quiet. The footsteps became louder, closer. Louder and closer. Fisch moved back behind Maggie, making himself small behind her petite frame, and pressed the business end of the knife against her side, angling upward toward her vital organs. A death blow if he needed it.

The footsteps stopped, and a figure appeared in the doorway. The light was dim. Fisch squinted to see who was there. He pushed the knife tighter against Maggie's body, causing her to wake from her unconscious state.

"Show yourself," Fisch yelled.

The figure stepped into the light.

CHAPTER 31

MINUTES BEFORE DODGE ENTERED the building where deputy Fisch was holding Maggie Rodstein, Chief Johnson received a text message. Before he could read it, Renquest's phone vibrated on his desk.

"It's Dodge," Renquest said. "What the hell is he doing?"

Chief Johnson raised his phone closer to his eyes and shook his head.

"He's doing Dodge."

"What the hell is that supposed to mean?"

"It means he wants to go it alone. He doesn't want to get anyone else involved. We call it a Dodge."

"He has a jacked-up move named after him?"

"Yeah, he does."

"Well, I call it bullshit," Renquest said. He was furious with his partner for not trusting him. The two men weren't always the best of friends and didn't see eye to eye on everything, but he always backed Dodge's play. "Where do you think he is going?"

"I am not sure, but it would be a place both men felt comfortable."

"Why would he give Dodge any say in where the meeting place?"

Chief Johnson said, "Fisch wouldn't have a choice. Dodge wouldn't agree to the meet if he didn't already know the layout or have some familiarity with the surroundings. Remember, this is all a con. He won't be giving that asshole what he wants, so this is likely to end once Fisch catches on. Dodge would want to know any escape routes and response time of local PD to his location."

Renquest shook his head and peered through the glass, separating the office from the bullpen area. "Where have those two crossed paths that would make him feel comfortable enough to meet without backup?"

Chief Johnson referenced the original crime scene, but Renquest said the department still had uniforms sitting on that location, so he would have known if anyone trespassed at the scene. They both agreed that the police station and the parole office were not a likely choice, for obvious reasons. That left just one place.

"The apartment building where Dodge was attacked," Renquest said.

"How would Deputy Fisch know about that place?" chief Johnson asked.

"Dodge told me the other day that he was sure it was Fisch who attacked him that night, or at a minimum set him up."

"He never told me that".

"He was going off a gut feeling. He was practically accusing a Deputy U.S. Marshal of murder and obstruction. He didn't want to say anything until there was more proof. For once, he was playing it smart."

Chief Johnson nodded.

"I have the address in my phone," Renquest said.

"Well, let's get down there and help out our boy before he does something stupid, like get himself killed."

The pair grabbed their jackets and headed out the door toward the parking lot and Detective Renquest's cruiser. He used lights without sirens until within three blocks of the building and parked a block away. Then the two men walked the rest of the way and used the cars parked on the street for cover. Chief Johnson checked for a window from the sidewalk. Renquest watched the two exits from the other side of the road, using vehicles for protection.

Chief Johnson knelt in front of the small window that opened into the basement room. The window had bars on it, not bars like a jail cell, but a latticework made of iron. Dirt and trash kicked up from rainwater draining off the roof and landing on the sidewalk caked the window in a permanent grime. He could make out three figures. One facing him and two with their backs to him. Two men and a woman. A woman was in a chair with the other man crouching behind her. Chief Johnson waved Renquest to the window.

"That would make the ones with their backs to us, Fisch and the hostage," Renquest said.

Chief Johnson looked at Renquest, "Maggie Rodstein?"

"Can't tell through this filthy window, but it sure looks like a young woman or teenager."

The two men needed to decide how this was going to play out. Renquest wanted both men to overwhelm Fisch with superior numbers. This plan would be the best way to make sure the hostage didn't get hurt, he insisted. More guns meant more chances to hit Fisch before freeing the hostage.

Chief Johnson wanted to enter the building as backup. Renquest would remain at the window, unseen, and fire from behind if things went sideways. Whoever stayed outside could call for backup and help paramedics to the scene. It was the safe play. The two men agreed on Chief Johnson's idea. Chief Johnson would enter the building, and Renquest would stay outside and call for backup if needed. Chief had not fired his weapon at anything other than a paper target in years. The idea of Renquest taking a shot with people in the line of fire raised Chief Johnson's confidence level.

Renquest watched as Chief Johnson stood and made his way to the basement door. When Renquest looked back through years of dirt and grime covering the window, his view of the basement room was blurred. He was in a prone position with feet and legs splayed out behind his torso, stomach first on the cold, damp cement, his weapon readied in a two-handed grip.

The right hand holding the Sig Sauer .45 caliber, with his left hand providing a stable shooting platform. Just like they taught in the academy.

"Move, damn it," he said, continuing to watch, waiting for a clear shot. Then he saw Fisch press the knife deeper into Maggie's side, causing her to shift in her chair. There was movement from the hall behind Dodge, then Chief Johnson stepped into the room, taking up a position at his trusted parole agent's side. The two men, guns drawn, stood facing him, but the chief quickly moved to Renquest's left, out of the direct line of fire. *Smart move*, he thought. But Dodge had moved closer, placing the most vulnerable part of his body in front of his .45's muzzle. The detective had no shot without the possibility of hitting one of his own.

—⁓—

"Chief, glad you could make it," Dodge said.

"Would have been here sooner had you told me about the plan," he said.

"Enough," Deputy Fisch screamed. "I told her you always have to be the hero, a knight riding in on a white steed to save the girl. And here you are, just like I said. And you brought a friend."

Dodge took one step toward Fisch and Maggie, hoping Fisch would overlook his tactical reposition. The chief took a cue from his movements and took one step right, increasing the distance between the two of them. The move was smart, one that would force Fisch to decide. There wasn't enough time to plunge the knife in Maggie's side, draw his weapon, shoot Dodge—who was the more substantial threat—then swing forty-five degrees to his left to fire at Chief Johnson. Dodge would pull as soon as Maggie fell, so Fisch needed to decide. Take out the biggest threat, stab Maggie, or shoot Chief Johnson. A decorated war hero and famous parole agent or the grizzled old veteran with the five-shot revolver?

Dodge needed to make a move. He dropped his weapon to the ready position, the muzzle still pointed lower at the target but never taking his eyes off of Fisch.

"Are you OK?" he asked Maggie.

The dirty rag stuffed in her mouth prevented any response, but she nodded her head, signaling she was OK. At least for the moment.

"Everything will be fine. I'll get you out of here. Just sit tight and try to relax." Dodge used the conversation with Maggie to cover his next one-step advance toward her and Fisch.

The chief slid one step farther to the right, increasing the muzzle swing distance even wider, preventing two shots at two targets from Fisch's position. Increased distance meant more time to move his shooting hand over the hostage's head while swinging toward the chief, leaving his right side open and vulnerable. All of his organs and essential parts a big red bullseye. One shot. One kill. No need for a head shot. The round would tumble around, tearing apart the lungs, liver, and kidneys. Death would be slow and painful, not instantaneous. Even if he survived the initial shot, complications from the bile and waste in the shredded digestive tract would cause horrible infections. He would die within days.

"If either of you takes one more step, I kill her. She will bleed out before the ambulance even leaves the station, and it will be your fault."

Dodge froze maybe eight feet from Maggie. He glanced at Chief Johnson, who stopped where he stood but kept his sight picture on the side of Fisch's head.

"This wasn't supposed to happen," Deputy Fisch said. "All she had to do was keep her mouth shut."

"She is just a kid. Your job was to protect her," Dodge said.

"You know nothing about her. Maggie Rodstein is no kid. She is a manipulative, petty bitch. You think I wanted this? She seduced me. Don't you get it? I am the actual victim here."

Acid bellowed up in Dodge's throat. His ears burned. He was used to offenders playing the victim card, but this time it pissed him off. This time it was a cop. Fisch was one of them. A protector.

"Victim blaming? At first, I thought you just made a horrible mistake. Something happened one time. You did your best not to let it happen again. Call it a momentary lapse in judgment. Shit happens."

Fisch said nothing.

"She is a beautiful girl. It must have been hard to stand close to her all day. It was bound to happen. Right?"

Fisch said nothing.

"But there is one thing I need to understand. Why kill the Parker boy? Did she tell him what you did to her, or did he figure it out on his own?"

Still, Fisch said nothing.

"You had to know locals would call me in on the Parker boy's murder. I would figure out you staged the crime scene. Moving the body post-mortem was a mistake. So was removing the underwear and redressing the victim. The whole thing was amateur hour."

The statement was an attempt to force a reaction, and the last statement about Kevin Parker's murder struck a nerve with Fisch. The knife at Maggie's side moved slightly away from her body. Not a significant sweeping movement. More of a twitch. A subconscious reaction to something banging around in Fisch's brain. A preemptive muscle move before the rest of the body is set in motion to perform a task.

Dodge never had time to bring his weapon level. It was over in less than a second. Fisch had tried to say something when part of his brain passed a message to his central nervous system. He needed to stand up to make his point. It was a typical response, as standing told others what you had to say was essential, but it was a poor decision for that situation. The round from Renquest's .45 caliber pistol penetrated the back of Deputy Fisch's head just above the spot where the spine met the brain. The central server room, where the mind processes commands and signals as electric impulses. The round tore through the medulla oblongata, separating it from the brain, canceling any traveling signals. Fisch collapsed to the floor before the glass from the shattered window hit the cement.

Dodge approached Maggie, and the chief maintained his cover position to the right of where Deputy Fisch lay motionless on the floor. As he got closer, he glanced at the lone window that adorned the wall behind where Fisch had stood just a few moments earlier. Glass lay in shards below the empty window frame. He could see Detective Renquest's face through the open window and sounded the all-clear.

Maggie's restraints were loosened and the gag was removed. Her eyes were full of tears as he helped her from the chair and held her arm as she stood. Dodge pulled a handkerchief out of an inside jacket pocket and handed it to Maggie. She was still shaking. Her right shoulder had speckles of blood on it, as did the side of her head. There were pieces of hair and skull fragments stuck to her right arm. There was brain matter stuck to her clothing. Maggie tried to wipe off the parts of Fisch that had attached to her after his head exploded.

Chief Johnson told his agent to get Maggie Rodstein out and up to street level. He stayed behind to secure the scene until local police took control and the medical examiner arrived. The pair walked along the long hallway, through the creaky metal door, and up the steps to where Detective Renquest was waiting. The street buzzed with emergency personnel already. There were two ambulances with red lights bouncing off the building walls on either side of the road. Dodge could hear sirens in the background. Most likely command staff from PD rushing to the scene after Renquest placed a call for help.

"I need to take her down to the station," Renquest said.

"Yeah," Dodge said. He felt Maggie grip his arm tighter.

Her eyes were wide, and her hands were clammy. The shock of what just happened had set in. Realizing Maggie had a reason to distrust the police made him angry and sad at the same time.

"It's OK. This is Detective Renquest. He is one of the good guys."

Maggie said nothing.

"He is the one that shot Fisch," Dodge said, pointing to the broken basement window. "He will take care of you. If you have any family he can call, just let him know who they are and where they live. Even if you don't have a phone number, he will find them."

Carefully pulling Maggie's hand free from his arm, he passed her off to Renquest.

"You can come to the station and see her once we finish debriefing her. It shouldn't take more than a couple of hours. I'll keep her at the station until a family member comes to pick her up," Renquest said.

Dodge nodded. He then walked to his truck, got in, and lit a cigarette. A quick glance at his phone to check the time revealed a text message from Anna. He still didn't have time to deal with her. He needed to write his after-action report and follow up with Maggie Rodstein to make sure she had some place to go, preferably with a family member. It was going to be a long night.

CHAPTER 32

THE SUN SHONE THROUGH THE BLINDS into the living room where Dodge lay, fully dressed save for his boots, sprawled on the sofa. One boot had found its way onto a chair and the other, turned sole up, was a few inches from being lost to the sofa monster.

Dodge completed his morning routine as usual. The late night meant he had slept later, so breakfast came first. It was comprised of two eggs, three pieces of bacon, a slice of toast, and a cup of coffee. After cleaning up and washing the dishes, he removed the clothes he had been wearing for well over twenty-four hours and stepped into a hot shower. The water ran over his body, rinsing off the previous day's grime. The smell of sweat and damp, moldy air clinging to his skin from that basement washed down the drain.

After changing into a clean pair of jeans and a T-shirt, he donned a sweatshirt and ball cap before sitting down at the makeshift desk in his dining room. The mail had been neglected, and evidence from the case had to be returned to the police evidence room. He felt like doing none of it. He wanted to have a drink and go back to bed. Instead, he started with the mail.

He sorted through the stack of unopened envelopes on the corner of the table. The first three envelopes went to the trash can sitting by the table. The next two envelopes contained the electric and gas bills. He placed them in the trash, as those two accounts were automatically deducted from his bank account.

A letter from his medical insurance company was set off to the side to pay later that day.

The last piece of mail was a large yellow document envelope from Hall and Hall Law Offices. Hall and Hall was a local firm, and Dodge had had a few run-ins with attorneys from their office during his career. He wasn't impressed with the quality of service they provided for criminal defendants. However, the cases were part of a contract with the county, which meant the firm received about a third of the fees it would receive from a private client. "You get what you pay for" was never more accurate than in the criminal justice system.

A knock at the front door caught him off guard. He wasn't expecting any visitors, so he tossed the envelope on the table before going to answer the door. As the door opened, he saw Anna standing on his steps. Her hair was down, covering half of her face. The jeans she was wearing had holes in the knees. A black sweatshirt hung over her upper body, making her look very ordinary. She exuded a girl next door quality. Her eyes were bloodshot, with small puffy bags under them like a person got when they have been crying or lacked quality sleep. Here, he assumed both were true.

Stepping aside, he motioned for Anna to come in. He said nothing as she brushed up against him on her way through the doorway. He wanted her to talk first. The same technique he used when interviewing a suspect. People would talk themselves into a corner because silence was uncomfortable. Maybe Anna would as well. She sat on the couch, and Dodge sat in the chair to her left. His weapon lay on the table beside him. *Never be too careful.*

Anna stared at her hands, which were shaking and red from her rubbing them. Two minutes passed before she spoke.

"I wanted . . . I wanted to tell you I was sorry."

Dodge said nothing. Simply nodding.

"I didn't mean to lie to you. I wasn't trying to trick you. I swear," Anna said. "I knew when we went to Kelly's apartment you would figure it out, and I would get caught."

Dodge said nothing. He could see her growing more uncomfortable in her skin as she talked.

Anna paused before continuing. "It was the key that gave it away, wasn't it? What you said about the way the key would face if a right-handed person, like you, had placed it above the door. You knew I was left-handed. It was careless on my part. I simply thought no one would ever notice something like that."

"I did," Dodge said.

"Kelly always said you were a brilliant investigator. I should have remembered that about you," Anna said.

She was again greeted by silence from Dodge.

"Then, when we were in the bedroom, you went over to the closet. There it was. Hanging right in front of your face. That damn blue dress. I don't know why I put it back right in the middle. I should have buried it in the back where someone, you, would have to look for it. I knew for sure you knew once you saw that blue dress."

Thoughts of Kelly's apartment flooded his head. Specifically the bedroom closet. The dress. It had been bothering him ever since the two of them had gone there. Anna was wearing the blue one on their date. He had never seen Kelly wear the dress before that day, so he didn't recognize it when Anna showed up with it on. His subconscious must have picked up on the dress hanging in the closet, but his conscience was slow to process the information and connect the dots. Anna had been in the apartment, took the dress, and returned it after wearing it while out with him. It all made sense now. He glanced over at his weapon on the table but chose not to reach for it at that moment.

"Why did you do it?" Dodge asked.

Anna sat on the couch, her hands folded on her lap, clutching her purse and staring at the floor.

"Why did you do it, Anna?" he asked again.

"I just wanted you to like me. Kelly always talked about you. Whenever we were together, you would come up. She would talk about how you saved her. About the times the two of you spent together all the years ago. Then she would cry when talking about how she fell back into drugs. Losing you to her demons was her biggest regret. When she died, I just wanted to meet you. The man she had admired and loved. Why shouldn't I get that, too?"

Dodge stared at Anna, watching her hands still clutching the purse, his own hand resting on the arm of the chair a few inches closer to his weapon than a minute ago.

"Why the blue dress?" he asked. "What made you go to Kelly's apartment and get the blue dress?"

"When she told me you two were seeing each other again, I became so jealous. I don't know why. I wanted her to be happy, but I guess not happier than me. After the accident . . ."

"Murder," Dodge interjected.

"After she died," Anna continued. "And after I met you, I wanted to make you like me. I knew I needed to remind you of her. I had the key to her apartment, so I took the dress out of the closet and put it on. I hoped it would make you think of her just enough to notice me."

"Why did you go back to the apartment and put the dress back? I would have never noticed it missing. In fact, I didn't even know the dress belonged to her. I had never seen her in that dress, and I had never been in her closet before that day."

Anna sighed. "I really don't know why I did what I did. The only thing I can do is say I am sorry. Sorry for everything. I never meant to deceive you. I just wanted you to like me."

Dodge leaned forward in his chair. "How do you know Jonathan Alber?"

Anna looked up at him. A look of puzzlement on her face. "Who?"

"Jonathan Alber," he said again.

"I don't know who that is. Am I supposed to know that person? Was he a client of Kelly's?"

Staring into her eyes, he almost believed she didn't know. "He is the man who pushed Kelly in front of the bus. He is responsible for Kelly's death."

"Did the cops catch him?" Anna asked.

"They did. And he gave up his boss. The actual person who was behind Kelly's murder."

"Was it someone Kelly knew? A customer of hers?"

"No. It was someone from the streets. Someone who was in rehab with Kelly," Dodge said. "Weren't you in rehab with her?"

"Yes, but only for a week. Kelly was graduating from the program when I entered. I only knew Kelly because we went to the same AA meetings. The program had meetings for anyone using the program and those who had graduated. The staff thought having ex-members come could help hold those in the program more accountable. Kelly was the perfect example of that. Kelly helped me stay clean. She was my sponsor."

"Do you see the problem here? The man who killed Kelly was hired by someone who knew her from her treatment days. You knew her from treatment. You admitted you were jealous of her, then you stole her dress to con me. I am having a hard time separating all these things from you," Dodge said.

Anna jumped from the couch. "You think *I* killed her!"

"Did you?" Dodge asked as he rose to his feet, moving to his right to put himself between her and his weapon sitting on the table behind him.

"How could you think that? I loved Kelly like a sister. She was there for me when no one else was. She pulled me out of the gutter and kept me clean. No matter what I did, Kelly never gave up on me. That is why I had the key to the apartment, and that is why she never talked about me. Kelly took her position as a sponsor seriously. She would never have betrayed that trust and outed anyone trying to get sober," Anna said as tears ran down her cheek. "I would never have hurt her. She saved my life."

Dodge's phone vibrated. He pulled the phone from his pocket. The number on the screen was from police headquarters. He grabbed his weapon from the table and stuffed it in his waistband. "I need to answer this call."

The voice on the other end of the line asked him to wait while connecting to Detective Hanson of the Homicide Unit.

"Dodge, this is Hanson. You got a minute?"

"I am dealing with something at the moment. Make it quick."

"I have Detective Keller with me as well. We wanted to let you know there was an arrest in the Gosling case."

"Jonathan Alber. I heard," Dodge said.

"That is true. The DA charged him with second-degree murder," Detective Hanson said. "He pled guilty this morning and will be sentenced next month."

Dodge turned back to Anna, who was still sitting on the couch, staring at him, a look of concern on her face.

"Do you know who hired him yet?" Dodge asked.

"This is Detective Keller," a voice boomed. "That is why we are calling. Alber gave up the person who hired him."

He reached to his waistband, touching the Glock. "What was her name?"

The phone went silent for a moment, then Hanson spoke, "How did you know it was a woman?"

"Lucky guess," Dodge said.

"Well, the guess was a good one. The plan is to have the woman in custody within the hour. We circulated her picture to the patrol guys this morning. Two officers said they knew her from the streets. Should make her easier to find."

Dodge squeezed the grip on his Glock. "Do you have a name?"

The phone went silent again. His heart pounded in his chest. He turned away from Anna, not wanting to spook her and provoke a fight. Or worse, pull something out of her purse and use it against him. After what seemed like an hour, Hanson came back on the line.

"The woman's name is Sharnay Gibson. She is a local prostitute with a rap sheet a mile long. B and E, drunk and disorderly, drugs, and assault."

"Are you sure it is her?"

"Yeah, the mope gave up all the details. Even gave us the phone number he used to contact her. He destroyed the phone, but the provider sent us copies of texts and phone call records. We also have him on tape purchasing the phone at a local convenience store a couple weeks ago," Hanson said.

"Why did this Gibson woman have Kelly killed?" Dodge asked.

"It's the same story as always: greed. The woman was in the same treatment facility with Kelly a few months back. During one session, Kelly talked about her plans after she was clean. She planned on getting out of the street life. Kelly had saved a decent sum of money over the years, despite a drug habit. When they got out of rehab, Gibson contacted Alber, who she knew from that massage parlor we busted him at and set the entire plan in motion. Greed. The oldest motive in the world."

Dodge thanked Hanson and Keller and realized he still had his hand on his weapon. Anna was staring at him with eyes wide as half dollars. He pushed his right hand into his pants pocket, far from his weapon.

"They caught Kelly's killer. Killers, really," Dodge said. "It was a guy named Alber and a hooker by the name of Gibson. Sharnay Gibson."

Anna stood up from the couch. Her purse strap clenched in her right hand, a grip so tight he could see the veins on the back of her hands. She stood in silence, staring at him. He had made a colossal error, one that if he was thinking straight shouldn't have happened. He let emotions get the best of him and accused an innocent woman of murder.

"I am sorry," Dodge said before Anna interrupted him.

"You're sorry? That is all you have to say to me?" Her high-pitched voice cracked with emotion. "I am not perfect. I know that. I have done a lot of things I am not proud of for sure. But the one thing I am most ashamed of, the one thing I thought I was most right about, was trusting you. I hope I never see you again. Go to hell."

On her way out of the room, Anna slapped him across the face. He could have easily blocked the blow, but he deserved it. The sting would remind him of the misjudgment for a few hours. Bourbon would help him forget. He rubbed his cheek as the front door slammed shut, then poured a double shot of Bourbon once he heard the door to her cab close and drive away.

Time to forget, he thought.

CHAPTER 33

IT HAD BEEN SIX MONTHS since the task force had closed the case on Deputy Fisch. The after-incident investigation lasted another month and a half. Dodge spent many of the days giving sworn statements to the U.S. Marshals incident response team and the FBI child exploitation unit. He and Renquest were locked out of most of the investigation once they filed their reports. Renquest got the worst of it. He was the one who had killed a Deputy U.S. Marshal. Justified or not, that was what could end a cop's career. Renquest had to sit at a desk for a few months, but the brass never wholly removed him from the task force. A sort of *insult* to the Feds.

Within headquarters, Renquest was a hero, but that didn't always translate down. Other cops wouldn't trust him in the future. He had committed the ultimate sin. He breached the "thin blue line" and killed another cop. Sadly, even when right, it could be seen as wrong to line officers. Renquest was a good cop, and he would be all right in the end. Besides, retirement was only a short five years away. And Dodge would make sure he was safe until then.

There was no court case for Fisch. Renquest's bullet denied lady justice that opportunity. Maggie Rodstein confirmed Fisch had killed her dad the day he kidnapped her. She also told investigators about the totality of how he had been sexually abusing her. At first, Maggie said, it was fun. She flirted with him, and he seemed to like it. But it didn't take long to turn much darker. He would come into her room when she was changing clothes or open the bathroom door when she was getting out of the shower. He had rules about her not locking doors. He said if somebody were to get into the house, he couldn't help her if her door was locked. The first time he raped her, she said, she fought him off for as long as possible. Finally, he threatened to kill her father if she didn't give into him. She said after that incident, she played along and acted as if she liked it just to protect her father.

The whole thing fell apart when Kevin Parker found out about what Fisch was doing to her. He took the phone Fisch had given her and said he would show it to her father. She begged him to return the phone and forget about the whole thing, but Kevin refused. At first, Maggie pretended she had lost the phone, a careless teenager mistake. But Fisch was enraged and threatened to kill her if she didn't tell him where the phone was. After he killed Kevin Parker, Maggie could get the phone back from Fisch. He told her that if that ever happened again, he would kill everyone, including her. And that was when she gave up the phone, a decision that sealed the fate of her father, the person she most wanted to protect.

Maggie claimed to know nothing of the two apartments Fisch staged for Dodge's benefit. Or the fate of Leonard Miller, the man who lived in them. As best he and Renquest could guess, Fisch searched for a sex offender no one would miss. It was easy. As a marshal, he had access to the sex offender registry information and quickly got court documents containing presentence investigations detailing the offender's entire history, including family members' names. Dodge guessed that Fisch had dismembered Miller's body and strewn it across a hundred square miles. No piece remaining larger than a human hand. Renquest thought the body was sunk into a local lake and, in time, would find its way to the top once its restraints slipped from the bloated and rotting flesh. None of it mattered in the end. Only Fisch and Miller knew for sure what happened between them. Fisch was dead, Miller was missing and presumed dead, and the task force had no leads on where to find

Miller, dead or alive. The task force would continue to search, but everyone knew they were likely not going to find Miller's body anytime soon.

—∿∿—

The sun was bright, and the sounds of spring were in the air. The temperature had risen to the mid-seventies during the day. A perfect day. Dodge sat in the captain's seat on his forty-foot sailboat, *Kelly's Dream*. He thought about Kelly a lot and how she had saved over two hundred thousand dollars. Her last few years in the sex for money world was as a call girl. She had the looks and the personality for success with private clients. No shortage of wealthy men wanted to have a beautiful woman attached to their arm. Kelly simply took advantage of that. He chose not to think about her sleeping with the men. It was a sign of respect. She did what she had to survive. He would fault no one for that. Kelly always said she could never repay him for saving her life. She lied. This was what the large manila envelope that sat on his desk for weeks contained. His salvation. The entirety of a working girl's life savings. But the last wish had one caveat. He had to spend the money on *his* dream. That dream was this boat, *Kelly's Dream.*

Dodge sat, taking in the sun and the smell of the bay before going to check his supplies in the cabin. The heads at DOC had given him a month off with pay. Add that to three months of vacation time built up, and he planned to take *Kelly's Dream* to an island somewhere warm where he would park in the harbor and spend his time fishing and sipping cold drinks. The simple life.

From below deck, Dodge heard footsteps approaching his boat from the dock. He glanced at his service weapon lying on the table, picked it up, and placed it in a cabinet above the tiny kitchen sink. He climbed the four steps that led to the cockpit, and as he transitioned from the darker cabin into the day's light, a silhouette appeared on the pier.

"Need some company?"

His eyes squinted as they adjusted to the light. The voice was familiar. Within a few seconds, he could make out Anna's face. She carried no bags, only her purse. He smiled.

"Looks like you're ready for a long trip," she said.

"Packed kind of light, aren't you?"

"It's a boat, so I brought a bikini."

"What if we stop for dinner?"

"Are we going to stop for dinner?"

"I'm not sure. I haven't planned it all out yet. Kinda winging it."

Anna put her hand out, and Dodge pulled her aboard the boat.

"I suppose we can pick something up in port for you to wear if needed."

Anna smiled. "*Kelly's Dream*. That's a great name."

"Now it's complete," he said.

Anna reached over and grabbed Dodge's hand. The two embraced before he resumed his captain's duties.

"Can you get the stern line?"

Anna reached for the rope that secured the boat's stern to the pier and pulled the loose end. Dodge fired up the small engine that provided power when not under sail and steered out into the harbor. *Kelly's Dream* passed the other boats moored to the docks and the group of live-aboard sailboats anchored in the deeper waters. *Kelly's Dream* moved through the gap in the stone walls built to protect the harbor from rough seas and into the open water. Neither was sure where they were going or what to expect from the other. They just enjoyed the moment. Deep down, they both knew it wouldn't last forever. It never did.

ABOUT THE AUTHOR

CHRISTOPHER (CHRIS) FLORY spent ten years with various correctional departments as a probation and parole officer, specializing in the supervision of sexually based offenders and criminal street gang members. He is currently employed as a contractor for the federal government as an intelligence analyst.

Trust Misplaced: A Paul Dodge Novel is the author's debut novel, though he has been featured in academic journals and professional conference papers while attending undergraduate (BA Indiana-Purdue University Fort Wayne 00') and graduate school (MA Purdue University 15'). He is currently working on the next book in the *Paul Dodge* series.

Chris now lives in Northern Virginia with his wife and dog Shadow. He enjoys spending time with his family, baking and outdoor activities.

Connect with Chris online at:
christopherflorybooks.com
Twitter: @AuthorFlory
Instagram: @authorflory.